fashionably fit, fatally flawed

A Michelle Kilpatrick Mystery
Book Two

sharon kay

hale & thornton press llc

Copyright © 2024 by Sharon Kay

This book is a work of fiction. Any references to historical events, real people, or real places are used fictitiously. Other names, characters, places, and events are products of the author's imagination, and any resemblance to actual events or places or persons, living or dead, is entirely coincidental.

All rights reserved. No part of this book may be reproduced in any form or by any electronic or mechanical means, including information storage and retrieval systems, without written permission from the author, except for the use of brief quotations in a book review. For information or to book an event, visit www.thesharonkay.com

Printed in the United States

Book Cover Design by Kay Meadows
www.kaymeadows.com

ISBN: 978-1-960581-02-0 (paperback)
978-1-960581-04-4 (ebook)

the michelle kilpatrick mysteries

Book One: The Peculiar Case of the Petersburg Professor

(takes place in October, 1974)

Book Two: Fashionably Fit, Fatally Flawed

(takes place in December, 1974)

Book Three: TBA

(takes place Spring 1975)

Book Four: TBA

(takes place Summer 1975)

fashionably fit, fatally flawed

who's who

The University of Petersburg

Commuter Lounge Gang
  Amy Brown (works as a waitress)
  Billy Carson (musician)
  Jimmy Gordon (political aspirations)
  Lawrence Jackson (Vietnam Vet/works at Police Station)
  Michelle Kilpatrick (works at Mae's Gift Shop)
  Rick McGuire (works at his mother's fitness center)
  Tasha Constantin (free spirited hippie)
  Todd Spratt (Beatles fan)
  Yash Sharma (party-lover)
  T.J. Wilson (Michelle's best friend)

***

The Kilpatrick Family

Mr. & Mrs Kilpatrick parents of
  Crystal Kilpatrick (married to Mel Weston)
  Mike Kilpatrick (married to Suzie Stewart)

Michelle Kilpatrick

The Peterson Family

Chauncey Peterson (father of Anne and Mae, founder of Petersburg Lumber Company)

Anne Peterson Ladd (Mae's sister) married to Burt Ladd

Mae Peterson Romano Miller Emerson (owner of Mae's Gift Shop) previously married to Anthony Romano, Johnathan Miller, and Nathan Emerson

Craig Miller (published mystery author & grad student) son of Mae Peterson and her first husband, Anthony Romano, adopted by Johnathan Miller after Anthony's death

Steve Goodright (son of Chauncey Peterson's sister and is a cousin to Mae and Anne) married to *Barbara Braxton*

words to ponder

"The best laid schemes of Mice and Men

Go oft awry."

Robert Burns

chapter one

Saturday, December 14, 1974

As I hurried down the wooden staircase, the smell of biscuits and bacon grew more intense with each step. Grabbing my coat from the front closet, I threw it over my arm and ventured into the kitchen, where my mom was flipping eggs in one pan while strips of bacon sizzled in the other. My eyes went from her to the golden-brown biscuits sitting on the counter. Despite being crunched for time, I draped my coat over a nearby chair, grabbed a biscuit, and leaned against the counter as I savored each bite.

Mom glanced over her shoulder. "Where are you off to, Michelle? Don't tell me you don't have time to sit down and eat. With Christmas break and no classes, I just thought—"

"I promised Rick I would drop off some cookies at his mom's gym this morning for tonight's Open House."

"Can't it wait until this afternoon? The weatherman said there were a lot of accidents this morning because of the snow and ice. You shouldn't be out there driving." Grimacing, she thrust her hands into her red apron.

I took a few slow breaths and considered how to respond,

but she continued her rant before I could say anything. "The snowplows won't even be here until later today. Why they think we farmers don't need to be out and about is beyond me."

"I know, but Rick—"

"Surely, he'd understand. Look out there!" Mom's eyes darted out the window to the shimmering trees covered in ice. Overwhelmed, she covered her mouth and shook her head.

I knew my mom was right. The weather was terrible. Yet, nothing she could say would dissuade me from driving to the Petersburg Health & Fitness Center this morning.

"I know it's bad out, but Rick's counting on me. I don't want to let him down. He and the guys from the Commuter Lounge were there for me during that whole Professor Ladd thing. Now, it's my turn to support him and his mother. I don't want to break my promise."

"There's supposed to be a lull in the storm between noon and suppertime. Why don't you go to the gym when you get off from work? The roads should be better by then."

"I'm not sure there's enough time to drive to the gym and then get back here to change for the Open House. Besides, you're the one who always says, 'Don't put off what you can do now.' I'm just following your advice."

Mom flashed the undeniable look of disapproval I had seen far too many times before, so I added, "It won't be bad. T.J. and I have driven in worse to get to the university. When you think about it, I'm only leaving a little earlier than I normally would for work—and I have to go to work. Mae would never let me call off this morning—not with Christmas so close." I paused, reading the concern on my mom's face. "I'll be careful, I promise."

My mother put the bacon and eggs on a white ceramic platter. "Go ahead and do what you want, but I don't think it's a good idea. Why you want to risk life and limb for some cookies is beyond me." She grabbed the Christmas potholder and pulled a fresh pan of biscuits out of the oven. After setting it on a trivet on the counter, she wrapped a warm biscuit in a paper towel.

"Here. Take this. Heaven forbid if you end up stranded on the road, at least I won't have to worry about you starving...freezing maybe, but at least you won't die hungry."

"I'll be fine." I gave her a quick peck on the cheek and, as I walked away, twisted the Eiffel Tower charm hanging around my neck. *I can't wait. Someday, I'll be on my own, traveling the world, and I won't have to justify my every move.*

The kitchen door swung shut behind me, and as I walked to the front door, my father was bent over the staircase. His lips were moving, but I couldn't hear what he was saying. He spotted me, straightened up, and grumbled. "That darn cat of yours is everywhere. It's a wonder I didn't trip on her when I came down the stairs."

As he went into the kitchen, I set my tray of cookies and biscuit on the small table by the door. I turned and saw Gidget, my silver-haired Persian, lounging on the bottom step. *So that's who Dad was talking to! I bet he was giving her some early morning lovin'.* Like me, Gidget knew she had him wrapped around her little paw. Her life of leisure was secure.

I slipped my peacoat over my white cable-knit sweater and black slacks and grabbed a scarf from the closet. Gidget's green eyes moved back and forth as she followed the tassels dangling from the end of the scarf, contemplating how to capture the dancing strings of yarn as I tied it about my neck.

"Sorry, girl, I don't have time to play." Unamused, she swatted my hand as I raised it above her head to pet her. "Okay, I promise we'll have a game of Chase the String later tonight, all right?"

Gidget squinted her eyes and glared. Forgiveness was not foremost on her mind.

With my purse slung over my shoulder, I wrapped my

arm around the tray of cookies, placed my biscuit on top, and carried them into the cold. The ice-melting salt crunched beneath my feet with each step toward the Orange Bomb—my trusty '68 Plymouth Roadrunner—parked under the basketball hoop.

Halfway between the front porch and my car, the earth beneath my feet crumbled, and I stumbled forward. One foot went to the right while the other veered left. I flailed my arms, attempting to regain my balance and keep the cookies from spilling off the tray and scattering on the ground. Splat! I saved the cookies, but not myself.

After catching my breath, I turned toward the house. Fortunately, no one—especially my mother—had witnessed my poorly executed gymnastics. She'd never believe I could drive safely to the gym if I couldn't even walk to my car.

I pushed myself up, brushed the snow off my coat, and gingerly moved forward. Once I reached my car, I gave the frozen door a couple of powerful tugs, climbed in—or, more accurately, fell in—and started the engine. As the defrosters did their job, I begrudgingly reentered the cold and cleared the windows.

Job completed, I hopped into my toasty vehicle and maneuvered up the plowed driveway. As my mother predicted, the snowplows had not yet been on our street. Squinting at the white landscape, I gripped the steering wheel and drove down the country lane.

Off to the side, a station wagon was stuck in a ditch. As my mother's words rang in my ears—"I told you not to go!"—I guided my car toward the center of the road, determined to avoid the same fate.

After a stressful ten minutes, I reached the highway on-ramp and exhaled a deep breath at the sight of the snow-free pavement ahead of me. Relieved, I loosened my grip, wiggled my fingers, and turned on the radio.

The D.J. introduced the next song—John and Yoko and the

Plastic Ono Band's "Happy Xmas (War is Over)." My thoughts drifted to Lawrence, the Vietnam War Vet in our Commuter Lounge group at the University of Petersburg. Former President Nixon signed a peace treaty last year, removing all U.S. forces from Vietnam. Our government continued to support the Thieu dictatorship in Saigon, and the fighting still raged between the North and the South.

Although I had always questioned our involvement in Vietnam, my father forbade the topic at home. There was no room for discussion. In my father's eyes, the U.S. could do no wrong, and questioning our leaders was nothing short of the actions of a traitor. Yet, I wondered, with the South poised to fall to communism, had it been worth it? How many of Lawrence's friends died in a war that might never have been possible to win?

My philosophical musings stopped as I turned into the fitness center's parking lot and passed a sleek black limousine on its way out. *That's weird!* Around here, I've only seen limos for proms, weddings, or funerals. In fact, the last time I saw one was at the cemetery the day Steve and Barb tried to kill me. *I suppose someone rich might use a limo if they came to town, but who would be visiting Petersburg? And why would they be at the fitness center?*

As I pulled into a spot in front of the building, I could see Rick, my friend from the Commuter Lounge, standing behind the desk. A cluster of plastic snowflakes dangled from the ceiling above his head. I chuckled at the sight of the Charlie Brown Christmas tree positioned in the center of the window with its lone red ornament and a crooked star. Rick's attempt at humor, perhaps?

After tightening my scarf and brushing the wayward strands of my blonde shag back into place, I inhaled the warmth before entering the frigid air.

Rick must have seen me struggling to reach the door on the not-yet-shoveled sidewalk. Smiling, he held it open. Once

I stepped inside, the heat enveloped me like a beloved blanket. Unable to see anything, I used my coat sleeve to wipe the condensation off my glasses.

After regaining my sight, what I saw pleasantly surprised me. My only other experience with an exercise facility occurred during my first year at the University of Petersburg when I was writing an article for the school's newspaper, *The Wildcats' Daily News*, about a student who had been an alternate on the U.S. '72 Summer Olympics weight-lifting team.

I remembered how the dimly lit windowless room with its black-matted floor felt claustrophobic. It reminded me more of a prison than a place where people developed muscular physiques and worked toward their Olympic dreams.

This room, however, was different. The festive holiday decorations and the sounds of the Jackson 5 singing "Santa Claus is Comin' to Town" made even this non-exercising girl want to work out.

"Rick, this is wonderful! When you said your mom was opening a health and fitness center, I had no idea what you were talking about. This is so cool!"

He beamed as he scanned the room. "Yeah, it is, isn't it? All those long hours Mom's been working have paid off."

"The place looks amazing!" I glanced around the room and then turned toward Rick. "Where should I put the cookies?"

His brown eyes widened. "On the counter's fine. I have no idea where my mom wants them, but I'll figure that out later." He paused, growing somber while looking me straight in the eye. "You just missed T.J. and Meg."

"Really?"

As if waiting to gauge my reaction, his gaze did not waver. "Yeah, did you know they were coming?"

I shrugged, trying not to convey my disappointment. "No. I haven't seen much of T.J. lately."

The corners of his mouth turned up into a broad smile. "I

guess everybody's busy with the holidays so close. Anyway, they dropped off some cookies they picked up at the grocery store. They left in kind of a huff though. Didn't even say goodbye." He eyed the cookies on the platter. "You make these?"

"Last night." I smiled slightly as I shuffled my feet, unsure how my cookies would compare with the ones T.J. and Meg brought.

"Don't misunderstand me. Store-bought cookies are good and all, but homemade is the absolute best. Mind if I have one?"

"No, go right ahead. I'm sure your mom won't miss a cookie or two." I laughed. "So, who came in the limo?"

Rick raised his arm toward the tray and then stopped mid-air. "What limo?"

"One was pulling out of the lot when I came in."

"That's strange. Nobody here came in a limo." Rick swayed his hand back and forth over the cookies.

As he deliberated about which cookie to choose, I stuffed my brown suede gloves into my coat pocket and smirked when he selected a green-iced Christmas tree.

Rick cocked his head. "What?"

"Oh, nothing, sorry." I grinned. "The icing color matches your sweater and green shirt. I didn't realize you were so into green."

He glanced at his attire and the cookie in his hand and laughed. "Guess you're right! The things you learn about yourself."

Turning around, I marveled at how the Christmas decorations hanging from the ceiling, the red cushy mats covering the exercise area, and the gleaming white walls created a winter wonderland-like vibe. Even the sparkling silver fixtures added a holiday element to the decor.

I was about to ask Rick a question when my roaming eyes stopped on a ruggedly handsome guy in the corner examining a treadmill. He had windswept, shoulder-length, dark blond hair, and his t-shirt accentuated his muscular build as he moved about.

Rick must have noted my lingering attention. "Paul's my mom's handyman. He's been here all morning, checking the equipment and making sure everything is ready for tonight."

"I can see why she hired him. I mean...I bet he's quite the worker." When I realized I was still staring at Paul, I spun away as my cheeks grew warm and glanced in the opposite direction. "I never understood why anyone would pay to exercise, but looking at what your mom has here, it makes sense. It's clean, bright, and, oh, my goodness, look at all the equipment! A person could work out here for hours."

Eight treadmills and ten stationary bikes lined the front wall, allowing patrons to gaze out the windows as they exercised. A strategic arrangement, I concluded, that created free advertising to the people passing by the building. The machines on the far end, however, puzzled me.

"What are those?"

Rick grinned. "Mom came across this new company out of Michigan that makes them. They're called incline trainers. A complete workout on one machine. Crazy, huh?"

"You're kidding? How?"

"By working on an incline and using bodyweight resistance—"

I glimpsed Paul, lifting the dumbbells out of the corner of my eye. "And so many weights to choose from!" I uttered.

"Yeah, Arnold Schwarzenegger has gotten a lot of guys into bodybuilding. Come on." He spun me around. "Let's go to the yoga and Jazzercise classroom."

"Great! I'd love to see it."

Rick held the door as I entered the hallway. After the door swung shut behind us, he pointed to the first set of doors, the cuffs of his green paisley shirt peeking out. "These are the restrooms and the showers for the women, and over here are the ones for the men."

I smiled.

"Guess you knew that from the signs, huh?" He looked down, and the corners of his lips turned up ever so slightly.

"Yes, but it's fun to get the entire tour," I said.

Rick led me to the next door. "Here's the classroom. The break room is across the hall, and the laundry room is at the end." He turned away, blushing. "I did it again, didn't I?"

"That's okay. You make an excellent guide." I grinned.

Our eyes met, and for a moment, things felt awkward. My eyes darted toward the floor, and Rick reached for the chrome doorknob. He twisted it, but the door didn't open. He tried again, but still, it wouldn't open. Shaking his head, he muttered, "Guess it's locked. Give me a minute, and I'll grab the key from the front desk."

Unsure how long it would take him to return, I sat on the floor to wait. As I watched him walk down the hallway, something seemed different, but I had no idea what it was. Then it hit me. His hair was longer—it fell past his shirt collar in the back. *How did I miss that?* Had I been so busy studying for finals at the Commuter Lounge that I never noticed his mullet? *So much for my powers of observation.* I smirked.

Without warning, voices came from the break room, startling me. Until that moment, I thought I was the only one in this part of the building, but obviously not. Seeing the door cracked open, I scooted down the hallway to peek inside and saw two women talking.

The woman facing me had long brown shoulder-length hair that merged with the thick fur of her mink coat, making it almost impossible to distinguish where one started and the other ended.

The other woman, whose back was toward me, had cascading blonde tresses that hit her waist. The bell-bottom jeans she wore under her blue wool car coat suggested she was close to my age.

"What's the meaning of this?" The woman cloaked in fur frantically waved a piece of paper.

"I don't know what you're talking about." The bell-bottomed blonde tossed her head to one side.

"Cut the innocent act. You know exactly what I'm referring to, and don't you dare even think about telling Marvin—"

"I don't know who wrote that note, but it wasn't me. If I wanted to tell Marvin your dirty little secret, I would have told him long ago. But now that you mention it, if you pulled a few strings to help me win the Miss States of America pageant, I could forget a lot of things. A win-win for both of us, wouldn't you say? I get the crown, and you get your precious Mrs. McGuire title."

The blonde marched toward the door, affording me a clear view of her heavily made-up face before she halted and swiveled back to face the other woman. Rick opened the hallway door, and my focus on the two women broke as he jingled the keys in the air.

With a broad smile, he inserted the key in the keyhole, but stopped when a door slammed shut behind us. We whipped around. The blonde-headed woman was standing in front of the now-closed break room door, tugging at her coat belt and murmuring to herself.

chapter two

The stunning blonde's gaze focused on Rick and a smile immediately replaced her scowl. "Hi, Rick! How's it goin'"?

"Okay." He nodded. "And with you?"

"Oh, just fabulous." She swayed from side to side, fluttering her long lashes.

Unfazed by the attention she was throwing his way, Rick responded in a business-like tone. "I didn't realize you were back here. Did you need something?"

The young woman's flirtatious mannerisms faltered for a moment, but she quickly recovered and resumed her previous demeanor by coyly twirling a strand of hair around her finger. "I just wanted to drop off some cookies for the Open House. I left them in the break room, if that's all right?"

"Sure." Rick cocked his head. "Hey, just curious, but how'd you get in? I didn't see you come through the front. Did Paul let you in the back door?"

She laughed, tossing her long blonde locks behind her shoulder. "Paul? He'd leave me out in the cold if he could. I came in with Elaine."

Rick narrowed his eyes and frowned. "Elaine's here too?"

"Yeah, silly. I followed her in the back door."

Rick raised his eyebrows. "Mom keeps that door locked. How did she get in?"

"With a key, of course." The blonde threw her hair back and grinned.

Rick shook his head. "Who gave her a key?"

"I don't know." She shrugged as her eyes drifted from Rick to me. A puzzled look came across her face as she rubbed her forehead.

Rick spoke up. "Shelly, this is Michelle, a friend from school. Michelle, this is Shelly. She'll be teaching the Jazzercise classes here and competing in the Miss States of America pageant as Miss Indiana in a few months."

"You got it." She flashed a pearly white smile.

Intrigued, I jumped into the conversation. "Mind if I ask? If you live here, how do you compete as Miss Indiana?"

"Easy peasy. I have an apartment near campus, but my permanent address is in Indiana."

"Makes sense." I nodded.

Shelly studied me for a minute. "You're that girl who found Professor Ladd's killer, right?" She tightened the lid on her harvest gold thermos.

"Yeah, but I didn't do it alone. Rick and our friends from the Commuter Lounge helped. It was a group effort."

"I remember you saying something like that in the article you wrote for the *Wildcats' Daily News*. Of course, the piece you and that hunk Craig Miller did for the *New York Times* was intense. Tell me, how did you ever concentrate on writing when you were with him? I'd switch my major to journalism if I could do some extra-curricular investigating with Mr. Famous Author turned grad student, if you catch my drift?"

My cheeks grew warm. "Yeah, it was an experience working with him."

"I bet that's an understatement." Shelly winked, grinning. "Will you be at the grand opening tonight?"

"Wouldn't miss it."

"Cool! See you then." Shelly took a step, stumbled, and leaned against the wall.

Rick tilted his head and asked, "Are you okay?

"I'm fine," she said, running her hand through her hair while looking slightly embarrassed. "This crazy headache of mine...makes me a little dizzy. Too much dieting, I guess."

"A diet, why?" Rick asked. "You look just—"

"I know," she smiled. "But I've got another ten pounds to lose before the pageant if I want to win." She tightened her coat belt, drawing attention to her tiny waist.

"I'll never understand pageants," he said, shaking his head. "Hey, sorry 'bout Paul yesterday. Sounded like he was giving you a hard time. I didn't know he was working last night."

Shelly waved her hand in dismissal. "No big deal. It's nothing I can't handle. Paul's finding it difficult to admit we're through, but I'm sure he'll get over it. I know I have." She checked her watch. "Love to chat, but I better get booking. I'm meeting someone for lunch, and I don't want to be late. But," she laughed. "I think I'll have more than a salad today. I've got to get rid of this headache so I can be in top form tonight to teach my class. Besides, I can always hop on the treadmill afterward and burn off those extra calories. See you guys later."

"You might want to go out the way you came in." Rick pointed to the back door. "Paul's in the front checking out the equipment."

"Thanks for the warning. I think I *will* use the back door. No need for more drama."

As Shelly headed down the hall toward the EXIT sign, the woman wearing the fur coat emerged from the break room. With her hand wrapped around the doorknob, she watched Shelly leave the building. Once she disappeared, the woman pulled the door shut, turned, and let out a loud gasp.

"Gracious me!" she exclaimed, her hand on her chest. "You about scared me to death!"

"Didn't mean to startle you," said Rick matter-of-factly.

"Quite all right. I guess I had my mind on other things." The woman fluffed the collar on her mink coat.

The tension between them made me uncomfortable. If I could have run away, I would have grabbed the keys from Rick and hid in the room behind me. Instead, I stood frozen, hoping their conversation would end.

Rick, however, was in no hurry to leave. He crossed his arms and scowled. "No offense, Elaine, but what are you doing here?"

"Well, it's lovely seeing you, too, Rick." Elaine's voice dripped with sarcasm as she crammed a piece of paper into her brown leather purse. She rubbed her fingers together and then wiped them with a tissue she retrieved from her bag. "I have no idea what I got all over my hands. Something must have spilled. You really need to do a better job of keeping this place clean if your mother expects to make a go of it. It's not good business to have guests leaving dirtier than when they came."

Rick said nothing but squinted his eyes.

Elaine continued, "I needed to talk to Shelly...pageant stuff. One of my girls is competing in the same pageant as she is. I suggested we all drive to nationals together to make the trip less expensive for everyone. And then—" She took a deep breath. "There was the matter of the dresses." She turned toward me and extended her hand. "Hi, I'm Elaine Anderson...Rick's soon-to-be stepmother. Oh, how I hate that phrase! It makes me sound absolutely evil." She leaned over and planted a swift kiss on his cheek. "Such a sweet boy."

Rick clenched his jaw, and his face grew red. "When did my mother give you a key?"

"That'll be the day." Elaine laughed. "No, dear, it was

your father's key. Your mother gave him one in case there was an emergency."

"Is he here?" Rick glanced around the hall.

"No, he had hospital rounds this morning. In fact, I'm off to meet him there for lunch, but don't worry, we'll be back for the grand opening." She sighed. "I don't know why, but your father's determined to support your mother. That's so sweet, considering everything. Oh, well, if we're all going to be family, we should try to get along, shouldn't we?" A crooked smile crossed her face. "Don't you agree, Rick?"

Rick said nothing as Elaine pulled a pair of brown leather gloves from her coat pocket.

"Well, I'm off. Tootles. See you tonight!"

Once she was gone, I turned toward Rick. "Your father's engaged?"

"Yes." He nodded in disgust. "I don't like that woman. What does my father see in her?"

"Besides being young and beautiful?"

"Yeah, besides all that." He lowered his head into his chest. "My cousin says I need to be nice to her because she works with a lot of beauty pageant girls, and she could introduce me to them. But I don't know. That type doesn't appeal to me—all that makeup." His eyes landed on my blue eyeshadow. "Not that makeup is bad. I mean, the way you wear yours is fine." Rick's cheeks turned scarlet red, and he quickly added, "Did you know Meg is Miss Ohio State of America? Elaine is her pageant coach."

"No, I didn't. I'm not surprised. Meg is so pretty."

"She's okay...again, not my type." He shrugged as he entered the exercise room. "This is where Shelly will teach the Yoga and Jazzercise classes. Mom will also use it for the orientation class for new members."

A Christmas tree stood in one corner, while another housed a pile of blue and red mats. I ambled over to the mirrored wall and glided my fingers over the ballet bar. "Taking ballet lessons has always been a dream of mine."

"Why haven't you?"

"Probably because my parents never considered ballet an important skill for being a farmer." I laughed.

"If it's something you want to do, you should go for it. Mom hopes to hire a ballet instructor next year, and when she does, I'll ask her to give you a discount for the classes."

"That'd be great!"

"Come on, let me show you the break room."

"Cool."

"Mom is planning to offer a course on nutrition in February, and when she can put in a full kitchen, she'll offer cooking lessons."

"Sounds like she's got a lot of neat ideas."

"She does, but it takes so much money. Luckily, Mom met this woman—Sarah—a few months back who's like a silent partner for the fitness center. Sarah's been encouraging Mom to move ahead with her plans, but Mom wants to wait to turn a profit before diving into another project. She doesn't want to overextend herself." Rick scanned the room, nodding with approval. "It'll take time, but she'll make it happen. Let me lock up the exercise room, and then I'll show you the break room in all its glory."

He looked across the hall and cocked his head. "Strange, but I thought Elaine closed that door when she left."

I expected the room to be empty, but when Rick entered the room, a man shouted, "Watch your step!"

It was Paul. He was in the back of the room. "Hey Rick, someone spilled something on that table over there by the lockers, and some stuff was on the floor. I just finished mopping it up, but it still might be wet. Be careful."

"Will do. I was going to show Michelle the break room. We won't be in here long," Rick answered. "I thought you were working out front on the machines."

Paul pushed up on his mop. "I got done out there, and I knew your mom wanted everything to be top-notch for tonight, so I stopped to check on things before I left." He glanced around the room pointedly. "Man, your mother would have flipped if she had seen the mess in here. Crumbs all over the place, half-empty bottles of sports drinks on the counter, and a stack of dirty cups by the coffee pot. Guess somebody got hungry and started celebrating early."

"Good thing you came by. Was anyone here when you came in?"

"No, Elaine was walking out as I came through the side door, but I don't think she saw me. She seemed preoccupied."

"Yeah, she was upset." Rick surveyed the platters of food on the table and then glanced at Paul, who was looking in my direction. "Oh, excuse my manners. Michelle, this is Paul. He's a chemistry student at U.P. He plans to be a doctor but moonlights as our resident handyman, janitor, and weight-lifting spotter."

"Busy guy," I smiled.

"I fill in where I'm needed. A jack of all trades, you might say."

"Nice to meet you, Paul." Our gazes collided. His intense blue eyes were hypnotic.

"And you as well." He stood smiling with his mop in hand, not once taking his eyes off mine.

"Uh, I...uh...hate to interrupt this little meeting," Rick stammered. "But we should probably go back up front so I can be there in case anyone else drops off some food."

"Yeah." I abruptly turned toward Rick. "Guess I better get going. Gotta be at work soon."

As we walked to the reception desk, Rick told me about Paul. "He's an okay dude and all, but from what I hear, a bit of a player...until he set his sights on Shelly. When she dumped him, you would have thought it was the end of the world. I'm sure he'll recover and return to his old ways. How does that saying go? Old habits die hard?"

"Hmm...too bad they broke up. They'd make a cute couple," I said as I tugged my gloves out of my coat pocket and pulled them taut over my hands. "Seven o'clock tonight, right?"

"That's right. I'm glad you're coming. It should be a lot of fun." He scanned the room, seemingly distracted.

"Everything okay?"

"Yeah. I wanted to introduce you to my mom. She was here earlier, talking to Sarah and her boyfriend. Man, it's hard to keep up with everybody nowadays."

"What do you mean?"

"First, my dad gets engaged to Elaine, then Sarah comes into our lives and becomes Mom's silent partner, and now this new fella of Sarah's is around all the time."

"Is that bad?"

"No, weird more than anything. Sarah hasn't known this guy for very long, and it seems they're getting serious. You'd think when people get older, they'd take their time with things. You know, act like mature adults instead of flighty teenagers."

"Are you talking about Sarah or your dad?"

Rick sighed deeply. "My dad and Elaine. This marriage stuff is happening too fast. He's not thinking clearly. The last thing I need is for my mom to start dating someone." He stopped. "I didn't mean that."

"I know," I replied softly. It was no secret Rick hoped his parents would get back together.

"It could still work out, I suppose. After all, they're not married yet—I mean, my dad and Elaine. Until they say, 'I do,' I guess there's still a chance."

As I buttoned my coat, preparing to venture into the cold, I peered out the window at the falling flurries. "I love the snow in December, but enough is enough! I bet we've got five inches already."

"It makes it much easier for Santa to travel in his sled," Rick laughed.

"True, and maybe if you're a good boy, Santa will bring you what you want this year."

"Man, if getting my Christmas wish depends on me being a good boy, I'm in trouble." His eyes twinkled as he escorted me to the front door. "Be careful...looks slick out there. See you tonight."

"You got it."

Rick locked the door behind me, and after taking a few steps toward my car, I turned back and glimpsed him heading for the hallway door carrying my platter of goodies. Shaking my head, I chuckled, wondering how many cookies would disappear before he got to the break room.

Brushing the snow off my windshield, I halfway expected to see the elusive limo, but I did not. Instead, I spotted Shelly and Paul standing near the dumpster. He was waving his hands, veins bulging in his muscular arms. Yet, Shelly maintained her perfect pageant-girl posture, standing face-to-face with him, grimacing, arms folded across her chest. When she tried to open her car door, Paul grabbed her hand away.

Despite my windows being cleared of all traces of snow, I kept moving my brush back and forth so I could inconspicuously watch them. Shelly finally got into her Volkswagen Beetle, and, for a moment, I thought the situation was under control. Then Paul pulled her back out.

That's it. This is getting out of hand! Armed with a long-handled ice scraper, I walked toward them and hollered, "Everything okay?"

Shelly looked my way. "Everything's fine...just having some car trouble, but all's good now. Thanks!"

From the look of distress on her face, she was clearly lying, but at least Paul had moved away from her vehicle. He picked up the garbage bag by his feet, threw it into the dumpster, and disappeared around the corner. Meanwhile, Shelly backed out of her parking spot, smiled, and waved as I headed to my Orange Bomb. I glanced over my shoulder. Paul was standing in the shadows, watching Shelly drive away.

chapter three

It never seemed to fail, but in December, people's anxiety about purchasing Christmas gifts was directly proportional to the amount of snow on the ground. With the latest snowstorm and less than two weeks until the big day, shoppers were in a complete tizzy, making Mae's Gift Shop a madhouse. Customers strolled up and down the aisles, selecting greeting cards and presents. Others walked around in a daze, unsure what to do next.

The monotonous routine of working retail had always been one of my least favorite things, but this holiday season, something had changed, and now, most days, I didn't mind being stuck behind the counter at Mae Emerson's store.

It wasn't only the busy holiday season that made the work more bearable, but, in large part, it was because of Mae's new positive outlook. She had closed her shop for a couple of weeks after her sister, Professor Anne Ladd, was murdered, and it was during that time that she gained a new lease on life. Our customers noted the change, too, but few understood why. Some credited it to Mae putting the past behind her. Others surmised it was because she took a much-needed break from the store. Both assumptions were correct.

Unbeknownst to many, Mae's hiatus from the store was a turning point in her life—she reconciled with her son, Craig Miller, and contemplated selling the store. However, Craig convinced her to hold off on finding a buyer until she had time to think more clearly. His advice ignited a newfound determination within her. She made a solemn promise to herself to cherish the blessings in her life and bid farewell to the painful memories that had haunted her for so long.

Much to her staff's relief, the Mae who reopened the store was pleasant to work with, unlike the old Mae, whom we could never please. Yet, despite the improved working conditions, I still eagerly anticipated the end of my shift.

Today, that moment arrived at four o'clock when Stacy walked through the door, ready to set me free from behind the cash register.

On my way to the back room to grab my coat and purse, I noticed the small plates and napkins in the Christmas tree pattern were gone. Mae disliked—no, hated, was a better word—empty shelves, so I took a few minutes to restock them before leaving for the day. No sense risking putting Mae in a bad mood—not now. Things were going too well.

* * *

As I pulled into my driveway, I smiled seeing that Dad had cleared the path from my parking spot to the house. My father made no secret of his disapproval of my decision to go to college. He wanted me to get married, live nearby like my brother and sister, and work on the farm. Yet, moments like this helped me remember that underneath his gruff exterior, he still cared, which was the important thing. We could work through the rest.

The front door barely closed behind me when my mother yelled, "Michelle, can you give me a hand?"

"Sure, I'll be there in a second. I just need to take my boots off and hang up my coat."

Walking into the kitchen, I saw several loaves of home-made bread sitting on top of black metal cooling racks scattered across the counters. The sink overflowed with dirty mixing bowls, measuring cups, and spatulas and only reinforced the obvious—my mom desperately needed my help.

"The ladies' quilting group from church is meeting tonight for our Christmas party. I made a loaf of banana nut bread to give to each person. Twenty beautiful loaves, if I do say so myself." Mom beamed with pride as she handed me a roll of red cellophane. "The scissors and tape are next to the stove."

I lifted one loaf close to my face. After deeply inhaling the scents of cinnamon, nutmeg, and bananas, I sighed. "This is heavenly."

Hesitantly, I returned the loaf to the counter and glanced around the kitchen before getting her the tape and scissors. "Did you make any for us?"

Mom looked up with a blank expression, yet her eyes twinkled. "I didn't know you liked my banana bread."

"I *love* your banana bread," I protested, absent-mindedly twisting the Eiffel Tower charm dangling from my neck.

Mom's shoulders dropped, and she laughed. "Don't worry. I didn't forget you. There are a couple of loaves in the pantry. I took them out of the oven about half an hour ago. I knew good and well if I left them out, *someone* would eat them before they cooled." She turned away, smiling as she cut a piece of cellophane and wrapped it around a loaf of bread.

"Who would do such a thing?" I chuckled as I handed her some tape, knowing full well I was the one notorious for eating hot bread fresh out of the oven.

I jumped. Something rubbed against my legs.

My mother's eyes grew large. "What's wrong?"

I glanced down and laughed as I brushed away several

long silver hairs on my pants. "Oh, nothing. It's Gidget. I didn't know she was in here."

I patted her head, suspecting the sweet scent of banana bread had awakened her desire for a saucer of milk. "You're hungry, too?"

Gidget meowed as I set the scissors and tape down and followed close behind me as I went to the refrigerator, where I pulled out the glass bottle of milk. Her purr grew louder as I placed the small plate filled with the white liquid on the floor.

Mom reached for the scissors and cut another piece of cellophane. "So, what are your plans for tonight? I hope you decided against going out again."

"Well...I'm going to give it a try. I told Rick I'd be at the Open House. The fitness center is so cool! He gave me a tour this morning when I dropped off the cookies."

"I wonder how well something like that will go over in this area?" Mom handed me a wrapped loaf to put on the counter and nodded toward the window. "Do you have to go? Just look outside. It's snowing again. A real friend would understand with the weather and all."

"The thing is, I want to go." I paused for a moment. "And what about you? You're going to your party tonight." I brushed my bangs out of my eyes and measured another piece of cellophane.

"Yes, but your father's driving me. Perhaps he could drive you, too? Is this fitness place close to the church?"

"No, it's in the opposite direction—near campus—but I'll be okay. I'll take it slow like I did this morning."

"Is T.J. going? Maybe you could ride with him?"

I sighed. "I'm sure he's going, but he's probably taking Meg, and I don't want to intrude."

"I don't think he'd mind. Why don't you call him?"

T.J. is the only guy my mom approved of me calling. Anyone else and she would have lectured me by saying things like, "You don't want to be known as being too forward. It's not ladylike. No self-respecting girl would ever call a boy." The funny thing was, not so long ago, I never would have thought twice before phoning T.J. and asking for a ride. It used to be so easy. After all, he and I have been best friends since first grade. But with Meg in his life, I didn't think he would appreciate a tag-a-long, and I didn't want to find out if I was right.

Adding to my aversion to calling him, I sensed that the gulf between us was growing wider by the day. Carpooling with T.J. to campus always gave us time to talk about anything and everything on our minds. It was our built-in bonding time. Unfortunately, finals this quarter had played havoc with our schedules. T.J. only had one day of exams—our photography final and his computer final. I, on the other hand, had four finals—one per day. Not riding together fueled my fears that our friendship was dissolving.

"I don't know," I said finally, shaking my head. "I'd feel weird asking him for a ride—besides, it's better if I drive myself so I can leave whenever I want. If the weather gets worse, I can come home early."

* * *

As I zipped my green velvet empire-waisted dress, I heard my parents getting their coats out of the closet. Realizing it was time for me to go too, I slipped on my black platform shoes and headed down the stairs, my feet barely hitting the steps. I threw on my coat and hat, locked the front door behind me, and turned to wave goodbye as my parents drove away.

My cheeks stung from the icy wind, but the inside of my car gave me quick relief. I switched on the defrosters, and after delaying the inevitable for as long as possible, I hopped out to scrape the snow off my windows. Once they were clear, I nestled behind the steering wheel and peeled off my wet gloves, draping them over the passenger seat. Hopefully, they would be dry by the time I got to the fitness center.

My father's tire tracks provided a path for me to follow on the country roads, which were blanketed in several inches of white fluff. However, when he turned toward the church, I was on my own to navigate the unplowed path in front of me. My jaw tightened with each mile, and I only relaxed when I reached the snow-cleared highway. Now, I told myself, the only thing I had to worry about was not sliding on the ice.

Of course, if I thought getting to the Open House would be the challenging part of the evening, I was wrong. It was finding a place to park. The lot was full.

On my third trip around the building, I spotted a pair of red taillights backing out of a parking spot, which I immediately claimed. As I got out of my car, I saw a limousine parked in the corner. *This is beyond weird.* With pen and paper in hand, I marched toward it so I could write down the license plate number. That way, I reasoned, I would know if I was seeing the same limo or a different one. My great plan, however, was to no avail. There was no license plate.

Disappointed and perplexed, I dropped the paper and pen into my purse and headed for the fitness center. As I turned the corner, I spied Rick holding the front door open for a trio of women wrapped in their scarves and knit hats. The sounds of Barbara Streisand singing "My Favorite Things" escaped from the gym into the night air.

Rick waved as he leaned against the open door. "Hey, Michelle. Glad you made it. This snow is something else, huh?"

"Yeah. Makes it feel like Christmas, doesn't it?" I unbuttoned my coat, glancing around the room for familiar faces.

Yash—another friend from the Commuter Lounge, wearing a black velvet blazer and looking the epitome of style

—was by the treadmills, laughing with two attractive girls. *He is so in his element!* Not far away stood a man in a green camo jacket. *I bet that's Lawrence. He never goes anywhere without that jacket.* A woman had her arm linked to his. *That must be his wife. At least, I hope so!* She was tall and model-thin, precisely the type of woman I imagined he would be with.

Rick excused himself to lead the trio of women around the fitness center. He beamed as he explained to them how to use the equipment. I recognized two of them: Mrs. Winterfield and her daughter, Elizabeth, both regular customers at Mae's Gift Shop. Rick's eyes met mine as he opened the door to the hallway. Grinning, he raised one finger and mouthed, "I'll be back in a minute."

After Rick and his tiny band of followers disappeared behind the door, an attractive couple by the stationary bikes caught my attention. The woman, about my mother's age, reminded me of my Barbie doll with her blonde bubble cut hairstyle. She wore a mink coat, like the one Elaine had on this morning. Silently, I chuckled, wondering what would happen if they bumped into each other while wearing identical coats.

The woman with the bubble cut walked alongside a gentleman in a leather vest as he examined the stationary bikes and treadmills. Caroline, whom I recognized from her picture hanging on the wall, soon joined them.

After chatting for a few minutes, the two women left, but the gentleman stayed behind. He stepped onto a treadmill and turned it on. As the belt picked up speed, I thought he might break into a fast-paced jog—a rather fun thought, considering his brown leather loafers were definitely not running shoes. However, to my disappointment, he abruptly stopped the machine, got off, knelt on the floor and looked underneath the treadmill for several minutes.

The woman with the bubble cut returned and he showed her something in his hand. Intrigued by their conversation, I watched them until the sound of a crashing tray diverted my attention to the other side of the room.

When I turned back, the woman and the man by the treadmill were gone. Hoping to find them, I scoured the room. But my gaze halted when the last person I expected to see came into view—Craig Miller.

Since writing our article about Professor Ladd, I hadn't seen much of him except when he stopped in at his mother's shop and, of course, in our investigative journalism class. There hadn't been a lot of time for socializing. He was focused on his new book, and I was juggling end-of-the-quarter projects while working extra hours due to the holidays.

It never crossed my mind to tell Craig about the Open House. I assumed he wouldn't be interested—he being the introverted writer type. Plus, I figured he might have his own gym at the Peterson Manor. Yet, there he was, lying on a weight-lifting bench with a heavy-looking bar raised above his chest. His neck and face strained as he lifted it higher. Paul stood nearby, spotting him.

A familiar voice behind me pulled my attention away from Craig.

"Hey, Michelle! How's it goin'?" T.J. grinned as he shook the snowflakes from his hair. Predictably, every strand went back into place, even the little swoop across his forehead. He looked Christmassy in his black pea coat and red scarf. His arm was draped over Meg's shoulder. "A lot of people showed up, didn't they? I wasn't sure if many would come with all the snow we've had today."

"Me neither, but it's a good turnout."

"I was hoping you'd be here." T.J. smiled bashfully. "I meant to call and ask if you wanted to ride with us, but time got away from me."

As T.J. spoke, Meg pulled his arm tighter around her shoulder and leaned against him. A smirk crossed her face.

"Guess you can blame me. I made him go shopping, and before we knew it, it was time to come here."

I half-heartedly muttered, "That's okay. No big deal," then returned my focus to T.J. "Did you find what you were looking for?"

He shook his head. "Meg and I spent most of the afternoon trying to find a dress for Meg to wear for her pageant. I haven't even started my Christmas shopping yet."

"For the Miss State of America pageant?" I asked.

Meg pulled away from T.J. and crossed her arms. "Yeah, how'd you know?"

"Rick introduced me to Shelly this morning, and she said she's competing in that one." Meg rolled her eyes, and T.J. tilted his head in confusion. "You were here earlier?"

"Yeah, I dropped some cookies off. Rick said I just missed you." I thought I saw a slight sign of disappointment on his face for not being here when I was, but I wasn't sure.

Meg leaned closer to T.J. and hijacked the conversation. "You said Elaine was still here?"

"Yeah." I shook my head. "But only for a few minutes. She was on her way out. Why?"

"Just wondering—" Meg tossed her long wavy hair behind her shoulder, "did she say anything about the dresses?"

"Only that she had talked to Shelly about them and something about traveling arrangements."

Before Meg could comment further, one of her friends pulled her away. "Come on, Meg. We're all going to try the Jazzercise class in the back. It'll be a blast."

Meg glanced at T.J., who nodded in return. "Go ahead. Enjoy your workout."

She grabbed my arm. "Why don't you come with us?"

"No, that's okay, but thanks!"

She gave a little pout, which I ignored. I was more than

happy to be alone with T.J. for a few minutes, and I think she knew it.

As Meg walked away, T.J. whispered, "You're lucky you weren't here when we were this morning. You missed all the excitement."

"What happened?" I leaned closer to T.J., thrilled to be taken into his confidence like old times.

chapter four

T.J.'s brown eyes widened, and, with Meg clearly out of earshot, he dove into his story. "Meg and Shelly got into a shouting match this morning about the evening gowns they're wearing for that pageant they're in. Elaine...you know she's engaged to Rick's dad, right?"

The loud music and bustling crowd faded into background noise as I stepped closer to T.J., hanging onto his every word.

"Well, Elaine is Meg's pageant coach. Man, I never even knew they had coaches for stuff like that. Anyway, Elaine found out that Shelly and Meg had the same color and style of dresses. Elaine told Shelly to wear a different one, but Shelly wasn't having it. I left and waited in the car, but when Meg came out, she freaked. Turns out Elaine backed down from Shelly and ended up telling Meg she had to buy a new evening gown."

"That's a bummer."

"Tell me about it. We spent the whole day shopping for a new dress. We even drove to Dearborn to check out their fancy dress shops. I couldn't believe it. Shopping for that crazy dress took the whole day."

"That doesn't sound like much fun. Did she find one?"

"Yeah, finally, but I've never seen Meg so mad."

I thought about pointing out to T.J. that his Miss Perfect wasn't so perfect after all, but—trying to be a good friend—I bit my lower lip and listened as he continued ranting about Meg's foul mood. "She said Elaine should have fought harder for her instead of giving in to Shelly."

I shrugged. "I understand why she'd be so upset, but what could Elaine do? I mean, she's not Shelly's coach. Could she really make her buy a new dress?" I paused, trying to gauge T.J.'s reaction. I didn't want to offend him by being unsympathetic about Meg's predicament. "I'm not trying to stick up for Elaine, but what else could she do?"

"Yeah, that's what I thought too, but when I tried telling Meg that, she only got angrier. I learned something interesting, though—Shelly had asked Elaine to be her coach, but Elaine told her 'No.'"

I said, "I wonder why? I can't imagine turning down clients and…money."

T.J. unbuttoned his coat, revealing his pressed red and green plaid flannel shirt—perfect for the holidays. "Meg said Elaine was too busy to take on more than one national pageant contestant, and she was already working with Meg. I don't think Shelly has a coach. Maybe that's why Elaine thought she could tell her what to do, but apparently, she was wrong."

I started laughing.

"What's so funny?

"Wouldn't you love to be a fly on the wall in the Jazzercise class Meg went to? Shelly's the instructor."

T.J. flashed the biggest smile I had seen on his face in a long time. "That would be verrry interesting!" he said, giving his best Arte Johnson imitation.

"I wonder who will survive—Meg or Shelly?" I chuckled.

"What I'd miss?" Rick asked as he joined us.

"Oh, nothing." I grinned. "Just wondering how the Jazzercise class is going. Did Mrs. Winterfield decide to stay and try it out?"

Rick smirked. "She was most intrigued. I think she would have tried it if her daughter hadn't been with her. Mrs. Winterfield finally agreed with Elizabeth that the class was a *little* beyond her, but she stayed to watch."

I glanced around the room filled with people talking and laughing. "Everything's going so well. I bet your mom is happy so many people showed up tonight."

Everyone seemed to be having a good time, especially Yash. The five girls surrounding him looked captivated by whatever he was talking about, and by the smile on his face, he didn't mind.

Within a few minutes, the door to the hallway opened, and a steady stream of women emerged. Shelly lagged behind, taking small sips from her thermos, her steps weighed down by her heavy gym bag. Her long blonde hair was pulled up in a tight ponytail and barely moved as she walked. With hunched shoulders and her head cocked to one side, all traces of the perfect pageant girl posture from this morning were gone.

I noticed Rick's eyes following her across the room. With furrowed brows, he lifted the sleeve to his shirt and glanced at his watch. "Shelly must still not be feeling well. She cut her class short."

Meg overheard his comment as she rejoined our group. "Thank goodness!" she huffed as she swooped up her brown locks in the back with both hands and held them against her scalp. "I don't think I could have lasted any longer. Shelly may be a royal pain, but she sure knows her stuff. She gave us quite the workout." Meg took a deep breath before releasing her hair, allowing it to tumble around her face. "I'm sorry if she's not feeling well, but seeing her struggle to power through was rather gratifying. If that's any indication of how she teaches when she's not at her best, no way could I keep up with her on a good day." She giggled. "But don't tell her I said that. I'll deny it if you do."

All eyes turned toward Shelly as she ambled over to the gentleman in the vest that I had seen earlier. They talked for a few minutes by the treadmill, but when Shelly shook her head, the man walked away. She placed her gym bag on the floor and put the thermos in the machine's cupholder.

I couldn't believe it. "Is she really going to exercise more?"

"Looks like it." Meg threw her head back and laughed. "I guess Shelly meant it when she said she had ten pounds to lose before she competes next month. You'd be surprised what girls like Shelly do to prep for a pageant. Everything for the crown. Me…there's a lot I'd do to win, but I draw the line at hurting myself."

Shelly wiped her flushed face with a towel and gingerly climbed onto the treadmill. After her first few steps, she wobbled. She stepped off, leaned against the machine, and covered her chest with her hand.

"Maybe she'll change her mind," I murmured.

Meg rolled her eyes. "I doubt it. She's obsessed about her weight."

"That's crazy! She's already so skinny." I shook my head as Shelly climbed back onto the treadmill.

"Like I said—" Meg sneered, "it's do or die for the crown with Shelly. Just look at her—not feeling well and running on that machine like her life depends on it."

Rick nudged me. "Don't forget to get some food. There's plenty on the—"

A scream from the direction of the treadmills rose above the chatter. Shelly was wildly batting the treadmill's console. Suddenly, she lost her balance and fell—her head hitting the floor with a thud. The black rope on the control panel caught my attention as it swung like a clock's pendulum, no longer attached to Shelly's waistband.

Rick's mother, Caroline, ran to Shelly, dropped to her

knees, and shook the girl's arm, trying to get a response. When there wasn't any, Caroline frantically scanned the faces staring at her. "Help! What do I do?"

Craig rushed to Caroline's side and took charge. "Somebody call 911. We need an ambulance!" His sandy brown hair hung over his eyes as he performed mouth-to-mouth resuscitation. He pleaded, "Hang on! Come on. Don't leave us now!" He held his ear close to her lips and then attempted CPR.

Rick ran to his mother's side, throwing his arms around her. She wilted into his slender frame.

Within minutes, two men in blue uniforms burst through the fitness center doors and dashed to Shelly. Craig moved away, and they took over administering CPR. Everyone in the room froze, watching as the medical team tried to revive Shelly.

A deep voice pierced the silence, "Police! Let us through!" A man dressed in a dark suit pushed through the crowd. I immediately recognized him from our previous encounters. It was Detective Douglas. Lt. Grogan followed close behind. They made their way to Shelly and the EMTs, and I glanced at the clock on the wall. It was 8:15.

Detective Douglas edged closer to Craig and appeared to be questioning him. Other than the commotion caused by the detective's arrival, the room remained still. Corporately, we all held our breath when the man kneeling beside Shelly turned toward his partner, looking physically exhausted. They switched places, and CPR resumed. Perhaps there was still hope.

Finally, to our horror, the EMT looked at his partner and shook his head. I knew at that moment it was over. I looked at the clock. Fifteen minutes had passed since their switch, making it well over half an hour since Shelly became unresponsive. I didn't need anyone to tell me hope had taken a holiday.

The EMTs placed Shelly's body onto a stretcher without

saying a word. Detective Douglas walked alongside them, peppering them with questions as they carried her to the ambulance.

Once the door closed, the stillness disappeared, replaced by the rumble of whispering and the shuffling of feet. My eyes locked with Craig's as he maneuvered toward me through the clusters of people. Despite appearing to move in slow motion, he suddenly stood in front of me.

His green eyes were tight with worry. "Are you okay?"

"N...n...no. What happened? How'd she fall?" I stammered.

Craig shrugged.

"She's dead, isn't she?"

"I think so. I couldn't detect any breathing, and I don't think the EMTs did either."

I took a deep breath. "It's not fair. It's just not fair." Tears welled up in my eyes.

Craig pulled me close. "It's going to be—"

Detective Douglas interrupted. "Mr. Miller, I have a few more questions.

"Yes, sir."

"Did you notice anything unusual before or after the accident?"

"You mean with her or with the equipment?"

"Either."

"No. I was putting my weights away when she screamed. That's when I ran over to help."

I spoke up. "Detective Douglas, why are you here? You only do murder investigations, don't you?" Stopping, I gasped. "Do you think someone murdered her?"

"Don't jump to conclusions, Ms. Kilpatrick. No one said anything about a murder. Lt. Grogan and I were down the street at the diner when the call came in about an accident. I told them we'd respond. Now, if you'll excuse me, I need to talk to the owner. Do you know who that might be?"

"Yes," I answered. "Caroline McGuire. She's over there." I pointed. "She's the woman with the dark wavy hair in the corner with her son, Rick."

As Detective Douglas approached Caroline and Rick, I whispered to Craig, "I hope she's not in trouble. I can't believe Shelly fell off the treadmill."

"I know. I overheard some people saying the belt was turning unusually fast, and Shelly seemed unable to stop it or slow it down."

"Oh, no!" I gasped. "Does that mean Caroline could be liable for Shelly's —?" I couldn't bring myself to say death.

"I'm sure she has an insurance policy that covers injuries on the property." Craig paused for a moment, thinking. "And since everything is new, I wouldn't think they could blame her for the equipment malfunctioning, but again, I don't know all the legal ins and outs."

My heart ached. Rick had been so excited about his mother pursuing her dream, and now this. I didn't even want to think about how bad things could get with the negative publicity.

Craig scanned the room. "Do you remember seeing a man in a gray suit, late forties or so?"

"Yeah, he was here earlier. It's hard to miss the only guy in the room wearing a suit. He was talking to Rick's mom. Why?"

"That was Mr. Langford. He owns the gym on the other side of town. He opened it over the summer. I've been going there to lift weights."

"Maybe he was scoping out the competition?" I stopped. "Wait, you don't think he sabotaged the treadmill?"

"Your gift of suspicion is incredible, Sherlock. I think that only happens in the movies."

"Maybe, but—" I gave the room a sweeping glance, "do you see him anywhere?"

Craig turned and studied the exercise area. "No, but that doesn't mean anything."

"Perhaps, but earlier tonight, some guy in a leather vest was looking under the treadmill Shelly used. Do you think he works for this Mr. Langford?"

Craig shook his head. "Everything doesn't have to be a conspiracy."

Lawrence and his female companion joined us, and we huddled for a few moments without saying a word. We watched as people gathered their coats and left after being questioned by Lt. Grogan and another officer who had recently joined them. The heavy shadow of death had replaced the festive spirit of Christmas. I desperately wanted to sit down and cry.

The dark-headed woman with Lawrence spoke, interrupting my thoughts. "Can you believe what happened? To see someone die right in front of you. How awful! I don't think I'll ever be able to forget it."

Lawrence turned away and withdrew into his world. I wondered what he was thinking. Was it about the war? He never talked about the horrors of Nam. How many people had he witnessed dying?

The woman grabbed Lawrence's arm and tugged him back into reality. "Aren't you going to introduce me to your friends?"

"Um, yeah. Michelle. Craig. This is my wife, Amanda."

"I've heard about you two. Lawrence helped you with that professor's death a couple of months ago, right?" Her brown eyes shifted from me to Craig and then back to me. "You're from the Commuter Lounge?"

I nodded.

"Do you run into Lawrence a lot there?" she asked.

I shrugged and replied, "Our paths sometimes cross, but not much."

Lawrence seldom talked about his wife, except I remembered him saying she was the jealous type.

"What a shame!" She smiled and pulled Lawrence closer.

Lawrence's cheeks grew red, and he changed the subject. "Craig, what did Detective Douglas want?"

As Craig detailed his discussion with the detective to Lawrence, who worked part-time at the police station, Yash and a few other friends from the Commuter Lounge surrounded Rick and T.J. near the reception desk. A few feet away from their group, another group formed, which included Elaine and, considering how closely they were standing together, a man I assumed to be Rick's father, Dr. McGuire. Across from Elaine was the woman with the bubble cut hairdo, a man wearing a heavy overcoat, Caroline, and Mae, my boss.

The two groups soon merged, and Rick and T.J. stepped away, joining our group.

"Is your mom okay?" I asked.

"She's trying to put up a good front, but she's having a rough time." He drew a deep breath, "Aw, man, everything she's worked for could go up in smoke."

Amanda piped up. "Yeah, when word gets out about this accident, who'll want to come here?"

My mouth dropped open. While what she said was true, I couldn't believe she'd be so cruel as to say it in front of Rick.

She looked at me and added, "Well, you know I'm right.

"But—" I interrupted.

Craig tightened his arm around me. "We're all upset. It's a lot to process."

We nodded in agreement, and the tension caused by Amanda's remark disappeared.

My gaze shifted back towards the group deep in conversation in front of the reception desk.

"Rick, is that your dad next to Elaine?

"Yeah, that's him."

"Do you know who that couple is they're talking to?"

"That's Sarah Bentley, Mom's friend, and the guy is Sarah's boyfriend, Carl Westwood. Mom said the police questioned Meg, and she told them the same thing she told us, that Shelly had been acting funny in class—having difficulty breathing, losing her balance—that sort of stuff." Rick shook his head as if looking for answers. "Maybe Shelly was so sick she couldn't figure out how to stop the treadmill. What if she made it go faster instead of slowing it down?" He paused. "Why did she have to work out when she didn't feel good?"

I placed my hand on his shoulder. "The police will find out what happened."

At that moment, I saw Carl remove his overcoat, revealing his brown leather vest. I looked at Craig and darted my eyes toward Carl, hoping he'd follow my lead.

"Rick, what do you know about Carl?"

"Not much. Mom said he's from London...moved here during the summer, and Sarah, as she says, is smitten with him."

"Why'd you ask?"

"Just curious, that's all."

Caroline glanced in our direction and motioned to Rick to join her.

After he left, T.J. leaned toward me and whispered, "Out with it. I can tell from that look on your face that it's more than random curiosity that's got you asking about Carl."

Craig chimed in. "Yes, do tell, Sherlock. What's going on in that head of yours?"

I looked back at the man in question. "It's probably nothing, but he's the man who was examining the treadmills and stationary bikes earlier tonight."

T.J. pursed his lips and looked at me questioningly. "Well, it is an Open House. Isn't that what people do at these things? Examine the equipment?"

"Yeah, but do they usually adjust the machine so that the next person who gets on it falls off and dies?"

chapter five

Sunday, December 15th

The phone rang in the living room as Mom and I cleared the lunch dishes. Grumbling, my father pushed his chair back from the kitchen table. "Can't a man even enjoy a cup of coffee after his meal on Sunday without being disturbed?" His feet pounded against the linoleum floor as he stormed out of the kitchen.

A few moments later, the words, "Michelle! It's for you," shot through the air. I let out an audible sigh as my shoulders sank under the weight of guilt that a phone call for me propelled my father into a foul mood.

"You better hurry," my mom said, raising an eyebrow.

I quickly placed my plate in the kitchen sink, rushed to the living room, and found my father with a deep frown etched on his face, holding out the receiver.

"Thanks," I muttered as I took it from him.

He, in turn, grunted and walked to his recliner, grabbing the newspaper lying on the coffee table.

"Hello?"

It was Lawrence. Confused as to why he was calling, I

tugged the phone cord toward the staircase and quietly perched on the bottom step, while he said, "Hey, I've only got a few minutes. I'm working this morning at the police station, but I thought you'd like to know the doctor at the hospital informed Detective Douglas that he has requested an autopsy for Shelly."

"Is that normal?" I asked. "I mean, she hit her head pretty hard."

"Douglas told me the doc said his initial impression was that Shelly died from a traumatic head injury, but he has some questions…something about her skin coloring. Douglas didn't go into detail. In other news, word is that Shelly's parents hired a lawyer to file a wrongful death suit against the fitness center."

"But it was an accident. Rick's mom is going to be devastated!" I exclaimed as thoughts about how this news would affect Rick's family raced through my mind.

Lawrence continued. "But that's not all—Douglas is deliberately being slow in turning information over to their attorney."

"Why would he do that?"

Instead of hearing Lawrence's reply, it was Detective Douglas's voice barking orders that came across the phone line. "I need those files now, Jackson. Do you understand me?"

I had never heard anyone call Lawrence by his last name before, so it took me a moment to make the connection that Lawrence and Jackson were the same person.

The rustling of papers ceased, and Lawrence's demeanor morphed from friendly to business-like when he returned to our conversation. "Hopefully, that will take care of your problem, ma'am. If we can help with anything else, give us a call. Have a good day. Goodbye."

I hung up the phone, guessing Detective Douglas was still standing near Lawrence.

As I returned to the kitchen, I marveled at Lawrence's skill at seamlessly turning our private conversation into a fake business call. His quick thinking was ingenious. It was imperative that Douglas be ignorant of Lawrence relaying information to me regarding Shelly's case. If he found out, the consequences could be dire for Lawrence.

The kitchen door swung shut behind me, and I spied my mom washing dishes and adding them to the neatly stacked pile on the rack. I grabbed the dishtowel on the counter.

"Everything okay?" Mom rinsed the soap bubbles off a dinner plate and handed it to me. "You're awfully quiet."

"I'm worried about Rick and his mom. I wish I could do something to help. Caroline's trying so hard to start a new life, and then this happens. It's not fair."

"Life's rarely fair. When life knocks you down, you have to pick yourself up and keep going."

"But having your dream destroyed when you're so close to reaching it is just plain cruel." I grasped my Eiffel Tower charm, unnerved by how quickly a dream could be destroyed.

"You ever think what that poor girl's parents are going through?" Mom sighed as she removed her Christmas apron and hung it on the nail by the door. She brushed her hair backward, tucking it behind her ears, revealing her Sunday-best pearl earrings, and then adjusted the skirt of her green dress, smoothing out a few wrinkles.

"I know. It must be hard." I let out a deep breath as I dried the last dinner plate and placed it in the cupboard. "I can't believe Shelly's gone. One minute, she was teaching a Jazzer-cise class, and the next, she was lying dead on the floor. No matter how much I replay the scene in my head, it doesn't make sense."

"Accidents happen—"

"But what if it was more than just an accident?"

She cocked her head, puzzled.

"Did I tell you that Sarah's boyfriend was fiddling around with the treadmill that Shelly fell off?"

"Who's Sarah?" Mom pulled a chair from the table, sat down, and cupped her chin in her hand.

"A friend of Caroline's, but that's not important. What was that guy doing to the treadmill?" I paused. "And then there was a limo at the fitness center yesterday morning and again last night. Isn't that weird? I could count on one hand the times I've seen a limo in Petersburg my whole life, and now three have crossed my path in just a couple of months."

"Three?"

"Yeah, there was one at the cemetery the day I was there with Mae."

"Seeing a limousine at a cemetery isn't that strange," Mom said.

"That's what I thought, but now I'm beginning to wonder. Every time a limo—"

Mom straightened up in her chair. "Really, Michelle. Don't go getting superstitious on me."

"Just because I don't think it's a coincidence that every time a limo shows up, something bad happens doesn't mean I'm superstitious, but I want to find—"

"You're not going to get involved with this whole mess, are you?" she asked, her eyes narrowing.

The phone rang as I considered how to answer her question without starting an argument. Mom dashed into the living room, probably more concerned about silencing the phone before it woke my father from his Sunday afternoon nap than with my intentions to start sleuthing. I peeked around the kitchen door as she snatched up the receiver, and I saw my father sleeping undisturbed in his chair with his newspaper scattered on the floor.

"And may I ask who's calling?" Mom pressed the phone against her ear. "Just a minute, and I'll get her." Covering the receiver with one hand, she mouthed, "It's for you." As I got closer, she whispered, "It's that Craig person. What would he be calling about?" She furrowed her brows and frowned, not attempting to hide her disapproval for the man she had never met yet vehemently disliked.

"I have no idea. Let's find out." I mischievously smiled as I took the receiver from her hand.

"Hi, Craig. What's up?" I carried the phone back to my spot on the stairs.

"I went to that gym across town I was telling you about, and guess who was there?"

"Not a clue." Leaning toward the railing, I glanced over my shoulder and chuckled. Although my mom had returned to the kitchen, she left the door partially open. If her intent was to eavesdrop discreetly, I wondered how that was working out between my father's loud snoring and my soft voice.

Craig continued. "Remember that guy in the leather vest last night—the one you said was checking out the treadmill? It turns out he's the brother of the gym's owner."

"You've got to be kidding!"

"No, I'm quite serious. His name is Carl Westwood. I asked around and discovered that Carl moved to England after college to study economics at Oxford and liked it so much he stayed."

"But you said his brother's last name is Langford—different fathers?"

"No. Nothing like that. Westwood is Carl's pen name. After graduating from Oxford, he started writing historical fiction for the fun of it. He used a pen name because he didn't want to diminish his reputation as an economist, just in case no one bought his books. When their father died earlier this year, Carl returned to Petersburg, and he's been here ever since. And before you ask, I have no idea why he's using his pen name rather than his real name. If I were a betting man, I'd say he's hiding something."

"Wow! You found out a lot this morning. Impressive."

"All in a day's work." He chuckled.

"Hey, before I forget, Lawrence called and said Shelly's mother and father may sue Caroline over the treadmill. There's going to be an autopsy, so it'll depend on the results, but apparently, Detective Douglas is delaying giving info to their lawyer. Why would he do that?"

"He's probably just making sure all the information is correct since there may be a lawsuit." Unlike me, Craig sounded indifferent about the entire matter.

"But if Shelly's parents sue Rick's mother—" I protested, the pitch of my voice rising. I paused, took a breath, and tried to regain control of my emotions, "she could lose everything."

"Unless we could prove someone *deliberately* tampered with the treadmill."

"And how are we going to do that?" I asked, exasperated.

"The same way you found out who killed Anne."

"By almost getting myself killed? No, thank you."

"No, Sherlock, by working with a team. Do you think your friends are up to solving another mystery?"

"If it'll help Rick and his mom, I'm sure they will."

"Good. How about we gather everyone tonight at my place? I'll provide pizza and drinks, and you provide the bodies, I mean, people. Sorry, bad choice of words."

I rolled my eyes and smiled. "Sure, I'll see who can make it. What time?"

"About six o'clock?"

"That should work, but...where do you live? Have you moved into the Peterson Estate?

"Yes, my things are here, but to say I've moved in would be an exaggeration." He laughed. "I've still got a lot of unpacking to do."

"Hey, I wanted to ask you about your mom. I was surprised to see her at the Open House last night."

"You know my mother." Craig laughed. "She likes to be

where the action is and doesn't want to miss out on an event that will have everyone talking."

"She certainly got that one right," I said.

"Yeah, that's for sure. Last night didn't quite turn out the way anyone planned."

I leaned back on the step. "I saw her with Sarah. Are they friends?"

He drew a deep breath. "Apparently, they knew each other years ago when they lived in Boston. Mom was married to Johnathan Miller at the time—the man she married after my father died. Anyway, Sarah's husband was a business associate of Johnathan's. They would all go out to dinner several times a year, but after Johnathan passed away, they lost touch. Mom was shocked to find out Sarah's husband had died a few years back and that she was living in Petersburg. Small world, isn't it?"

"That's for sure. Strange that they both ended up in Petersburg. It makes sense why Mae moved here. I mean, she grew up here, but what brought Sarah to the area?" I asked, my curiosity getting the better of me.

"Sarah's son works for a local law firm, and she wanted to live closer to him."

"Wow, the world really is a small place."

After ending my call, I unplugged the phone and carried it to my room, where I moved the vanity to get to the wall jack. While tugging on the vanity, I sensed something standing behind me. Startled, I spun around and jumped, finding myself face-to-face with my mother.

"Didn't mean to scare you," she said apologetically.

"That's okay. Guess I was in deep thought."

"Why? What did *he* want?" She turned her head slightly and squinted her eyes.

"Oh, not much. Craig wants to invite our group from the Commuter Lounge over to his place tonight for pizza and asked me to tell everyone."

"Just for pizza? He didn't say anything about that girl's death?" She looked me squarely in the eyes.

"He's worried about Rick and his mom and wants to help if he can."

"And by *help*, does that mean getting you involved?"

I shrugged. "I think he just wants everyone's input on how best to help them."

"Well, make sure you don't get caught up in all this. Somehow, when this Craig guy is involved, things get dangerous."

"I have no intention of putting myself in harm's way." I grinned. "Which is why I brought the phone to my room to make some calls. I don't want to risk waking Dad and making him mad."

Mom smiled and nodded before leaving.

When I closed my bedroom door, I accidentally woke Gidget from her nap on my bed. She sat up, her big round eyes intently watching my every move as I reached for the telephone cord and connected it to the jack on the wall. Despite her cute and innocent appearance, her expression was undeniably melancholic, as if she longed for something.

"Have I been neglecting you today?"

She narrowed her green eyes.

"Fine. I can bring the phone over there. We can make calls together."

I plopped beside her on the comforter and dialed T.J.'s number, rubbing her head as I waited for him to answer.

After the fourth ring, I thought perhaps no one was home, but as I lowered the receiver to hang up, T.J.'s father answered, "Hello."

"Mr. Wilson, this is Michelle. Is T. J. around?"

"Michelle. How are you? It's been a while since we've seen you."

"Yeah, life's been kind of busy lately. You know, school and work."

"I understand, but don't be a stranger, ya hear. Wait a minute, and I'll get him."

I missed going to T.J.'s house and hanging out together. We used to watch T.V. or listen to his newest record album. Sometimes, we'd sit in the family room and talk for hours on end, but those days seemed over now that Meg was in the picture.

The wave of despair that threatened to overwhelm me vanished at the sound of T.J.'s voice as he asked, "Hey, what's up?"

I leaned back on my pillow and told him what I had learned from Lawrence and about Craig's offer to meet at his house tonight. "I'll call Rick and Lawrence. Could you give everyone else a call?"

"Sure," he said. "You can always count on me. Don't ever forget that." After a brief pause, he added, "Listen. Just be careful with Craig. Don't let him put you in any danger, okay? And....promise me you won't go off by yourself this time."

Remembering the look on his face when I almost got myself shot trying to solve Professor Ladd's murder, I nodded. "I promise...having guns waved in my face is not something I'm in a hurry to do again."

"Cool. As long as you promise." He exhaled deeply. "Hey, do you think you should call Rick first and make sure he and his mom are all right with us getting involved before we invite everybody?"

"You're probably right. I don't think they'd have a problem with it, but it's better to be safe than sorry."

I smiled as I hung up the receiver. *T.J.'s worried about me...maybe things aren't as bad between us as I thought.*

I rubbed behind Gidget's ears and became lost in the sound of her purr until a bird flew by, and the purring stopped. She snapped upright, whipped her head towards the window, and meandered closer for a better look.

Meanwhile, I dialed Rick's number, but when there was no answer, I left a message on his answering machine. While waiting for his return call, I flipped through the latest issue of *Glamour* and found an article on quick beauty remedies for the holiday season. Before I could finish reading it, there was a knock on my door. Gidget turned her head away from the glass and glared at the doorway.

"Come on in," I shouted.

My mom stepped in and stopped under the ceiling light. "Was that T.J. you were talking to a few minutes ago? I thought I heard you say his name. Is he doing okay? He hasn't been around much the last few months."

"T.J.'s fine." I chuckled as Gidget jumped to the floor and playfully pawed at the shimmering reflections coming from the rhinestones on my mother's cardigan. "We haven't had much time together with finals and all, and when he's free, he's with Meg."

"Do you think it's serious between them?"

"I don't know." I shrugged. "Most of the time, they seem to get along good enough, but then there are days like yesterday and…well, who knows?"

She sat down on the bed next to me. "What happened?"

"Well, Meg is Miss Ohio States of America, and she and Shelly had evening gowns that were too similar for the national pageant they were both in. Meg ended up having to buy a new dress. T.J. said he had never seen her so angry, and it really bothered him." I cocked my head. "But I'm sure they'll work it out."

"Perhaps he'll come to his—"

The phone rang, startling Gidget, who was still trying to capture the mysterious moving specks.

"Maybe that's Rick," I said.

Mom looked puzzled.

"I called him earlier and left a message." I picked up the

receiver, and when I heard the voice on the other end, I mouthed, "It's Rick."

As Mom went downstairs, I returned to my comfy spot on the bed. "Would it be all right with you and your mom if we got everyone from the Commuter Lounge together to brainstorm ways to help her? Craig's offered to have us all over at his place tonight."

"I don't see why not. It'll be nice to get out of the house. Between my dad, Sarah, and her lawyer son stopping by, it's been like we have a revolving front door around here. Strange, but in a weird way, I think it's helping my mom feel better. At least she knows she has people who believe in her."

I patiently listened as he rambled on about the day's events. I gathered he needed someone to talk to, and I was more than happy to oblige. When our discussion of solving crimes morphed into the new James Bond movie, his mood noticeably brightened. *Man With the Golden Gun* was coming out later in the week, leading us to debate who played the best 007—Roger Moore or Sean Connery. Ultimately, we agreed it was too early to tell since Moore was a relative newbie, having only played the secret agent once.

"You know," Rick said, "the only viable solution is to see the *Golden Gun* after this mess with the fitness center is cleared up. You wanna go?"

"Yeah, that sounds like fun!"

I hung up, baffled. Did he just ask me on a date, or were we going to the movie as friends? Sometimes, this whole relationship thing with guys was so confusing.

Not sure what to make of it all, I pushed it to the back of my mind and called T.J. to tell him it was okay to call everyone about tonight. "Sarah's at his house and volunteered to stay with his mom while he's gone. Perfect timing!"

"I'm glad Rick and his mom are cool with us helping," T.J. said.

I wholeheartedly agreed. "It would be so awesome if we

could figure this whole thing out and clear the fitness center's name before Christmas. Wouldn't that be the best present ever?"

"Guess we better get crackin' then. Nothing like a deadline to motivate the troops." T.J. laughed. "You wanna ride with Meg and me to Craig's house? No sense both of us driving."

"Sure, that'd be great."

I stared at the Edgar Degas poster of *The Ballet Class* hanging on my wall and leaned against my pillow. I was looking forward to this evening and seeing everyone. Yet, I suddenly felt anxious about seeing T.J. and Craig. But why? T.J. was my best friend since first grade. And Craig? Although I didn't know him well, I found him intriguing. As much as I wanted to ignore my connection with them, I couldn't deny it existed.

chapter six

T.J. convinced his father to let him borrow the Ford F-100—his father's pride and joy—since our country roads were still not plowed by the time we had to leave for Craig's house.

As I climbed into the truck, T.J. was beaming, sitting in the driver's seat. My short legs struggled to maneuver around the tools his father stored on the floorboard in the backseat. T. J. often said his dad wanted to be prepared for any emergency, and seeing everything stashed in the back, I believed he had succeeded. Should the Cold War escalate, Mr. Wilson would be more than ready.

It didn't take long, however, for me to regret agreeing to ride with T.J. and Meg. Neither one said anything to me except for the obligatory greeting of "hello" when I got into the car. After watching Meg whisper in T.J.'s ear several times and the glances they exchanged, there was no doubt I was the proverbial third wheel.

Meg turned toward me and flashed a victor's smile before settling her head on T.J.'s shoulder. Everything in me wanted to tell her to back off...that she had won, but I stayed quiet, knowing I had never been competing with her for T.J.'s affections. After all, T.J. and I were just friends, right? Nothing more and nothing less. *So why does Meg infuriate me so?* I stared out the window and quietly sang "A Holly Jolly Christmas" with Burl Ives. A single tear trailed down my cheek.

After the longest thirty minutes of my life—or at least it seemed that way—we passed through a black, wrought-iron gate. We proceeded down a long driveway lined with evergreen trees. At the end of the drive, the imposing brick Georgian house, the Peterson Manor, stood before us. The view was breathtaking. The house was three stories tall, with chimneys at both ends and an elaborate doorway. I felt like Elizabeth Bennet in *Pride and Prejudice* when she saw Mr. Darcy's Pemberley for the first time.

T.J. and Meg led the way to the massive porch flanked by two stone lions standing guard. T.J. raised his fist to knock on the door but stopped when he caught sight of the brass door knocker—a lion's head. With a mischievous grin, he turned toward Meg. "You don't suppose it will turn into the ghost of Jacob Marley, do you?"

After giving the door knocker a couple of swift raps, he waited. The door opened just as he raised his hand to strike again. I expected to see a butler attired in black tails, but, to my disappointment, it was Craig clad in jeans, a white button-down oxford shirt, and a blue tweed blazer. Not quite as impressive, I mused. However, whatever letdown I felt gave way to unbridled delight when I spotted the Christmas tree adorning the entryway. The ornate spiral staircase, draped with evergreen garland and red velvet bows, stretched to the third-floor balcony while Craig's sandy blond hair glistened under the crystal chandelier. I stood still, awestruck.

"Michelle...Michelle?" Craig's voice jarred me back to reality.

"Oh, I'm sorry. Yes?" I said.

His eyes twinkled as he extended his arm. "May I take your coat?"

Charmed by his old-fashioned manners, I smiled and

slipped my arms out of my coat, taking in the woodsy scent of his cologne.

He hung our coats in the nearby closet and explained, "My great-grandfather built this house in 1900. Not much has changed since then, so I want to remodel it this spring. Bring it up to the 1970s, if you know what I mean. I want to keep its architectural heritage but make it feel more like a home instead of a museum."

"It's beautiful!" I exclaimed. "I wouldn't change a thing."

"I'm glad you like it. I was afraid you would think it was too much."

"Quite the contrary. It's perfect!"

"The old house has great bones, doesn't it?" Craig smiled. "Let me take you guys to the family room, and I can show you what I've done there. Excuse the boxes everywhere." He started down the hallway, scooting a few moving boxes closer to the wall as he went by. "Some of my stuff from my apartment arrived yesterday, and I haven't had time to unpack them."

"Are you giving up your place in New York?" I asked as I walked beside him.

"No, not yet. I'm still thinking about it. Between meetings with my agent and doing the talk show circuit when I write a new book, I'll be in the city several times a year. Staying at a hotel is an option, but I enjoy having my own bed to sleep in, so I'm leaning toward keeping my place for now, but I can always sell it if I change my mind." He laughed. "Although my friends in real estate cringe whenever they hear me say that. They think I'd be a fool to let it go now because they're convinced prices will skyrocket in the Big Apple." He tilted his head to one side and raised his eyebrows. "It might be an investment worth hanging on to if nothing else. We'll see, but first, I want to give the Peterson Lumber Company my best shot. Who knows? I may be so bad at running the business my grandfather founded that the board might pay me to stay away." He chuckled.

Craig opened a pair of wooden doors and ushered us into a darkly paneled room. A crackling fire welcomed us, illuminating two symmetrically arranged brown leather Chesterfield sofas with matching armchairs on either side. A beige and black Persian rug covered the floor.

Instinctively, I began untying my brown leather oxfords, wet from the snow, before stepping onto the tapestry. T.J. and Meg followed my lead and slipped off their loafers.

Craig smiled warmly. "It's all right if you want to leave your shoes on. I'm sure this rug has seen much worse than snow."

My cheeks grew hot, embarrassed by feeling like I had committed a faux pas. All I could think of was my parents and how they freaked out whenever someone tracked dirt onto their carpets—and they weren't even super nice floor coverings. *Do people with money not mind getting their expensive rugs dirty, or is it just Craig?* Maybe he didn't realize how much rugs cost. But surely he did. If I knew Persian rugs were pricey, he had to know.

Trying to push my embarrassment aside, I turned toward T.J. and Meg and took their shoes from their hands, placing them next to mine in front of the fireplace. "It'll be nice to have warm shoes to wear when we go home."

"Warm feet, happy heart, or something like that," Craig joked.

I squinted and shook my head, grinning. "What are you talking about?"

He laughed. "Oh, I don't know. But, changing subjects, what do you think of my new furniture? They delivered it Friday."

Meg ran her fingers along the arm of the sofa. "Genuine leather."

T.J. rolled his eyes as Craig said with a fake sigh, "I'm glad I didn't pay through the nose for vinyl."

"It looks nice." I nodded. "You did a good job."

"I wish I could take credit for it, but the interior decorator put it all together. Words I can craft, but room decor is beyond me."

The doorbell rang.

"Pizza and drinks are in the kitchen." Craig pointed toward the door on the other side of the room. "Help yourselves, and I'll see who's at the door."

I followed T.J. and Meg as they strolled arm-in-arm into the kitchen. With their heads close together, they laughed and joked as they headed for the pizza on the countertop. As I placed my slice of pepperoni pizza onto a paper plate, Meg whispered something to T.J., and he abruptly pulled away. A chilly tension filled the room.

Craig soon entered, followed by Lawrence, Amy, and Yash.

"Need something, T.J.?" Craig asked.

T.J. looked around the kitchen. "Do you have anything besides soft drinks?"

"Not tonight. I thought it would be better to keep our heads clear. That way, I don't have to worry about anyone drinking and driving on those roads. I've already had enough of that in my family."

Craig didn't have to say another word. We were all aware that despite his father's death being wrongly attributed to alcohol, the accident had made him keenly aware of the dangers of drinking and driving.

The doorbell chimed again, and within a few minutes, everyone from the Commuter Lounge group who was in town over the holidays had arrived. T.J. and Meg settled on the floor in front of the fireplace while Rick and Yash sat on one sofa, and Lawrence and Jimmy took up residence on the other.

Tasha surveyed the room until Yash scooted over, making room between him and Rick on the couch. She sank into its cushion, cross-legged with her dark green maxi peasant dress almost touching the floor. Jimmy commandeered an armchair, and Amy positioned herself on the chair's arm, draping her arm around his shoulders.

I studied my seating options and saw two possibilities—a spot on the floor near T.J. and a cozy-looking cushion next to Craig's chair. After deliberating momentarily, I turned toward T.J. but stopped when I heard a thumping sound. Craig was tapping the floor next to the cushion by his chair.

"Why don't you sit here? Or, if you prefer, you can have my chair, and I'll sit on the cushion."

Revamping my seating plan, I said, "No, don't do that. The cushion will be fine."

Craig kicked off our investigative jam session as I nestled into my seat. He picked up a small yellow writing tablet from the table next to him and retrieved a pen from the pocket inside his blazer. "Rick, how's your mother doing?"

"She's upset and…. worried, really worried." Rick tugged at the sleeve of his brown paisley shirt. "With all this publicity about the accident, she's concerned no one will come to the fitness center, and she's got a three-year lease, plus all that equipment she bought. It's not looking good with Shelly's parents possibly filing a wrongful death lawsuit against the place."

"That's why we're here," Craig stated matter-of-factly. "To put our heads together and see if anything was amiss that might have led to the treadmill malfunctioning." He looked everyone over in the room and then refocused his attention on Rick. "Your mother had everything inspected before the Open House, right?"

Rick's face flushed red, and his brown eyes widened as he glared at Craig. "Of course she did. My mother would never cut corners and put people at risk."

Craig shook his head and waved his hand. "Look, man, I'm not saying your mother did anything wrong, but this is a question that needs to be asked so we can get to the cause of the problem. All right? Are we cool?"

Rick slumped back into his seat. His eyes locked on Craig's face. "Sure. I'm just tired of everybody accusing my mom of doing something wrong."

"We're on your side," I said softly, hoping to diffuse the situation. "Craig is just trying to gather all the facts so we can figure out what happened."

"Exactly," said Craig. "That brings me to my next point. Lawrence, is there anything on the autopsy report?"

"No." He pushed his round wire-rimmed glasses up the bridge of his nose. "That'll take a few more days, but I'll let you know as soon as I hear something."

"Okay. I guess since we don't know if Shelly had any preexisting conditions that may have led to her falling off the treadmill or being physically unable to stop the machine, we'll assume she died from head trauma like the doctor originally thought."

"We'll have a definitive answer when the medical examiner releases his report," said Lawrence as he unbuttoned his camo jacket and headed to the kitchen.

"Is there anything we can do in the meantime?" asked Amy, leaning on Jimmy's shoulder and swinging her jean-clad legs. "Or do we just sit and wait?"

"For starters, I think we need to investigate Mr. Langford and Carl Westwood," I stated.

"Why Carl? What'd he do?" Rick's eyes narrowed.

"Right before Shelly's accident, he gave the treadmill quite the once-over."

"Maybe he was curious about how it worked? There's no crime in that, is there?" Rick shook his head, and his posture grew rigid.

Despite Rick not appreciating my suspicions about Carl, I

pressed on. "What's the big deal about checking him out? Don't you think it was strange he was on the floor looking underneath the treadmill—"

"Plus, there's the fact that Carl is Mr. Langford's brother," Craig added.

"Who is this Langford?" T.J. asked as he leaned toward Craig.

Lawrence, holding his plate as he stood behind the couch, answered. "He's the guy who opened that gym across town at the beginning of summer."

"How do you know about Mr. Langford?" I asked.

"From one of the reports I read this morning." He smirked.

"But these two dudes have different last names," piped Amy as she straightened up and fluffed her long, light brown hair over her shoulders.

Craig spoke up. "Carl's an author and uses Westwood as his pen name, although I'm not sure why he's going by that name in Petersburg. We need to check that out as well. It seems we've got a couple of different angles to follow up on. Where should we start?"

I thought for a moment. "Until we learn otherwise, let's assume someone caused the treadmill to malfunction. We can look into Mr. Langford's gym and see how it's doing financially. You know, find out if he had a motive to sabotage Caroline's business." I shrugged and continued. "Maybe no one was supposed to get hurt. Maybe he simply wanted to have people question the safety of Caroline's fitness center so they would go to his gym instead."

Yash, our resident business major, spoke up. "If they've only been open a few months, it's doubtful they're turning a profit...most businesses take three to five years before they're in the black."

Nodding, I added, "Good point. Perhaps we should look into whether Mr. Langford borrowed any capital to start his gym and, if he did, who gave him the loan. And—" I paused briefly, "maybe find out how much his monthly payments are and if he's keeping up with them?"

Yash lowered the zipper on his pullover sweater and added, "Yeah, and is he bringing in enough money to cover his other bills, or is he using money he has in savings?"

"For the sake of argument," Tasha said as she adjusted her skirt, "even if this Langford dude is strapped for money, it doesn't prove anything."

"True, but if I learned one thing from investigating Professor Ladd's murder, it's to follow the money," I said.

T.J. rubbed the stubble on his chin. "And exactly how are we gonna do that?"

I looked at Craig. "Do you think you could talk to Burt Ladd? Since he was married to your aunt, maybe he could help? He's still the district manager for Petersburg Savings & Loan, right?"

Craig nodded.

I continued. "If Mr. Langford didn't get the money from Burt's bank, then perhaps he'll have some ideas on where to look or who loaned him the money."

"I'll ask Burt. I haven't spoken to him since Steve and Barb's arraignment for Anne's murder, but it might be a good opportunity to get better acquainted with him. We got off to a rocky start, considering he didn't know I was Anne's nephew and thought we were having an affair."

I nodded. "Yeah, that was a bit awkward."

Craig winced and then turned toward Lawrence. "Can you find out if Mr. Sam Langford or Carl Westwood has a criminal record?"

"Shouldn't be a problem."

Craig continued. "If we can prove Mr. Langford is financially in trouble with his gym, we can establish a motive and opportunity for tampering with the treadmill." He glanced in my direction. "You might have been right about the brothers working together."

"You're agreeing with me?"

"For the time being." He smiled.

I wanted to respond with something clever, but I was at a loss for words. Instead, I just stared into his green eyes and grinned. For a moment, it felt like time had stopped. I looked around the room and saw all eyes fixed on us.

Luckily, Yash diverted everyone's attention when he rose from his seat. "Has anyone checked out the rest of the exercise machines to see if anyone tampered with them?" He raised his can of orange pop to his lips and took several swigs while we looked at each other and shook our heads.

"Sounds like we need to check out all the equipment at the fitness center. How do we do that?" I asked, exasperated.

Rick was silent for a moment but then spoke up. "We could schedule a maintenance call with the installers. I have no idea how long it would take for someone to come out or how much it would cost, but I can look into it."

"Maybe my dad and I could help," Jimmy volunteered as he sat up, forcing Amy to remove her head from his shoulder. He pushed up the sleeves of his blue cardigan sweater. "He and I have worked on enough cars. We can check for anything that looks out of place or suspicious. We might not be experts on treadmills, but we can narrow down any equipment that needs a professional inspection."

"Do you think your mom would be okay having Jimmy and his dad look things over?" I asked Rick.

"I don't see why not. There shouldn't be a problem if they don't work on anything."

Jimmy nodded in agreement. "We'll make sure not to void the warranty."

Lawrence and Yash carried their empty dishes to the kitchen while Tasha followed close behind. T.J. went to talk to Rick.

Craig nudged me. "What's wrong? You look like you're in deep thought."

"There's got to be something else—"

"We're checking out the money—"

"And all the equipment." I stopped mid-sentence and strode over to where T.J. and Rick were discussing something in hushed tones. "Rick, tell me about Paul. The guy who works for your mom at the fitness center."

"I don't know much about him. He's a senior at U. P., studying to be a doctor...has an apartment...and, as you know, used to date Shelly until she dumped him for some other guy." He shrugged. "That's about it."

Amy slipped next to Rick. "Paul and my brother are friends. They're both pre-med students, so they study together at our house on the weekends. I can tell you that Shelly really hurt him when she broke things off. He hoped they could get back—"

Rick interjected, "I don't want to say anything that might incriminate the guy 'cause he's been a big help to my mom, but I overheard him and Shelly arguing the other day. It was intense. He said the only way she would ever be out of his head was if she was dead."

I cringed. "That sounds a little cryptic."

Amy grabbed Rick's arm. "I can't believe Paul would hurt her."

"I agree," Rick replied. "I don't think he meant it. People say a lot of things they don't mean when they're angry."

"But sometimes they say exactly what they've been thinking. Could he have tampered with the treadmill?" I asked.

Rick shook his head. "I don't think he'd do something like that, and even if he wanted to, how would he have known which treadmill Shelly would get on or if she would even get on one that night?"

I raised an eyebrow. "Did Shelly often exercise on a treadmill?"

"Hard to say since we just opened." Rick sighed. "I know she tried them out when they first came in, but other than that, I don't know. She might have stopped by and used them when Mom was at the fitness center and I was in class."

"Well—" I said, "considering the fight I witnessed between Paul and Shelly in the parking lot yesterday morning, I wouldn't rule out his involvement with the treadmill. Of course, he wasn't the only one upset with Shelly."

T.J. asked. "What do you mean?"

I turned toward Rick. "Do you remember when you went to get the key to the Jazzercise room?"

He nodded.

"I overheard Elaine and Shelly fighting…something about a piece of paper and info Shelly had on Elaine. We should probably find out what that was all about."

"It's no secret Elaine's not my favorite person," Rick said, "but I can't imagine Elaine feeling threatened by Shelly. Even if Elaine wanted to get back at her, she wouldn't know how to sabotage a treadmill."

"Could she have hired someone to tamper with it to cause trouble for your mother?" Amy asked.

"Wow!" I said. "We have no shortage of suspects, do we? I guess the only way to narrow the list down is to look at all the evidence. We've got Jimmy and his dad checking the equipment at the fitness center. Craig will investigate Mr. Langford's finances." I scanned the room. Lawrence was talking to Yash. "Lawrence can keep us posted on the medical examiner's report, and Rick, maybe you can keep an eye on Paul. Amy, can you check with your brother to see if Paul has been acting funny or has mentioned anything about Shelly or her death that seemed a little off?"

"What do you want me to do?" asked T.J.

"Would you mind checking out Carl? The library may have some articles about him since he's an author."

"What am I looking for?"

"I'm not sure," I shrugged. "But I'm most curious about his life in England, why he moved back here, and how he met Sarah."

"Unless the library has a British gossip section, I don't think I'll find it there." He laughed.

"No." I grinned. "Probably not, but that reminds me of something else. I need to talk to Mae and Mrs. Winterfield and see what they know. Plus, I want to find out what Shelly had on Elaine."

T.J. raised his brow. "And *how* are you going to do that?"

I paused for a moment and then scanned the room. "Where's Meg? I think I need to become a beauty contestant."

<h1 style="text-align: right">chapter seven</h1>

Monday, December 16th

With my mom's afghan securely tucked around me, I curled up in the recliner and looked out the picture window. My parents would soon be home from their last-minute Christmas shopping, making me all too aware that I had procrastinated calling Elaine all morning. It was now or never if I wanted to use the phone before they got back.

The problem was I had doubts about the plausibility of my concocted story. Yet, it was the best I could do. I took in a long breath and dialed her number.

"Hi, Ms. Anderson? This is Michelle Kilpatrick—a friend of Rick's. We met the other day at the fitness center."

"Yes, Michelle. What can I do for you?"

"I was wondering if I could meet with you and discuss the possibility of me entering a pageant."

"Was there a particular system you were interested in?"

"Well, I know I'm not ready for the major pageants like Miss USA and Miss America, but Meg Hathaway mentioned there were smaller systems that might be a better fit for me. I'm studying to be a reporter at U.P., and I thought doing pageants might help me develop more confidence, but I have no idea where to begin."

Despite Meg's run-down on the ins and outs of pageantry, there was no doubt I was out of my depth. Before last night's meeting at Craig's house, I had never considered doing a pageant. The only thing I knew about pageant contestants was that they were statuesque beauties, and, unfortunately, I was neither tall nor beautiful. As I tapped the pencil's eraser against my notepad, I listened to Elaine Anderson, all the while wondering if I could convince her I had what it took to compete.

"Pageants can certainly help women build their confidence. The interview sessions would be beneficial for you. Granted, you wouldn't be the one asking the questions, but you could learn how to conduct yourself and think quickly. Listen, I'd love to chat, but I'm on my way to a meeting. Why don't we have a late lunch at Grayson's, and we can talk at greater length about what is involved with being in a pageant and the financial commitment required. Would one thirty work for you?"

"That'd be great. Thanks. See you then." I hung up the phone, and Gidget jumped onto my lap, purring as I ran my trembling hand through her soft fur. "I'm in trouble, girl. Calling Elaine was the easy part but getting her to talk about Shelly and Caroline is an entirely different matter."

I stared out the window, letting out a heavy sigh as I clutched the Eiffel Tower charm dangling around my neck. Could I pull this off?

***

As I entered Grayson's, my glasses fogged up. Unable to see anything, I stepped away from the door, wiped my lenses against my coat sleeve, and knocked the snow off my boots. When the room came into view, I spotted Elaine giving a slight wave from a table in the back of the restaurant.

The hostess, with her bleach blonde curls cascading below her shoulders, was studying something on the wooden podium in front of her, but glanced up as I returned a wave to Elaine. "Are you meeting someone?"

"Yes, she's right over there," I said, pointing in Elaine's direction. "The woman with the dark hair in the black turtle-neck sweater."

The hostess put her pen down. *"You're* with Ms. Anderson?

"That's right."

"Really?" For a moment, she looked like she didn't believe me. "Mmm…may I take your coat?"

"No," I shook my head. "I'll keep it with me."

With narrowed eyes, she gave me the once-over. "As you wish. Now, if you'll walk this way."

Between chuckling as I remembered Dr. Frederick Frankenstein mimicking Igor's awkward gait in the new *Young Frankenstein* movie when he was told to "walk this way," and being distracted by a Cherry Jubilee Flambé about to go up in smoke, I forgot to pay attention to where I was walking.

The hostess's voice jolted me back to reality before I bumped into her. Frowning as she pulled out a chair at Elaine's table, she said, "Here you are. Your waiter will be with you shortly."

"Glad you could make it." Elaine looked up from the menu she had been reading and smiled, oblivious to my near-catastrophic entrance. The soft layers of her brunette hair framed her face as her eyes locked onto my coat.

"Wasn't there someone available to check your coat?"

"Yes, but I wanted to keep it with me."

With her pursed lips, she muttered, "How quaint."

My shoulders sank. *Nothing like getting off on the wrong foot.*

Trying to regain my composure, I smiled as I slipped out of my coat, draping it over the back of my chair. "Thanks for meeting me today."

"My first appointment in the afternoon canceled last night, so it worked out perfectly." Elaine's eyes returned to her menu, where they stayed until the waiter came to our table and asked if we were ready to order.

With a coy smile, she looked directly at the 20-ish-year-old man, who happened to be tall, dark, and handsome. "Yes, I'll have the chef's salad with ranch dressing on the side...and anything else you might suggest." Elaine bowed her head, looking up at him with her emerald green eyes.

A slight blush came over his cheeks as he asked, "And...would...would you like something to drink?"

"A cup of coffee. Thank you."

He dutifully turned toward me and, without so much as a smile, asked, "And for you?" His fingers drummed impatiently against his leg as he waited for me to reply.

"I'll have the flounder with a plain baked potato...and a diet pop, please."

Elaine chuckled as she watched the waiter walk away from our table. Once he disappeared around the corner, she turned her full attention to me. "Why do you want to enter a pageant?"

I leaned back in my chair. "I'm a little shy, and I thought doing pageants might help me come out of my shell."

The waiter returned with our glasses of water and my soft drink, serving Elaine first. I sipped the bubbly caramel-colored liquid, trying to quench the dryness brought on by a severe case of nerves. Her disapproving gaze left no doubt I was not up to her standards. How was I going to segue into a discussion about Shelly if she ended our conversation because she did not see me as a potential client?

I set my glass down and cleared my throat. "Ms. Anderson, I just want to improve myself. I want to graduate and get a job that lets me see the world. Is there anything wrong with that? And I've never thought about entering a pageant because I didn't think ordinary girls like me could enter them."

"First, please call me Elaine, and second, why do you think you're ordinary?"

"Well, for starters, I'm not tall and I don't think I'm beautiful, but Meg said you could help me with my appearance."

"Come, come. I'm not a miracle worker, but with proper training and money, a lot is possible. You understand competing in pageants is an investment—clothes, coaching, travel expenses, and entrance fees? Did Meg mention any of that?"

"No."

"I didn't think so." Her eyes darted to my weather-worn leather bag hanging over my coat.

Ignoring her condescending attitude, I leaned forward. "That's why I wanted to meet with you—to find out whether this is something I could pursue."

Elaine sat back in her chair. "I see."

She took a bite of her salad, and I seized the moment to change the subject. "Are you from around here?"

"No, I grew up in a small town in Indiana and moved to Petersburg a couple of years ago."

"Indiana? Anywhere near Indianapolis? That's such a cool city!"

"No, I'm afraid not. I grew up in Bicknell. It's about two hours southwest of Indianapolis." Elaine flipped her hair and drew a deep breath. "Before I was born, it was a big coal mining town, but about fifty years ago, the mines started closing, and a lot of people moved away. Bicknell is trying to come back, but I suppose it will take time."

"What did you do in Bicknell?"

The color drained from her face as she stumbled, trying to come up with an answer. "I...I got an education degree at

Vincennes University." She paused and pushed the salad around with her fork. "When I moved back to Bicknell, I wanted to find a teaching job, but when nothing opened up, I took odd jobs. Then, some friends from the university who were into pageants asked me to help them prep for the interview part of the competition. One thing led to another, and I started my own business as a pageant coach. The best decision I ever made."

"What made you decide to move here?"

Elaine took a bite of her salad and glanced out the window, where the snow-covered trees glistened in the afternoon sun. "Several girls I coached were from Ohio and Michigan. So, when looking for a change, it seemed the logical choice."

When the waiter stopped at our table and asked if we wanted any dessert or needed anything else, he and Elaine shared flirtatious glances. After he left, she chuckled. "Boys… some of them are so easy to manipulate. A little smile here, a glance there, and they're eating out of your hands." Elaine's ruby red lips formed a half smile before starting her well-rehearsed monologue about the different pageant systems and their requirements, emphasizing the amount of money needed for each one.

"Before we proceed, I need to know your level of commitment to pageantry. I could have you ready for some of the mid-size pageants in six months if you are willing to lose… let's say….maybe ten pounds and start a workout regime with a trainer. If not, perhaps one of the smaller ones. Regardless, you will need a new wardrobe for interview, as well as for swimsuit, evening gown, and the talent segment. You do have a talent, don't you?" Elaine picked up her cup and peered at me over the rim.

Her words cut through the air like a sharp blade, and my stomach clenched tightly as her eyes looked straight through me. I sat up and shifted in my seat. "Of course, I have a talent. I...I just haven't decided which one I want to use."

Elaine smirked but remained silent as she took a sip of her coffee. The click of her cup on the saucer echoed in my ears as I desperately searched for a way to shift the conversation away from my lack of pageant suitability to her relationship with Shelly.

"Like I said earlier, I think doing pageants would help with my confidence and my public speaking skills. Even though I only met Shelly once, she impressed me with a confidence I wish I had." I paused. "It was so sad what happened. What a terrible accident!"

Elaine held her cup in mid-air as she stared out the window, saying nothing for a few moments before she set it down.

"Yes, it is a shame. Shelly was a talented young woman."

A thought came to me, and I wasted no time playing my hunch. "Paul must be taking it pretty hard."

"I'm sure he is. They had been dating for quite a while."

"Mind if I ask how you know Paul?"

She froze and shot me an icy glare. "I don't know him well. I run into him sometimes at Dr. McGuire's office. Paul is researching the effects of various toxins on the human body, and Marvin is helping him with it. We chat occasionally. That's about it."

"Any idea why Shelly broke up with him?"

Elaine grimaced. "Probably because she was nothing more than a money-grabbing social climber."

"But wouldn't dating a doctor be a step up?" I stopped, remembering that Elaine was, in fact, engaged to a doctor. "I...I...mean, a guy who wants to be a doctor."

"Common misconception that all doctors are rich. If only that were true." She attempted a half-hearted smile. "But the problem with Shelly was that while she worked to advance her social standing, she didn't care who she hurt." Elaine breathed in deeply. "Shelly made a lot of enemies along the way, but that's what happens when you focus on yourself and put your desires above everyone else's. Paul is better off without her. It may just take him some time to realize it."

"Do you think someone could have tampered with the treadmill to hurt Shelly?"

Elaine snapped up in her seat. "I wouldn't think so. Seems like a far-fetched idea to me."

"You're right. I'm just having a hard time believing a brand new treadmill caused Shelly's death."

Elaine leaned over the table. "What else could it have been? Have you heard something from the police? You and that detective on the force are friends, aren't you?" She tapped her chin thoughtfully.

"Friends is a bit of a stretch. Our paths crossed while we each tried to find Professor Ladd's killer." I paused. "But, no, I haven't heard anything. Call it my gift of suspicion. It gets me curious when someone has enemies and then dies under unusual circumstances." I drew a deep breath, mustering the courage to continue with my probe for information. "Plenty of people didn't like Shelly. Even you said you didn't get along with her...and then there are the rumors."

Elaine slammed her fork against the plate. "What is it you're trying to say?"

Stalling for time so I could choose my words wisely, I took a sip of my diet pop. "It's probably just a baseless rumor."

Elaine cradled her chin in her hands while keeping her eyes focused on mine. "Oh, do tell. There's nothing better than juicy gossip."

I glanced around the room, ensuring no one was listening, and lowered my voice. "Well, word is Shelly found something from your past and was using it to blackmail you."

Elaine rolled her eyes as she leaned back in her seat. "Is that all?" She laughed. "Please, that couldn't be further from the truth. I have no doubt Shelly was capable of blackmail, but don't believe everything you hear—I was not one of Shelly's victims."

"Oh, good, I'm glad." I feigned relief. "Being blackmailed would be horrible." I smiled. "How long had you known Shelly?"

"Long is such a vague word." Elaine returned to staring out the window, leaving her statement hanging in the air. After a few seconds of silence, she shifted her weight and started again, her voice low and hesitant. "Our paths crossed from time to time since I moved here. I coached Shelly for two, maybe three, pageants—strictly a business relationship. We spent our sessions practicing how to walk on the stage, different poses to strike, and how to answer interview questions. There wasn't much time for idle chitchat. Sorry, but most of what I know about Shelly comes from other people's opinions of her."

She paused and looked me squarely in the eyes as she rubbed her finger against her chin. "Tell me, why did you contact me about being your pageant coach?"

"Meg and I were talking about pageants last night, and when I mentioned I might want to try one, she recommended that I call you. Rick overheard our conversation and gave me your number."

"I'm surprised Meg suggested you call me, considering how upset she was with me the other day. I was under the impression she was thinking about dropping me as her coach." Elaine crossed her arms and leaned back in her chair. "Fascinating. And Rick? You say *he* gave you my number?"

She paused while our server removed the empty plates from our table and inquired if we wanted dessert, to which we both replied, "No."

After he left, Elaine continued. "That Rick would give you my number surprises me as well."

I shrugged. "Guess he was trying to be helpful."

"Seems a bit strange, wouldn't you say?"

"Why?" I shifted in my chair, feeling the unease rising between us.

"Two people who are upset with me suggest you hire me as a coach when, until last night, you've never thought about doing a pageant. Am I missing something?" She took a sip of coffee and stared at me.

I shrugged, trying to appear unconcerned while wondering how to prevent Elaine from discovering my ruse. Despite wanting to end this topic, I forced my gaze to meet hers. "I think they knew I was excited about doing something new. The way Meg described pageantry made it sound so enticing."

Remembering Shelly was from Indiana, I saw a way to change the subject. "Did Shelly live near Bicknell?"

"Not too far away."

"Was she easy to get along with when you first met her, or did she always like to manipulate people by holding things over their heads?"

Elaine's eyes grew wide as she shifted in her seat and set her coffee cup on the table with a thud. Her voice quavered as she glanced at her watch. "I would love to stay and chat longer, but I didn't realize it was so late! I have another appointment in half an hour."

She raised her hand and waved to the waiter, who soon appeared at our table with a black folder, which he placed before her, flashing a broad smile.

I reached for the folder. "I can take my bill."

"Oh, no. My treat. Besides, it's tax-deductible—a business expense." Elaine laughed and placed thirty dollars in the folder. She stood up and tugged at one of her sleeves. "Think about what we've discussed, and if you want to compete, call me and let me know your level of commitment. We'll look at the pageant schedule and find one that's a suitable match."

I swallowed hard, feeling stuck between the proverbial rock and a hard place. I didn't want to compete in a pageant, but I also didn't want to close the door in case I needed to talk to her again. "Sounds good. Thanks so much for all the information. I have a lot to think about."

I trailed behind Elaine and waited as she got her coat from the hostess. After she hurriedly buttoned her navy-blue wool coat with a large golden YSL embroidered on the front, she covered her eyes with a pair of oversized, black-rimmed sunglasses. We exited through the double doors and parted ways. I went to my faithful Orange Bomb, and she to her white Lincoln Continental. As I brushed the snow off my car's windows, I kept an eye on Elaine as she cleared hers. *I wonder where her appointment is? Dare I follow her?*

In spy mode, I followed Elaine as she drove to the other side of town, staying far enough behind her so she wouldn't notice me. When she finally stopped at Langford's Fitness Club, I pulled into the strip mall lot across the street. Elaine sat in her car until a vehicle parked next to her. A man emerged and walked to the sidewalk. I gasped. It was Carl Westwood. He and Elaine embraced and then disappeared inside the building.

I have to talk to Lawrence—now!

chapter eight

The drive to the police station only took about ten minutes. At three o'clock in the afternoon in Petersburg, traffic was almost nonexistent. I chuckled, thinking that our version of *rush hour* was having to sit through two red lights. Not exactly the same inconvenience experienced in the big city, but still, we complained.

When I stepped inside the brick building, I did a double-take after wiping the fog off my glasses. The festive décor caught me off guard. I never expected the place where the men in blue worked to be transformed with holiday cheer. Even Lawrence, wearing a red tie decorated with green Christmas trees, surprised me. He reminded me of one of Santa's elves as he sorted papers with his wire-rimmed glasses halfway down his nose.

"Hi, Lawrence! How's it going?"

He peered over the rim of his glasses and, with the slightest of smiles, said, "Not bad. Still snowing, I see. What brings you here?"

"Would it be possible for you to get me some information on Shelly? She was from Indiana in a city close to Bicknell. Can you find out which one?"

Lawrence pushed his glasses up. "I'll ask Detective Douglas when he gets back, and I can let you know."

"Thanks. So, is he heading up the case?"

"Yep, that's what I heard when I came in this morning."

"But he only handles murders, right?"

Lawrence nodded.

I leaned over the counter. "Is it officially a murder investigation? Did the medical examiner uncover something suspicious?"

Lawrence shook his head. "Not that I know of, but Douglas has his doubts about her death being accidental."

"Really?"

He laughed. "Don't act so surprised! Even you have questions about the accident."

"True, but for Douglas and me to agree on anything is nothing short of a Christmas miracle." I chuckled.

Lawrence picked up a stack of papers and sorted them into three piles. "We won't know anything until the M.E. releases his report later this week. But maybe things will move faster since Shelly's family and their attorney are putting pressure on the guy to finish quickly so he can release Shelly's body." He stopped sorting his papers and glanced up. "As far as Douglas is concerned, the cause of death is undetermined until we get the official findings."

I nodded. "Do you think Shelly could have had some kind of underlying medical condition that contributed to her death?"

"That's probably why Douglas wanted a copy of her medical records, but from what I've heard, nothing is out of the ordinary about her health. Shelly's last physical was two weeks ago, and her bloodwork was unremarkable." Lawrence resumed sorting the papers while I stood, deep in thought.

I said, "When Shelly climbed onto the treadmill that night, she was exhausted and seemed to struggle to keep her balance.

I know she was trying to lose weight for the pageant, but I remember thinking she probably had a good workout teaching her class and could surely skip…." I paused and ran my fingers obsessively over the silver chain around my neck. "Hmmm…."

"What?" Lawrence's eyebrows came together, puzzled.

"Rick said Shelly cut the class short that night. I really have to talk to Mrs. Winterfield. Hopefully, she'll stop in at Mae's soon. She was in Shelly's Jazzercise class that night, and if anyone noticed something unusual with Shelly, it would be her. Mrs. Winterfield never misses anything."

***

Driving home, I turned on the radio and listened to Christmas music to clear my head of all the murder stuff occupying my thoughts. It was hard to enjoy the holiday season being absorbed in death. For a few minutes, I wanted to forget Shelly's fatal accident. Yet, no matter how loudly I sang with Elton John's "Step into Christmas," the image of Shelly's body being wheeled out of the fitness center haunted me. The only way to save the holidays was to find the cause of her death.

As I turned into my driveway, I saw my tire tracks from this morning covered by the day's snowfall. Fortunately, the caution tape streamers my father tied to the wooden stakes outlining the driveway made getting to my parking spot under the basketball hoop manageable.

With the front porch steps buried under snow, I gingerly slid my foot across each one until I found a secure foothold and then searched for the next one. After knocking the snow off my shoes, I hurried inside, where the aroma of a pot roast and homemade bread enveloped me like a warm, fuzzy blanket.

I followed the scent to the kitchen and found my mom and dad eating. In unison, they looked up.

"Cut it a little close, didn't you?" My father growled as he pointed at his watch. "You're lucky there's any food left." He grabbed a knife, cut a piece of roast beef, and put it on his plate.

The rooster clock hanging on the wall revealed the cause of his angry mood. It was ten minutes after four. I was late for the four o'clock suppertime my mom had planned so we could all eat together, and my father, a stickler for punctuality, had no tolerance for late arrivals.

"Guess I lost track of time."

"You have a watch, don't you?" My dad asked between bites.

I shook my head. "Yes, I forgot to look at it."

"Forgetting seems to be a habit with you," he muttered as he reached for the bowl of mashed potatoes.

I took a deep breath and pulled out my chair. "Supper smells delicious, Mom."

As I cut a piece of the roast and spooned some potatoes and carrots onto my plate, Gidget rubbed against my legs— her ploy to get fed. Despite her loud purring, I couldn't give in to her request now, not with my father already upset with me. I gently patted her head, hoping to divert her attention, but it was neither love nor attention she craved. In a daring move, she stood on her hind legs and stretched her paws onto my lap to better make her point.

"Must that cat always be in the kitchen when we're eating?" my father grumbled.

Ignoring his comment, I kept my eyes fixed on my plate. Despite his gruff talk, I knew he had a soft spot for Gidget. After all, he chose the silver-haired kitten and named her after a character from the T.V. show by the same name. More than once, I had spied him slipping her a spoonful of vanilla ice cream when he thought no one was looking, but I would never tell.

After dinner, my mom and I cleared the kitchen table, and

my father retired to the living room. Soon the sounds of "Deck the Halls" from his Guy Lombardo Christmas record filled the house. But before the song finished, the shrill ringing of the telephone broke the holiday mood. The record stopped, and my father shouted, "Michelle! Phone!"

I dried my hands on the hand towel hanging on the oven door and hurried into the living room. He handed me the receiver as I asked, "Who is it?"

"How should I know? Do I look like your answering service?"

Fortunately, he did not see me roll my eyes as I turned away and put the receiver to my ear. "Hello?"

It was Craig. "Your idea about checking out Sam Langford's finances was spot on. Burt told me Langford took out a loan with Peterburg Savings & Loan. He couldn't tell me any specifics, but I got the distinct impression this guy might have a cash flow problem. We need more info on his finances."

"How are we going to do that? It's not like he's going to tell us." I tugged the phone to my perch on the stairs.

"No, but he might share his financials with a potential investor."

"Any idea who that investor might be?" I laughed, knowing full well Craig had something planned.

I listened as he painstakingly explained his idea, and as crazy as it sounded, I agreed it was worth a try.

"Good, glad you're on board because I've already scheduled to meet Langford at his gym tomorrow."

"What time?"

"Noon." He paused. "Why?"

"I don't work until tomorrow night, so I can go with you."

His tone grew serious. "I think I can handle this on my own."

"I'm sure you can, but that's not the point. Rick is my friend, and I'm not going to let you leave me out of this investigation. I'm going with you."

He said nothing.

I looked around the living room and, not seeing my father, continued. "Craig, we can go together, or I'll meet you at the gym. Which way do you want it?"

"Fine," he grunted. "But how am I going to explain why you're with me? Most men don't even take their wives to business meetings, let alone some random girl."

My blood pressure began to rise. Sometimes, Craig was such a jerk! I ran through potential scenarios until I landed on one—not perfect, but plausible.

"What if I was your fiancé? You know, a modern woman who *is* involved with her future husband's finances. That would work, wouldn't it?"

"Why, Michelle, I had no idea you cared. Are you proposing?" There was mischief in his voice.

"Oh, get over yourself. I'm simply trying to come up with an idea so your plan will work. Got any better ideas?"

chapter nine

At eleven-thirty sharp, Craig pulled his silver Jaguar into my driveway. Had my father been home, Craig's punctuality *and* his choice of vehicles would have impressed him. Why, it was only the other night that Dad and my brother Mike were talking about their dream cars—each having a soft spot for such "fine pieces of machinery." My father would have approved of Craig without hesitation. After all, any man with a car like that must be outstanding, he would say. My mother, however, was a different story as she regularly voiced reservations about the man she blamed for getting me involved with murder investigations.

Unlike T.J., Craig did not honk his horn and wait for me in the car. Instead, I watched from my bedroom window as he got out of his Jag and walked toward the porch. I ran downstairs, threw my black pea coat over my green pantsuit, and grabbed my scarf as he knocked on the door.

"Wow, right on time," I said as I stepped outside.

"Didn't want to keep you waiting." Craig smiled. "Watch your step. It's icy," he warned as he offered his arm and helped me down the steps. After escorting me to his car, he opened the passenger door like the perfect gentleman. All his attentiveness made me uneasy. How could the guy who threw a fit yesterday about me going with him be so considerate today? Sometimes, the many sides of Craig made my head spin.

After he climbed in and fastened his seatbelt, he handed me a small black velvet box sitting on the dashboard.

"What's this?"

He smiled. "If we're going to pull this charade off, we need a convincing story. Open it."

Craig's grin widened as he watched me remove the lid. Before me was the most exquisite ring I had ever seen. I didn't know what to say or what to do.

Craig could not contain his delight. "Try it on. If you're going to be *my* fiancé, you've got to have an impressive ring."

I gingerly placed it on my finger and held my hand in front of my face. "It's beautiful!" The solitaire diamond ring fit perfectly.

Craig's eyes brightened. "My mom gave it to me a few months ago. My father gave it to her. I'm glad it fits because I had no idea what I would do if it didn't. Guess that's the problem with these quicky engagements," he chuckled.

I raised my hand closer to my face and marveled at what was before my eyes—the largest diamond I had ever seen in my entire life.

Barb—the wife of Mae's cousin Steve Goodright—used to wear some impressive diamond rings when she came to the shop. Of course, that was before the police arrested her for the murder of Mae's sister. As disturbing as that incident was, I couldn't help but smile as the diamond cast sparkling dots of light on the dashboard when I wiggled my finger.

Craig laughed at the showy display. "So, I guess it's safe to say you like the ring?"

"What's there not to like? It's beautiful, but don't think it gets you off the hook for not wanting me to come with you." I crossed my arms and leaned into the door.

Craig turned toward me. "I was only trying to protect you because I don't know how messy this might get. I mean, if Mr. Langford is involved with—"

"Yeah, yeah, yeah. I get it, but I can take care of myself, and if this Mr. Langford had anything to do with Shelly's death, I want to help catch him."

During our drive, we planned how we were going to get the financial information we needed. Craig would take the lead, considering he was the one with the money, and I would pretend to be the fiancé he insisted on including in the decision-making.

"There is something—" he said, "I think your fiancé idea provides an excellent cover, but to make it work, I think we shouldn't tell *anyone* our engagement is all an act. That way, no one will let the truth slip out. With any luck, we won't have to keep this charade up for long."

I shook my head. "I think it'd be okay to tell my parents what we're doing. Who would they tell? And if T.J. found out we were engaged, he'd be hurt that I hadn't been the one to tell him. Think about it—what if Mr. Langford tells his brother, who tells Sarah, and she tells Caroline? You see what I mean? Our engagement is bound to get out. Petersburg is a small town. People talk."

Craig took a deep breath. "I understand your concern, but I think it is best for all concerned if we act like our engagement is real and we don't tell *anyone* anything to the contrary. Otherwise, our cover may get blown, and our plan won't work."

I looked out the window and weighed my options. Keeping a secret from my parents and T.J. felt dishonest. Yet perhaps Craig was right. Maybe, I told myself, I would be protecting them in some way. Against my better judgment, I told him I agreed.

When we entered the fitness club, a tall brunette standing behind a gingerbread house on the counter greeted us.

"Hello. I'm Craig Miller. I have a twelve o'clock appointment with Mr. Langford."

The receptionist called Mr. Langford, and he appeared in the hallway within a few minutes. I recognized him from the Petersburg Health & Fitness Center's Open House. Dressed in his charcoal herringbone suit with his tanned face and dark wavy hair, he reminded me of Dean Martin. With such distinguished looks, he was a hard man to forget.

Mr. Langford gave us a friendly smile and shook Craig's hand. "Mr. Miller. Nice to meet you."

His gaze shifted to me and lingered. "We've not met before, have we? You look familiar."

I momentarily hesitated and then extended my hand. "No, I don't think so, but Craig has had nothing but good things to say about your gym." I slid my arm through Craig's, making sure my ring was visible.

Craig glanced at me with a big smile. "Mr. Langford, this is my fiancé, Michelle Kilpatrick."

Craig gazed into my eyes so tenderly I thought my heart would melt. I felt the heat crawling up my face and quickly reminded myself he was playing the part of a man in love. Or was he? Was there more to this ruse than I thought?

Craig patted my hand and whispered, "Are you okay?"

Despite feeling lost in a fog, I nodded and smiled. I never knew how to read Craig or all men, for that matter. Just like my relationship with T.J., I sometimes questioned if Craig and I were friends or if he felt something more toward me. Add to that the times when I just plain wondered if we were even on speaking terms. I berated myself for being so confused about such things. Someday, I told myself, I'd figure it out.

Mr. Langford brought me back to reality as he congratulated us while we walked to his office. "I didn't know you were dating anyone. The rumor mill in this town usually gets going when it involves someone from the Peterson family. Well played."

If he only knew. I chuckled. But for now, it was time to put on my game face. After Caroline's name was cleared, there would be time enough to figure out where I stood with T.J. and Craig.

Mr. Langford took our coats and hung them on the stand by the door as he directed us to the two chairs in front of his desk. After taking his seat, he focused on Craig. "Please call me Sam, and may I call you Craig? And it's Michelle, right?

Craig and I nodded.

"Good. Dispensing with formalities always makes doing business much easier. But before we begin, let me ask you a question. Why are you considering investing in my business? To my knowledge, you've never expressed an interest in my gym other than occasionally coming here to work out?"

Craig replied, "As I'm sure you're aware, I've come into an inheritance from the Peterson Estate. I want to generate some passive income, and I believe that fitness centers are the wave of the future. I want to get in on the ground floor. Currently, Petersburg has two fitness centers, and, well, I'm not sure how long the other one will be in business, which brings me to yours." Craig pulled out a pen and mini notepad from the inside pocket of his tweed blazer.

Satisfied with Craig's answer, Mr. Langford laid out his five-year plan to expand his gym's services. His six-month marketing strategy included buying additional radio spots, newspaper ads, and increasing the gym's visibility in the telephone book.

After finishing his well-rehearsed presentation, Mr. Langford gave Craig several documents, which after reading, he passed to me. While I read page after page filled with charts, graphs, numbers, and more legal phraseology than I ever cared to read, Craig went through his list of questions with Mr. Langford.

After handing me the last paper, Craig put his notepad and pen back in his pocket. His face grew stern as he looked at Mr. Langford. "I realize you've not been open a year yet, but how are the finances?" His brow furrowed as he asked, "When do you expect to show a profit?"

Mr. Langford opened a desk drawer and pulled out another folder. "As I'm sure you already know, most businesses don't make money in the first three to five years." He paused. "But I plan to beat those odds. I believe we can turn things around within the next twelve months with new equipment, more personal trainers, and an aggressive advertising campaign."

"That soon?" Craig said with a hint of skepticism.

Mr. Langford removed some papers from a folder and handed them to Craig. "As you can see from the projections, turning a profit next year is within realistic expectations. With your investment of $20,000 and 10% ownership of the gym, Mr. Miller, you should start seeing a return on your money in the next 12-15 months."

"With your profit estimates, have you accounted for the competition in your market share? Even if the new fitness center doesn't survive, I'm sure someone else will open one. Can Petersburg support two or three fitness centers?" Craig passed the latest set of papers to me.

Mr. Langford sat straight up in his desk chair. "To be honest, I didn't expect the challenge of another gym opening in this area so soon after I opened mine. But if we can stay ahead of the competition with what we offer, we will grow quickly." He tilted back in his chair. "Don't misunderstand me. I'm sorry for Caroline, but this presents a golden opportunity for us. Her gym is getting terrible press since one of her employees died because of faulty equipment, and I have no reason to believe the story will go away anytime soon. She's finished. If we move on this, we can make my gym a premier fitness club, which might detour anyone from opening another gym in the area." He leaned back in his chair with his hands clasped behind his head, his smile broadening.

"Apparently, you've thought of everything," I muttered offhand.

"That's my job," he said, lowering his arms and leaning over his desk. "I didn't start this business to lose money."

Craig stood, breaking the tension in the room. "Thank you, Sam, for your time and answering my questions. Michelle and I will discuss it, and if we decide to proceed with investing, I'll pass these financials to my accountant and lawyer."

Mr. Langford stepped around the desk and, flashing a wide smile, offered Craig a handshake. "If you need any additional information, call me. I'm sure you'll find everything satisfactory." He directed a focused gaze toward me and added, "As will you, Michelle."

Mr. Langford returned his attention to Craig, who was holding my coat as I slipped my arms into it, and said, "I look forward to doing business together, Craig."

Except for saying "goodbye" to the receptionist, Craig and I did not say a word as we left the building. But as soon as we were inside his car, Craig couldn't contain his curiosity any longer. "So, what did you think?"

"My gut feeling tells me Sam Langford is in financial trouble based on how pleased he was about Caroline's business possibly failing."

"I agree, but that doesn't prove he sabotaged Caroline's equipment."

"No," I conceded, "but you have to admit, he had motive and opportunity. He was at the Open House, and his brother was fiddling around with the treadmill." My brain spun through the events of that evening. "Carl was talking to Shelly right before she got on the treadmill—the very one he had been looking at so closely. Do you suppose he maneuvered her to use the machine he tampered with?"

Craig lifted one eyebrow and shot me a sidelong glance. "That's quite a stretch. I'm not saying you're wrong, but it seems farfetched." He turned the key in the ignition, and the wipers swiped across the windshield as the snow fell. "What do you say we stop by the police station and see if Lawrence is working? Perhaps he's uncovered something about Sam Langford or his brother, Carl. And, who knows, the medical examiner's report might be back by now. Do you have time?"

I looked at my watch. It was a little after one o'clock. "Sure, but I've got to be home by four, so I can change for work. Your mom called me this morning and asked me to come in a little earlier."

"Things must be hectic at my mother's store now that Christmas is almost here."

"That's for sure. A few months ago, I thought Mae might have to close her gift shop because business was so bad, but hopefully, the holidays will be busy enough to turn everything around."

"Mom told me that the layoffs at the car factory, plus not getting the money from Steve, hurt her cash flow quite a bit."

"Yeah, and all that publicity about her cousin Steve and his wife getting arrested for her sister's murder and the attempted murder of Bob Lane. Plus, the revelation that Steve was embezzling money from the family's lumber company was all too much! People didn't know how to act around Mae in the beginning, so I think a lot of them just stayed away." I shook my head. "It certainly wasn't good for business."

Craig pulled into the parking lot behind the police station, shaking his head in amazement. "Hard to believe that was only a couple of months ago."

"It's crazy, but it's almost like people got so caught up in the holidays that they forgot all about the drama surrounding Mae. You know, I don't think anyone has even brought it up since the middle of November. I hope it stays that way." I sighed and, after a moment, smirked.

"What are you smiling about?" Craig asked, squinting his eyes as if trying to read my mind.

"Mrs. Winterfield. She knew all along that Mae was part of the Peterson family and that you were Mae's son, but she never let on. Honestly, I don't think Mrs. Winterfield's life as a housekeeper for your grandfather, the illustrious Chauncey Peterson, is the whole story. I'm convinced she was a spy in her younger years." I mused, my voice low with suspicion.

"Who's to say she wasn't? Maybe...Mrs. Winterfield still is," chuckled Craig.

I snickered as I put my hand on the door handle, my mind racing with possibilities. "With any luck, you might be right."

"Huh?"

"I'm hoping with that spy background of hers, Mrs. Winterfield noticed something during Shelly's Jazzercise class."

Before stepping out of the car, Craig grinned mischievously and gave me a knowing wink. "Only one way to find out—ask her."

chapter ten

I steadied myself against a gust of icy wind and pulled my scarf tighter around my neck, burrowing my chin and nose deep into the woven fibers as I climbed out of Craig's car. Winter's chill stung my exposed cheeks, and I longed for the warm breezes of summer.

It took a moment to find Lawrence once we walked into the police station. He was hidden behind the miniature Christmas tree on the counter, talking on the phone.

Craig and I chatted as we waited for Lawrence to finish his call. Detective Douglas was no where in sight, and I hoped we could get in and out before he knew we were there.

As soon as Lawrence hung up the receiver, Craig asked him, "We were in the area and wondered if you found anything on Sam Langford or Carl Westwood?"

Meanwhile, as I removed my gloves and stuffed them into my coat pocket, a tiny red Christmas bulb lying beneath the tree caught my attention. I picked it up and hung it on the last empty branch.

"I didn't find anything on Langford. However, I discovered that his brother, Carl, was charged with assault about a year ago. The guy he hit dropped the charges. Other than that, I've got nothin'."

"Any idea what the fight was about?" I asked as I fluffed the branches on the tree. When I realized the display of sparkles on the counter was coming from Mae's diamond ring, I shoved my hand into my pocket. Crisis averted.

Lawrence, oblivious to my actions, continued. "Carl had invested his life savings into the stock market, and when it crashed, he took it out on his financial advisor."

Craig rubbed his chin. "The guy probably had quite a few clients upset with him. Last year was brutal, and the market still hasn't recovered. Any news from the medical examiner?"

"Now *that* I can help you with," Lawrence's eyes lit up, and he grinned like the Cheshire Cat from *Alice in Wonderland*. "The ME discovered that something besides falling off the treadmill may have contributed to Shelly's death."

"An underlying health condition?" I asked.

"Listen, I've probably said too much. Nothing is definitive until he finishes the report." Lawrence explained. "Hey, I almost forgot to mention I found out where Shelly was from— Bicknell, Indiana." He stopped as his eyes darted to the side.

I looked over my shoulder. *Oh, no! Detective Douglas is coming over here.*

The detective stopped beside me, his dark brown eyes boring into mine. "Is Lawrence getting you what you need?"

"Yeah, I think we've got everything."

"And what exactly might that *everything* be, Ms. Kilpatrick?"

I bit my lower lip, contemplating how I should answer. No way was I going to tell him we were looking into Mr. Langford, his brother Carl Westwood, and the ME report and risk getting Lawrence into trouble. *Think, think, think.* I cleared my throat. "We were in the neighborhood, so we thought we'd stop by and say 'Hi.'"

"Uh, huh? Just make sure you're not trying to involve yourself in my cases. Understand?"

My eyes narrowed. "Of course, Detective. I've learned not to interfere with you and your unit. After all, you're the professional."

Sensing my sarcasm, Craig reached over and grabbed my arm. "Michelle, I hate to rush you, but we need to go if you're going to make it to work on time. Merry Christmas, Detective Douglas. Lawrence."

As Craig and I headed to the car, I breathed a sigh of relief. "That was close."

Craig nodded. "I thought the way you handled Douglas was quite impressive." An amused smirk played across his face as he opened the car door, and I slid onto the red leather seat.

"Not that, silly. I forgot I was still wearing your ring. At least I realized it before Lawrence saw it. Not sure how I would have explained that." I laughed.

Craig's eyes twinkled as he flashed a playful grin. "That would have been most interesting, indeed."

I gazed at the ring as he walked to the driver's side. *I wonder what it would be like to be engaged to the famous mystery author and heir to the Peterson fortune.* Before my imagination got too carried away, I remembered how he tried to keep me out of the Langford investigation. *Nope.* I shrugged. I didn't need someone to *protect* me. I needed someone to work *alongside* me.

Craig tugged at his seat belt as I slipped the ring off and put it back in its box. "Should I put it in the glove compartment?

"Why don't you keep it with you?" He paused and then grabbed my hand and smiled. "The ring suits you."

I pulled my hand away. Despite the engagement idea being mine, I never thought about the consequences of our ruse or dealing with a ring. There was the real possibility people would get hurt by the lie I had concocted. It was all wrong. And then, as if that wasn't enough to make me uneasy, another horrible thought crossed my mind.

"What if I lose it?"

"You won't."

"But—"

"Relax. It's insured. And you need to wear it in case you run into Langford."

I looked him in the eyes. "I think that's highly unlikely. We don't exactly move in the same circles."

"While that may be true, I think you're right that he'll tell Carl, and who knows who he will tell."

Realizing that the deceitful web I had spun could quickly get bigger made me feel like I was sinking into quicksand with no way to escape.

Craig reached over and gave me a hug. "It'll be okay. We only need to keep up appearances until we get the info from Mr. Langford and Rick's soon-to-be stepmother. Remember, we're doing this to help Rick and his mom."

"I know," I sighed. "But how am I going to explain this ring?"

"You're a quick thinker. You'll think of something." He grinned. "I wouldn't be engaged to you if you weren't."

***

Mae's Gift Shop was bustling with activity when I walked through the door for my shift. Poor Stacy had a long line of customers waiting to be rung up, but at least they were laughing and smiling. The Christmas Spirit was alive and well.

Despite Craig wanting me to wear the ring to work, I left it at home. I wasn't going to lie to Mae about why I was wearing the ring she had given her son. That was too much. The lies had to stop somewhere. Until someone asked me about my engagement, I wasn't going to bring it up.

I stashed my coat and purse in the back room and dashed to the register to help Stacy. We had a system when we worked together at the cash register—I bagged the purchases while she rang up the sales.

When it came to greeting cards, my job was to slip the envelope inside the card, making it easier for Stacy to see the price and guarantee that the envelope was the correct size. We didn't want our customers to get home and discover their card didn't fit in its envelope.

After an hour of non-stop customers, the line dwindled to just two, so I left the cash wrap to refill the card racks but changed course when I found Mrs. Winterfield lingering by the candles.

"Mrs. Winterfield! How are you? I didn't expect to see you tonight. It's getting dark so early."

"Yes, dear, it is, but I'm doing well in spite of it." She chuckled. "However, it will be nice when the days are longer again."

I smiled. "I agree. Winter is bad enough without the days being even shorter because of that silly time change."

"I don't go out much in the evenings during the winter, but Elizabeth had to come into town tonight, so I came with her." Mrs. Winterfield leaned on her cane.

"Sounds fun." I paused. "How did you like the Open House the other night? I mean, before poor Shelly...." My voice drifted off.

"Wasn't that awful?" Mrs. Winterfield moved her white-haired head from side to side. "They say death comes in threes."

My eyes narrowed. "What do you mean?"

"First, it was Mae's sister, and now Shelly. She was a great-niece to Mae's second husband."

"Mae never mentioned being related to Shelly. In fact...neither did Craig."

"I'm not surprised. Mae doesn't like to talk about her

personal life, and, in Craig's defense, he might not have known. My understanding is Shelly's mother didn't have much to do with the Miller family. Shelly's parents moved to Indiana years before she was born. But putting all that aside, I never would have suspected tragedy coming to one so young. I had just seen her teaching that exercise class, and I don't know what it was, but I didn't think she looked well. For someone in such good shape, she was huffing and puffing, having a terrible time. Near the end of class, she grabbed her stomach. I thought maybe she had pulled a muscle with all that hopping about. Poor girl. I felt bad for her."

Mrs. Winterfield lowered her voice. "Have they determined it was the fall that killed her? That's what I heard—head trauma of some sort, I believe. The talk is the machine she was using went haywire. I do hope that wasn't the case. Someone said Shelly's parents are going to sue Caroline. Sweet Caroline, that's the last thing she needs."

"Do you know Caroline?"

"Oh, yes, dear, years ago her mother and I belonged to a ladies' group at our church. We would meet every Tuesday night and make quilts. Caroline was just a little tyke. Elizabeth looked after her in the church nursery."

"Is there anyone in this town you don't know?" I laughed.

"Not many, dear, not many at all." She smiled, her eyes twinkling with secrets. I looked around the shop. Mae was still on the floor helping customers. Since no one was in line at the cash register, I concluded it was safe to talk to Mrs. Winterfield for a few more minutes. As long as I looked like I was helping one of her favorite customers, Mae wouldn't accuse me of socializing while on the clock, and it would give me time to ask Mrs. Winterfield more questions about that fateful night.

I picked up a vanilla-scented candle and inhaled its sweet scent. "I love candles in the wintertime. Vanilla has got to be my favorite scent. It makes me feel so warm and cozy. Do you have a favorite one, Mrs. Winterfield?"

The elderly woman leaned on her cane and pointed at a candle on the shelf. "I'm rather partial to these cranberry-scented candles this time of year. They remind me of the bread my mother used to make at Christmas."

I picked up a burgundy cranberry candle and sniffed it. The sweet holiday scent was magical. Mrs. Winterfield's eyes lit up as she motioned for me to move the candle closer to her face. A satisfied smile graced her lips as she inhaled deeply.

Returning to our conversation about the Open House, I asked, "Do you think Caroline will be okay? I hope her insurance will cover any settlement if her equipment caused Shelly's injury."

"Oh, I'm sure she has good insurance. It's the money for operating costs I worry about. Her friend Sarah Bentley was going to invest in the business, but now, after this, I'm not sure what will happen. Elizabeth said Caroline hopes the publicity about the accident will die down in a couple of weeks. Still, that may not be true if there's a lawsuit."

"It sure is a mess. But going back to Sarah, I thought she already invested in the fitness center."

"Oh, no, dear. Sarah was going to invest in the business initially." Mrs. Winterfield lowered her voice. "But, according to my niece, who works at the bank, when Caroline was able to obtain a loan without Sarah's investment, Sarah decided to wait until after the grand opening before writing a check. My understanding is Caroline was going to use the money from Sarah to buy more equipment, hire another personal trainer, and do a big advertising campaign. I think Caroline let everyone believe Sarah was still on board because she firmly believed Sarah would come through with the money. Now, don't quote me on this, but rumor has it Sarah is having second thoughts about investing."

"But Caroline needs her help now more than ever."

"That's true." Mrs. Winterfield shook her head. "But I don't think it's going to happen."

"Why? Won't Sarah stand by her word? They're friends, right?" I paused. "I've heard money is no object with her."

"True, but money and friendship rarely mix, and besides, they haven't been friends very long."

"When did they meet?"

"I'm not sure. Maybe this past spring? Caroline had been inquiring about a space to rent when Sarah's son, an attorney for the firm that represents the shopping center, introduced the two of them."

"For some reason, I thought they had known each other longer, but I remember Rick saying something along those lines. I didn't realize how short a time."

"Yes, when Caroline told me about her new friend wanting to invest in her fitness center, it surprised me. It all seemed a little too easy, but I suppose Sarah's son saw an excellent investment opportunity for his mother. If it was strictly a matter between Caroline and Sarah, I'm sure Sarah would have gone through with investing in the beginning as planned."

"Is someone else involved?"

"Carl Westwood." Mrs. Winterfield's eyes narrowed. "I don't trust that man. Caroline says that since he and Sarah began dating, she thinks he has been trying to talk Sarah out of investing in her business. Now it looks like he may have finally won."

chapter eleven

As I pulled into my driveway, the front porch was awash in a red glow thanks to the Christmas lights strung around the house's windows and bushes. The scene was quite welcoming. It was good to be home.

The day had been productive. After all, Craig and I had gathered a great deal of information from Mr. Langford and Lawrence. An unexpected bonus had been talking to Mrs. Winterfield at Mae's shop about Shelly and Caroline. Still, it had been a long day. I wanted nothing more than to eat, unwind, and go to bed.

My heart skipped a beat as I walked into the house. Something was amiss. The two brass table lamps in the living room were on, but the T.V. was off. *That's weird! Where is everybody?*

My father usually enjoyed relaxing in front of the T.V. at night. Not having to get up early during the winter months, he caught up on the shows he had missed in the fall, like *Hawaii Five-O* and *Marcus Welby, M.D.* When the late-night news ended, he'd sit in his recliner and read biographies about famous Americans until he fell asleep. But tonight, he wasn't in his chair.

I wandered into the kitchen, searching for either of my

parents. Instead, I found a note under an orange cat magnet on the refrigerator—"Went to Crystal's house."

Although it was unusual for my mom and dad to make an unscheduled trip to my sister's house, I welcomed the time to myself. I microwaved some leftovers I found in the refrigerator and returned to the living room, plopping onto the sofa.

Gidget was sleeping in the corner chair with her tail enveloping her face, forming a furry cocoon. Despite wanting to give her a loving squeeze, I fought against the urge. She, too, deserved some alone time.

I reached over to grab the afghan lying at the opposite end of the sofa when my gaze landed on an index card peeking out from under the phone—"T.J. called."

I checked the clock—nine thirty-five. With my mom and dad gone, I could call T.J. and not cause drama on my home front, but that might not be true for T.J. His parents frowned on calls after nine o'clock. *Oh, how I wish he had a phone in his room—with his own number!* I had no choice. I would have to wait until morning to call him.

There was, however, one person I could call without upsetting his parents—Craig. Clad in my crocheted cape, I paced back and forth. I didn't have any information that couldn't wait until the next time I saw him, but at the same time, I had an undeniable need to hear his voice.

Confidently, I dialed Craig's number but regretted my decision when he answered. Muffled voices in the background made it clear I had interrupted something.

"What do you need, Michelle?" He snapped.

"Ummm...sorry to...I'm sorry to bother you," I stammered. "Sounds like you're busy. I can talk to you later. It's not that important."

"Why did you call?"

"It was a silly idea," I muttered. "It can wait."

As I pulled the receiver away from my ear so I could hang

up, he said, "Michelle, hang on. What were you going to say? Are you still there?"

"Yeah, I'm here."

"So, what's up?"

"Mrs. Winterfield came into your mother's shop tonight, and she said Carl Westwood has been trying to convince Sarah not to invest in Caroline's fitness center—"

"But I thought she had already invested in it," he interrupted.

"That's what I thought too, but, according to Mrs. Winterfield, Sarah was waiting until the fitness center opened before giving Caroline any money. I can't believe I forgot to tell you this, but after my lunch with Elaine the other day, I followed her and you'll never guess where she went?"

A woman's husky Brenda Vaccaro-like voice muttered something to Craig, to which he replied, "Sorry, but I need to take this call in the other room. Would you mind hanging the phone up after I pick it up in the study?"

After a slight pause, he said, "Michelle, give me a minute. I'm going to switch to a different phone."

As I listened to the hushed voices in the background for what seemed like an overly long time, I started to think Craig had forgotten me. I tapped my foot and glanced around the living room until he finally said, "I've got it."

There was a loud click.

"Okay, Michelle, I'm back."

"Sounds like you've got a lot going on tonight."

"My agent and lawyer are here. We're ironing out some contract issues. Not a fun way to spend the evening, but it has to be done. Now, where were we? Oh yeah, you followed Elaine."

"That's right, I followed her to Langford's gym, and Carl met her in the parking lot, where they shared a rather long hug before going inside. Do you think they might be an item?"

"I have no idea. Perhaps they're friends. I mean, isn't he seeing Sarah?"

"Maybe he's two-timing her."

"Be careful about jumping to conclusions. Don't forget, not that long ago, people thought Anne and I were having an affair, and nothing could have been further from the truth. And do you remember when Amy was convinced that Burt and Betsy were an item? If we learned anything, it was that things aren't always as they seem."

"Okay," I half-heartedly agreed. "I'll give you that, but I still think we should keep tabs on them. And don't you think it's interesting that Elaine and Shelly are both from Bicknell, Indiana? I'm more convinced than ever that Elaine knew Shelly better than what she's letting on."

"The plot thickens."

I exhaled deeply. "It sure does. Did you know Shelly and your stepfather, Johnathan Miller, were related? She was his great-niece."

"No. Mom's never talked much about Johnathan's family." He paused. "Although now that you mention it, I remember her saying Johnathan had an older sister he hadn't seen in a long time. Huh? Maybe that's where Shelly comes in. How'd you find out anyway?"

"Mrs. Winterfield—"

"Say no more. Is there anything that woman doesn't know about my family?"

"For real! I'll see if I can find out more about Shelly from Mrs. Winterfield...she's like the keeper of family secrets, isn't she?"

"I know you were joking when you said she might have been a spy in her younger years, but the more I learn about her, the more I sometimes think you might be right."

"You got to admit she's a good source for information. And speaking of information, I hope the medical examiner releases his report soon."

"I'm sure it'll only be a few more days. These things take time." Craig paused. "Do you know if Jimmy and his father have examined the fitness center equipment yet?"

"No news yet, but I'll call him in the morning and see what's happening. How 'bout with you? Any new information on your end?"

"I called my friend in London, and he's going to do some digging around about Carl."

The garage door opened, and Gidget's ears perked at the sound of the motor.

"Listen, I've got to go. My parents just got home."

"Gotcha. We'll talk later."

"Hey, good luck with your agent and your lawyer."

He laughed and hung up.

What was I thinking? Mr. Waynesworth was his attorney, which meant the alluring voice belonged to his agent. If her sexy voice was any indication of how she looked, I imagined she was gorgeous. Why would I want to wish him luck with her? At least, I consoled myself that Waynesworth would keep Craig's focus on legal matters. But then again, why did that even matter to me?

My hand had barely left the receiver when my mom and dad walked through the kitchen door into the living room.

"You're still up?" Mom asked as they headed toward the coat closet.

I shrugged and replied, "Just trying to destress a bit." I pulled the afghan tighter, my head spinning with thoughts of Craig and his agent while questioning at the same time why it bothered me.

Mom stopped behind the couch. "Do you want a bedtime snack? Crystal sent home some shortbread cookies she made this afternoon."

"No, that sounds good, but I think I'm going to go to my room and try to get to bed early tonight."

As tired as I was, I couldn't sleep until I sorted some

things out. I pulled my red and green plaid flannel jammies from under my pillow and, as I put them on, mulled over the new information I had learned relating to Shelly's accident.

Armed with my notebook, I snuggled under the covers and got to work. First, I drew a chart with four columns and labeled each with the names of the people I suspected played some part in the treadmill mystery—Elaine, Paul, Carl, and Mr. Langford. My next step was adding a row for motives and another for opportunity.

Filling in the motive row was easy. Everyone on my list had one for killing Shelly or hurting Caroline's business. No love was lost between Elaine and Caroline or between her and Shelly, for that matter. Paul was the ex-boyfriend whom Shelly had hurt when she broke up with him. Carl and his brother, Mr. Langford, had a business that Caroline's gym might threaten.

I removed my necklace and set it on the nightstand as I contemplated who had the opportunity to tamper with the treadmill. A question mark went under Elaine's name. She was at the fitness center that morning, but did she have the know-how to do it? Paul certainly did, as did Carl and his brother.

I stared at the rows of names with the information written under each one, twisting the pen between my fingers. *Should I add a column for Sarah?* She was, after all, dating the brother of a competitor and was withholding funds for Caroline's business. Maybe she was working with Carl to take Caroline down. I added her name.

I looked at my chart. Was I being foolish for spending all this time on something that was an unfortunate accident? Yet, my instincts told me there was more to Shelly's death than anyone suspected. Until the authorities ruled out foul play beyond any doubt, in my mind—to quote the great detective Sherlock Holmes—"the game's afoot."

I reached over and disturbed my favorite sleeping ball of

fur, who had followed me to my room and found a cozy spot to nestle on my bed. While I found it therapeutic to pet Gidget, her snarl let me know the feeling wasn't mutual.

Overwhelmed by melancholy, I grabbed my journal from my nightstand. Inspired by the poetry of Susan Polis Schutz and E.E. Cummings, I found solace in writing free verse poems. Sadness and confusion poured from my heart onto the lines of the paper.

why is it

when i am with you

i don't know how to act

yet

when i am away from you

all i do is

r

e

a

c

t

I put my pen down, turned off the light, and raised the shade on my window. I gazed at T.J.'s house and wrestled with my feelings. I was jealous of Meg. There, I said it. I knew T.J. and I were friends, but maybe I wanted more. Maybe I didn't. The problem was I didn't know what I wanted, and as long as Meg and T.J. were an item, I could never sort out my feelings for T.J.

And then there was Craig. We grew close while investigating Professor Ladd's murder and afterward writing our newspaper article. Yet, until Shelly's death, I hadn't seen much of him. He was friendly enough, and although we usually sat by each other in class, he never mentioned getting together. I rationalized he was finishing his novel and learning the family business—the Peterson Lumber Company

—all things that take a lot of time, but the fact was, he never called.

Now that Craig and I were spending time together again, he was always on my mind. When I thought of T.J., I thought of Craig. Was it possible to have feelings for two guys at the same time?

chapter twelve

Wednesday, December 18th

"Hi, Mike. What brings you here so early?" I was puzzled seeing my brother sitting at the kitchen table. During the winter months, he rarely showed up at my parent's farmhouse before ten o'clock in the morning. With no work in the fields, he and my dad filled their days with repairing tools and chipping away at my mom's ever-growing to-do list.

"Today, Dad and I are going to wallpaper the dining room." Mike lifted his mug, which was shaped like Santa's face, and stopped mid-air. I wasn't sure if he was trying to make a point or waiting for Mom's reaction. Either way, he looked rather cute holding the mug Mom made in her ceramics class a few years ago while eleven other Santa mugs sat on the shelf, staring at us.

"Miracles never cease to happen!" Mom exclaimed as she turned toward us, gripping a plate in her soapy hands. "You two promised to have it finished in time for Thanksgiving—"

"But we will have it done before Christmas! We're only a month late; gimme a break!" Mike laughed.

Dad, sitting at the head of the table, peered at me over his morning newspaper. "If someone hadn't been so busy with school, we wouldn't have been so short-handed, and then we could have had it done in time, but—"

Mike stood up, threw his arm around me, and gave me a bear hug. "But we made it work. We got the harvest in on time, and today we'll get Mom's wallpaper up—it all worked out. So, sister of mine, how'd fall quarter go?"

"Fingers crossed it went well. I won't know until after Christmas when they mail out the grades. The powers that be like to make us worry over our break, you know." I smiled as I whispered "thank you" to my brother for rescuing me from my father's rant about school interfering with me helping around the farm.

Gidget nudged the kitchen door open while letting out a loud "Meow."

"Would somebody shut that cat up?" my father growled.

I scooped my beloved ball of fur into my arms and gave her a long, squishy hug before setting her down and getting the milk out of the refrigerator. Something about the label caught my attention. "What's this? Two percent?"

Mom laughed. "I thought cutting back on whole milk over the holidays might help me not gain so much weight over Christmas."

"I'm not sure how Gidget will feel about this," I said, grinning. But any doubts I had vanished as she lapped up the white liquid in her saucer, showing no signs of disapproval. Maybe, I mused, she, too, was watching her calories. After all, Dad had been eating ice cream at night, which meant she had too.

"Feed that cat while you're at it. She's probably hungry, and we don't need her making a lot of racket," my father barked—his irritation came through loud and clear, perhaps a little too loud and too clear to be believable.

I glanced at Mike, choking back his laughter.

Unintimidated by my father's stern tone, Gidget purred as

I dropped a few handfuls of dry cat food into her bowl. She knew Dad was all bark and no bite when it came to her.

"Did you see the note that T.J. called last night? It's been a while since we've seen him. Did you guys have a fight or something?" Mom asked as she gathered the remaining breakfast dishes from the table.

"Oh, what's this? A lover's quarrel?" Mike smirked.

I swatted his arm. "Nothing like that—T.J. and I are just friends, and besides, he's got a girlfriend."

"Which doesn't mean a thing," my mother said as she sat down. "T.J.'s had girlfriends before, but none have ever lasted. Mark my words; this one won't either," she said with a knowing smile.

I lowered my gaze, trying to hide my hope that she was right. "He probably called about something he discovered about Shelly's accident."

"Oh, no, please don't tell me you're involved with all that," my mom moaned.

"We're just helping our friend Rick."

Mike raised his brows.

"Rick's mother owns a fitness center, and one of her employees died during the Open House," I said.

"Yeah, I read about that," Mike said as he returned to his seat. "You're a good friend, Sis."

"Thanks! And you're a good brother." I gave him a peck on the cheek. "Guess I better call T.J. so I don't lose my good friend status." I chuckled. "Is it okay if I take the phone to my room?"

Mom nodded as I left the kitchen.

I dialed T.J.'s number and was relieved when he was the one who answered. Despite knowing Mr. and Mrs. Wilson since I was six years old, they still made me nervous. Especially since they, like my parents, were not supporters of the women's lib movement. In their minds, any girl who called their son was manipulative and would lead him down a path of destruction.

"What's up? I got your message that you called last night," I said.

"Yeah, I need to talk to someone. Listen, wait a minute." I heard T.J. ask his mom if she would hang up the receiver after he got the phone in his dad's office.

I waited, listening to the silence.

"Thanks, Mom, I got it."

Click.

"Okay, Michelle. I'm all set. You're the only one I can talk to," he paused, "but something strange happened yesterday."

"What happened?"

"When I was at Meg's house, we started talking about Shelly's accident. And get this…Meg was almost gleeful that Shelly was dead. I mean, she didn't even pretend to be sad about it. I get they were rivals, but to be happy about Shelly's accident was just plain weird."

"Yeah, it is. How strange!"

"But even stranger was when I questioned Meg about her reaction."

"What do you mean? What'd she do?" I pulled the phone over to my bed, laid down, and leaned against the pillows.

"Meg said she didn't think how she felt was wrong, that Shelly had been a real pain and the world was better without her. She sounded so heartless. I couldn't believe it!"

Although I agreed that Meg's reaction to Shelly's death was strange, I contemplated how to respond. Should I try to offer an explanation in Meg's defense, or should I use this opportunity to dismantle her perfect persona further? I rubbed the Eiffel Tower charm between my fingers and stared out the window while debating what to say next.

"Michelle? You still there?"

"Yes…yes… I'm here," I replied, twisting the phone cord. "I was trying to think about what may have caused her to say those things. Obviously, she and Shelly weren't friends. I mean, Meg did have to buy a new dress because of her. Who knows what run-ins they may have had in the past? Maybe Meg was just glad that she didn't have to deal with Shelly anymore. What bothers me is—"

"What?"

I stopped myself and shifted my thoughts. "Never mind. It's not important."

"You don't think Meg had anything to do with Shelly's accident, do you? Just because they were competitors doesn't mean she'd do anything to hurt her."

"No, of course not. I'm sure Meg wouldn't know how to tamper with a treadmill. She'd probably have to hire someone to do that."

As soon as the words left my mouth, I regretted saying them. I got out of bed and started pacing. A void hung in the air, and I didn't have to see T.J. to know he was getting ready to defend Meg against my *wild* accusations. And I was right.

"Meg might be glad Shelly is dead, but she's *not* a murderer," T.J. said.

"Of course, she's not. I'm sorry. I just want to figure out what happened . Sometimes, I say things before I think them through."

"Yeah, I get that, and if we're going to solve the treadmill mystery, we have to look at everything and everyone who could have been involved. Speaking of everyone with a motive—how's it going with Elaine and the beauty pageant stuff? Has she talked you into competing yet?"

"Don't be ridiculous! I'm definitely not pageant material."

"Don't say that."

"Seriously, T.J.," I laughed. "But I did learn about a connection between Elaine and Shelly."

"Like, duh, they were both involved in pageants."

"No, more than that, silly. They're both from Bicknell, Indiana."

"You're kidding. Do you think Elaine and Shelly knew each other before they moved here?"

"That's my guess. When I met Elaine at the restaurant, she skirted around the whole issue of how well she knew Shelly." I took a deep breath. "And I tell you, it may only be a gut feeling, but I'm convinced someone intentionally tampered with the treadmill. I need to call Jimmy this morning to see what he and his father found out about it and if they have questions about any other pieces of equipment."

"You'll let me know what they find out?" T.J. asked.

"Sure —"

"Listen, don't tell Meg I told you what she said about Shelly." He sounded panic-stricken.

"What? That she was happy Shelly was dead?"

"Yeah. Exactly. If Meg found out, she'd be furious with me. Okay? Let's keep it between the two of us."

"Yeah. I won't tell anyone."

"Not even Craig?" he asked sharply.

"Of course. Why would I tell him? This is between you and me."

"Good. There's something about that guy I don't like."

"Like what?" Although I was not surprised to hear T.J. say he didn't like Craig, I wondered why he had such a negative opinion of him. Granted, Craig and I had disagreements from time to time, but I had never seen him do anything to provoke T.J.

"I don't know. I'm afraid Craig's leading you on," T.J. said.

"Leading me on? Don't be ridiculous. He's only hanging out with me because we're trying to get information to help Rick's mom. I'd hardly call that leading me on." I chuckled.

"Yeah, but sometimes the way he looks at you. I don't like it. I mean, I don't want you to get hurt."

"Craig Miller and I are...well, we're like business

associates. We work together. That's all. He's not leading me on, and he will definitely not hurt me."

"Okay, if you're sure."

"I'm sure. Don't worry."

As I hung up the phone, I glanced back just as my mom placed her hands on my shoulders.

"Who is going to hurt you? Is someone threatening you?"

I put my hand on hers and gave her a reassuring smile. "No. No one is after me. T.J. is concerned that Craig will hurt my feelings, that's all."

"Why would T.J. worry about that?"

"Who knows?"

"It sounds like he might be jealous of this Craig person," she smiled. "I've seen T.J. and you together. A bit of jealousy might be what T.J. needs to wake him up before he loses you to someone else."

"I'm sure that's the last thing on his mind. You forget he's got Meg."

"Maybe," she paused, flashing a mischievous grin, "and maybe not." She turned and went downstairs.

Between my mom convinced T.J. likes me and T.J. thinking Craig is leading me on, you'd think my dance card would be full. So why am I sitting at home all alone?

I closed my bedroom door. I needed time to regroup.

If T.J. knew about my fake engagement to Craig, he'd blow a gasket. I could hear him now: "How did you let yourself get tangled up in this mess?" No, he'd come right out and say I was living a lie, and he'd be right. What had I done? I created this ridiculous story all because I didn't want Craig to meet with Mr. Langford without me. In the end, my lie could destroy my friendship with T.J., and he'd never trust me again. Still, I couldn't worry about it now. I had to call Jimmy. The sooner I solved this mystery, the sooner this charade could end.

Jimmy's phone number was in my address book, but

when I couldn't find it in my desk drawer, I remembered I had put the book in my purse. I reached into my bag, but I came up empty-handed. My only recourse was to dump the contents onto my bed—crumbled papers, pens, lipstick tubes, paperclips, and loose change.

As I sorted through the pile, Gidget got up from her morning nap to investigate. She purred and pawed at the messy treasure trove while I searched for the elusive address book. Finally, I found it underneath my wallet. A few moments later, Jimmy was on the phone.

"Hey, Jimmy, have you and your dad had a chance to check out the equipment at the fitness center?"

"You timed that right—we just got home from going over there."

"What did you find out?"

"From what we could tell, all the machines seemed to be in order, except one."

"Which one?"

"The treadmill Shelly was using. It was missing some screws. We looked all around but couldn't find them anywhere."

"Do you think someone removed them?"

"Possibly, or maybe someone rushed through the installation and didn't finish the job properly. It happens."

"But the other machines were okay?"

"As far as we could tell."

"Okay. Thanks for your help, and tell your dad thanks, too."

I hung up the phone and felt the sun's warmth shining through my window. If I only looked at the sky and not at the snow-covered ground, I could pretend it was a warm summer day. I thought how easy it was to be deceived when you don't have all the facts. *How unnerving!*

Gidget snuggled against my pillows—sleeping—having

apparently become bored with my scattered belongings. I took advantage of the lull in her curiosity and sorted through the pile on my bed, throwing a few things away, removing the duplicates, and tossing everything else back into my purse before she decided to reclaim the discombobulated mess.

I laid down next to her, grabbed my crime notebook off the nightstand, and added a column for Meg's name with the notation: Did she hire someone?

Gidget peered at me with slivered eyes, her tail wrapped under her chin.

"Let's keep this between us, okay? T.J. doesn't need to know I added Meg as a suspect."

She closed her eyes. My secret was safe.

When I opened my door, a heavenly aroma greeted me. I followed it to the kitchen, where I found my mother taking a tray from the oven.

I deeply inhaled, trying to identify the delicious smell. "What kind of cookies?" I asked.

"Hungarian Walnut." She shut the oven door. "Your father wants to make his Peanut Brittle tonight, so I thought I better get my baking out of the way this afternoon."

"Are you making anything else?"

"Some Opera Fudge, those Thimble Cookies you like, and—"

The back door to the kitchen opened.

"Crystal!" I exclaimed. "I didn't know you were coming over today."

"And good to see you too, Sis. I thought I'd stop by and help Mom with the baking." She hung her coat on a chair. "Plus, if I help make the cookies, I won't have to make dinner tonight 'cause I won't be hungry." She chuckled.

"Poor Mel. What's he going to eat?" my mom said, frowning.

"My dear husband is at his mother's house helping her

put up her Christmas tree. I'm sure she'll feed him more than enough."

"Have you had lunch?" Mom asked before she stepped into the pantry.

"No, I had a late breakfast."

"Okay, but if you get hungry, there's some chicken and dumplings on the stove. Get yourself a bowl. You, too, Michelle," she said as she carried a bag of flour to the table. "It's just us for lunch. Your father and Mike needed a break from putting up the wallpaper, so they went out to look for a tree."

Crystal wandered to the stove and lifted the lid off the large pot. "Chicken and dumplings—just what the doctor ordered."

"I thought you weren't hungry?" I laughed.

"I'm not, but warm soup sounds good. It's freezing out there!"

"Stay in the kitchen for very long, and the heat from this oven will warm you up in no time." Mom pulled a fresh tray of golden-brown Hungarian walnut cookies from the oven and set it on the stove.

Crystal turned toward me. "Want some soup?"

"Sure. Sounds good," I said.

"Mind if I turn the radio on, Mom?" Crystal asked as she reached inside the cupboard door for two blue stoneware bowls.

"No. Go ahead. Get something Christmasy."

Mom loved Christmas music, especially Bing Crosby's "White Christmas" and Nat King Cole's "The Christmas Song." Although Mom claimed she was not a big Elvis Presley fan, Crystal and I smiled at each other as we watched her swaying and mouthing all the words to his "Blue Christmas" as she mixed the sugar and butter together for the Thimble Cookies.

By the time Crystal and I finished our soup and rinsed our bowls, Mom had the latest batch of cookies on the cooling rack and the Thimble Cookies ready to go into the oven.

Crystal pulled a rubber band from her coat pocket and gathered her long brown hair into a ponytail. "You gonna help us?"

"Sure. I've got nothin' going this afternoon."

"Do my ears deceive me? Nothing on your calendar today? This is indeed a special occasion." Mom chuckled.

Looking past my mother's shoulder, I noticed Crystal stepping out of the pantry, struggling to carry bags of white sugar, brown sugar, and confectioner's sugar.

"Here, let me help you with those," I said, taking two bags and setting them on the kitchen table.

The afternoon went unusually well. Never once did my mom mention her frustration that I was too busy with school to help around the farm, or that she thought my dream of being a freelance reporter was ridiculous. Instead, we laughed, danced, and baked to our heart's content. Crystal made Mexican Wedding Cookies and finished the Raspberry-Filled Thumbprint Cookies while Mom made White Chocolate Opera Fudge.

After leaving my sugar cookie dough in the refrigerator for thirty minutes, I rolled the dough to cut out the star shapes. Crystal promised to help me decorate the cookies once they cooled. She had far more patience than I did in executing the fine details of decorating with Royal Icing.

The doorbell rang just as I started mixing the batter for the brownies.

"Now, who in the world could that be?" My mother wiped her hands on her Christmas apron and headed for the door, fluffing her hair as she went.

Crystal and I tiptoed to the kitchen door, which Mom had left slightly ajar. We looked at each other and started giggling when we realized we were holding our breath so as not to make any noise. Consumed by our laughter, we almost got hit by the door when Mom returned to the kitchen.

"Michelle, there's a young man to see you. He says he's a friend of yours from school. He's in the living room."

chapter thirteen

Crystal shimmied her shoulders and winked. "Ooh, la, la… a gentleman caller."

"Shhhh." I laughingly scolded her as I left the kitchen, unsure who was waiting for me in the living room.

"Lawrence! What brings you here?"

He stopped wiping the condensation off his wire-rimmed glasses. "Sorry to stop by unannounced, but I couldn't call you from work. I didn't want anyone at the police station to overhear me talking."

"Wow, that sounds ominous. Wanna sit down?"

Holding the lenses up to the sunlight coming through the window, he scrutinized them before putting them back on. "No, I've got to get home. The wife is waiting for me. We've got Christmas shopping to do. But I wanted to tell you that the medical examiner's report came in around noon, and, get this, Shelly suffered a traumatic head injury, but that's not what she died from."

"What then?"

Lawrence shook his head. "Someone poisoned her. Granted, the treadmill may have malfunctioned, but it's also likely she lost her balance because of the poisoning. She had enough arsenic in her system to kill her whether or not she fell and hit her head." Lawrence shrugged. "If it hadn't been for the witnesses saying Shelly had been tired and complaining about a headache that day, the ME might not have run the tests for poison substances. The report says she was given a couple of substantial doses that day."

"Arsenic, that's crazy!" My mouth dropped open. I had been so convinced she died from a traumatic head injury that I hadn't thought about any other causes. "It's like something from that old movie, *Arsenic and Old Lace*." I thought for a moment. "Wouldn't she have noticed her drink or food tasting funny?"

Lawrence shook his head. "Not necessarily. Arsenic has no taste or smell. Chances are she'd never notice."

The doorbell rang.

"Unreal," I said as I mulled over the poison info as I went to answer the door.

Craig was on the porch—an unexpected turn of events.

"Ummm, come on in. Join the party," I said as I held open the door.

"Thanks. Sorry to drop—" His eyes darted to Lawrence, who was buttoning his coat. "Hi, Lawrence. I didn't mean to interrupt anything. I should have called. I can come back later."

"No, man, I'm on my way out. Got to meet the little lady and do some Christmas shopping. Michelle can fill you in on the ME report." Lawrence turned toward me. "Call me tomorrow if you have any questions. I don't have to be at work until three o'clock, so I'll be home all morning."

As I stood at the door and watched Lawrence walk to his car, all I could think about was Shelly's poisoning. I looked over my shoulder to say something to Craig, but he was nowhere to be found. Baffled, I went into the kitchen. He was sitting at the table with a cookie in one hand, a glass of milk in the other and a plate piled high with cookies in front of him.

"Here you are!" I exclaimed. "I wondered where you went."

"Your sister was kind enough to invite me back here and—"

"Get you some cookies?" I smiled.

"Really, Michelle, your friend here—" Crystal grinned. "Well, aren't you going to introduce us?"

"Crystal, this is Craig Miller, a *friend* from school. Craig, this is Crystal, and my mother—" I glanced around the kitchen. "Where's Mom?"

"She's in the basement trying to finish that quilt she's been working on for the women's group at church," Crystal said. Positioning herself behind Craig's chair so he couldn't see her, she mouthed, "He's cute."

Craig spotted my eye roll in Crystal's direction and turned to see what was happening behind him.

Crystal ignored his glance and gushed, "So, you're the Craig Miller that Michelle has told us so much about."

"She's mentioned me, has she?"

"Not that much. Maybe just in passing." I shrugged nonchalantly. "So, what brings you here?"

"Michelle," Crystal said, "that's no way to talk to our guest."

Craig laughed. "No, it's okay."

Crystal continued. "First, you leave poor Craig alone while you're at the door, and now you give him the third degree about why he's here. It's a good thing I invited him into the kitchen for a cookie or two while he waited. As they say, the way to a man's heart is through—"

Craig flashed his pearly white Hollywood smile, obviously enjoying how uncomfortable my sister was making me. I squinted my eyes and glared at him.

He laughed. "Normally, I don't just drop in on people, but I had some news I wanted to tell you in person."

A glimpse at Crystal's face told me she was reading way

too much into Craig's surprise visit—something I'd have to straighten out later. For now, I avoided looking at her any longer and instead focused on Craig. "Did you find out something about Shelly or the fitness center?"

He nodded. "But first, what did Lawrence say?"

Crystal adjusted her ponytail and returned to her baking while I recounted the ME's discovery of arsenic in Shelly's system.

Craig stroked his chin. "Arsenic? Not very original, but one of the easier poisons for someone to get their hands on."

I motioned toward the kitchen door. "Why don't we go into the living room, and you can fill me in on your news."

Crystal's face dropped, but any disappointment she felt about us leaving the room faded when Craig got up and thanked Crystal for the cookies. When he kissed her hand, she blushed. I couldn't believe it. Craig Miller, who can be incredibly charming when he wants to be, had swept my level-headed sister off her feet.

"Cool it, Romeo," I said as I nudged him. "She's a married woman."

While Crystal muttered something about it being okay, I tugged Craig's shirt sleeve and led him into the living room.

"So, how'd it go with your agent last night?"

"It was a long night. All I did was listen as Waynesworth and Suzette hammered out the details. My big job was signing the final contract. Was I ever wrong when I thought negotiations would get easier when I became more successful! But, hey, I guess that's life." Craig sat on the couch as I claimed the recliner. "Anyway, I wanted to stop by and tell you what my friend in London found out."

"Do tell." I threw the afghan over my lap.

"As we know, Carl Westwood attended Oxford and was a well-respected economist. For fun, he started writing historical fiction under the pen name of Carl Westwood. He didn't want to tarnish his reputation as an economist if the books didn't sell, but he needn't have worried. His writing was well received. With the extra income, he delved into the, shall we say, riskier ways of making money—playing poker with his stockbroker, George Terrell. Unfortunately, his luck with poker was as bad as his luck with the stock market. To make a long story short, his father had to bail him out several times until finally, he cut off all funds, but Carl couldn't stop gambling...and losing."

"That had to make for some interesting family drama." I shifted in the recliner and pulled the afghan tighter around me.

"That's putting it mildly," Craig muttered.

"Why? What happened?"

"Carl cracked. He started gambling even more—poker, horses, soccer. If you could bet on it, he tried it. Anything to recoup his losses, but lady luck was not on his side. He got into a fight with Terrell—accused him of cheating at cards."

"Was he?"

"We'll probably never know the answer to that one, but Terrell agreed not to press charges if Carl signed a promissory note to pay him the money owed *and* agreed to leave the country."

"So, that's how he ended up here." I smoothed out the afghan as Gidget contemplated jumping on my lap.

Craig cocked his head as he watched her leap into the crocheted blanket and then paw it until she found the perfect spot in which to lie down. "Does she do that often?"

"What?"

"Curl up like that?"

Nodding my head, I patted her and grinned. "Yes, especially when there's good gossip."

Craig leaned forward to get a closer look at the purring ball of fur.

Gidget raised her head and looked at him. Craig reared

back. "I've never had a cat. They scare me. You never know what they're thinking."

"I think it's safe to say she wants you to continue with the story."

"Then I guess I better continue," he said as he shifted his eyes from me to Gidget and then back to me. "You'll be glad to know that I did some digging around and discovered that Carl and Sam's father died the day of Carl's fight with Terrell."

"Perhaps Carl's grief pushed him over the edge." I rubbed behind Gidget's ears as she purred, listening to every word.

"Perhaps, but that brings up the will." Craig's green eyes twinkled.

"What did you find out?"

"Nothing yet, but I'm on it. I'm going to pay a visit to the Probate Court."

"Well, regardless of what the will says, we know Mr. Langford is having money problems, and it sounds like his brother is as well." I took a deep breath. "Not knowing how much Carl is involved with Langford's fitness center, I don't know if getting rid of Caroline's business would benefit him, but it would help Mr. Langford." I paused and glanced out the picture window. "I'm not sure it matters. Even if the brothers were behind tampering with the treadmill, it doesn't mean they poisoned Shelly."

Craig sat straight up. "Or does it?"

"What do you mean?"

"I was curious about a few things, so I went to Langford's gym and invited the receptionist out for lunch."

"And she went with you?"

Craig smirked. "Don't act so surprised. Why wouldn't she want to have lunch with me?"

I shook my head and raised my eyebrows. "We've only been engaged for a day, and you're already cheating on me. Is this the way it's going to be?" I threw my hand over my forehead and leaned back, feigning despair.

Unamused by my antics, Gidget got up in a huff and moved next to Craig.

"Now see what you've done. You've upset the cat." Craig laughed.

"I'm sure she'll recover. So, tell me, what happened at your *lunch*?" I paused. "Hey, didn't it bother her that you're engaged?"

"I don't think it bothered her at all," he grinned. "Besides, I told her it was a business lunch, and that I wanted to talk to some of the employees before I decided whether to invest. So, you see, Sherlock, you're not the only one good at snooping. Anyway, during our conversation, she told me there was a rumor Shelly dumped Paul for Carl."

"That can't be right. He's dating Sarah."

"Perhaps, but it seems he's been playing the field."

"Sarah would be furious if she found out." I got up and walked around the room, thinking aloud. "But why would Carl do that?"

"Why wouldn't he? Shelly was young and good-looking."

"That is so disgusting! But what if Carl was only dating Sarah for her money? Oh, my goodness." I grabbed my Eiffel Tower charm and twisted it. "What if Sarah knew about Shelly and got jealous?"

"Or—" Craig asked, "What if Shelly threatened to tell Sarah...and Carl had to stop her?

After Craig left, I returned to the kitchen, where Crystal was baking more cookies.

She turned the music down on the radio. "Where's Craig?"

"He went home."

She laid her hand on my arm, her eyes narrowed. "What did he say? You look upset." She guided me toward the kitchen table and pulled a chair from under it. "Come here and sit down."

"Craig didn't do anything; I'm upset with myself. I've been so focused on the treadmill and its effect on Caroline's business that I never thought about someone only wanting to murder Shelly. It seems she was involved in a love triangle." I shook my head. "But I don't get it. If someone wanted her dead, why tamper with the treadmill when they were already poisoning her?"

"What's this about a love triangle?" My mom asked as she came into the kitchen from the basement, cradling a quilt in her arms.

As I told her about Craig's discovery that Carl had been cheating on Sarah with Shelly and that someone had poisoned the beauty queen, her eyes widened in horror. "Do you think someone would kill her because she was seeing this man?" She gasped.

Mom placed the folded quilt on the table and sat down. She cupped her chin with one hand. "On *Days of Our Lives*, even though Julie was in love with her mother's husband, Doug, she never considered murdering Addie. But, come to think of it, I guess she didn't have to. The writers got rid of Addie by having a truck hit her. Problem solved." She ran her hand across the quilt. "I just can't believe anyone around here could resort to murder, even if someone cheated on them."

"People do strange things when they're jealous," Crystal said.

"But to kill that girl?" Mom continued, her brows furrowed. "You know, Michelle, this isn't your problem. Don't get caught up in this mess. Let the police do their job. Your father and I need your help more than they do." She walked to the counter, picked up the bag of chocolate chips, and poured them into the mixing bowl.

Crystal leaned over the table. "Have you ever thought

perhaps someone wanted to kill Shelly *and* destroy your friend's business?"

"Crystal," Mom snapped. "Don't go encouraging her to get involved! Mercy me. The two of you will be the death of me yet."

Crystal and I exchanged glances and giggled.

Taking advantage of the break in the tension in the room, I said, "I think I'll call T.J. and tell him what Craig and Lawrence found out. It's been a busy news day around here."

Mom smiled. "Sounds like a good idea. In fact, why don't you invite him over? It would be nice to see him again."

"Three guys in one day. My, my, we're going to have to bake more cookies." Crystal chimed, sporting a mischievous grin.

***

T.J. was happy to accept my invitation to come over and sample our homemade Christmas treats. His mother's idea of having holiday treats in the house was to fill Christmas tins with chocolate-covered graham crackers, chocolate chip cookies, and shortbread cookies she bought at the store. Despite living on a farm, baking was not her forte. Mrs. Wilson delighted in warming up pre-made pies and claiming to anyone who would listen that the pies were home-baked. After all, she reasoned, she had baked them in her oven at home.

Over the years, however, T.J. had become a connoisseur of all things baked from scratch, thanks to my mother. She loved spoiling him with her home-cookin'.

As T.J. reached for another Norwegian Walnut cookie, I told him about Crystal's idea that Shelly's poisoning and the treadmill malfunctioning might have both been intentional.

T.J. mumbled through a mouthful of food, "I don't think anyone would go to all that trouble to kill two birds with one stone." He looked down for a moment and shrugged. "I think it was carelessness by the installers or the manufacturer that caused the treadmill to go bonkers. I don't think there was any ill-intent involved."

"Maybe," I reached for a piece of Opera Fudge. "But what if Paul planned to hurt Shelly because she dumped him? He did look over all the equipment before the Open House."

"Yeah, but we keep coming back to how would he have known which machine she would use. And, even if he did, I'm not sure he would know how to sabotage it, so it would throw her off. He's a pre-med student, not a mechanical genius."

"Perhaps the poison was his doing? What if he wanted to kill Shelly, but a different person wanted to destroy Caroline's business, and the two crimes overlapped? I don't know. I'm just thinking out loud and throwing out ideas."

"I get that, but I still think the treadmill acting up was an accident," T.J. said as he eyed another cookie.

"But what about Carl looking underneath the very piece of exercise equipment that Shelly used?"

"A weird coincidence? I guess you'll have to ask him. I'm sure there's a reasonable explanation, but I don't think it matters. We need to forget about the treadmill and focus on the poisoning."

I squinted my eyes in disgust. Sometimes, T.J. could be so obstinate. I almost told him he was being blind to the facts, but fortunately, before I said anything, I realized my facts were products of my gut instinct, nothing more. I knew T.J. well enough to know my intuition would not sway him.

"Okay, I agree. We need to focus on who poisoned Shelly, but I'm not giving up on my treadmill theory. I still think someone purposely tampered with it."

T.J. shook his head and muttered something about me being stubborn.

Takes one to know one. I chuckled.

The door to the basement swung open. Mom had an armful of Christmas-decorated tins. She placed them on the counter, walked behind me, and put her hands on my shoulders. "T.J., would you like to stay for supper?"

"Thanks, Mrs. Kilpatrick, but I better be getting home. My mom will be expecting me."

"We'll have to make it another time, but don't wait too long. We miss seeing you, don't we, Michelle?"

The heat ran up my face and I hoped T.J. didn't notice, but he did.

He smiled at my mom. "Yes, we'll make it soon—" Then he turned toward me and finished. "I miss seeing you all, too."

chapter fourteen

Crystal and I cleared the dinner dishes while Dad bustled around the kitchen gathering the ingredients for his legendary Christmas peanut brittle. When he started whistling, that was our cue to leave. We joined Mom in the living room so the King of the Kitchen could create to his culinary delight.

Scattered across the living room floor were six boxes of Christmas decorations, plus the artificial Christmas tree box perched in the corner. My allergy to pine trees necessitated decorating the inside of the house with fake greenery. Dad, however, insisted on cutting down a pine tree every year. After all, he'd say, "Christmas isn't Christmas without a real tree." The compromise—his tree proudly stood in the screened-in porch behind the kitchen.

The three of us got to work, putting out the candles and Christmas knick-knacks and assembling and decorating the tree. Everything came to a stop, though, when it was time for the two-hour *Little House on the Prairie* special to begin.

Mom and Crystal were giddy with excitement. Other things, however, were on my mind. "Would it be okay if I took the phone upstairs? I need to make a call."

"Go ahead," Mom said as she snuggled on the couch with

her afghan. Her thoughts were on her show, not who I was calling.

Relieved not to have to justify my actions, I glanced at Crystal in the recliner. She appeared quite content with a blanket draped over her lap and a bowl of Mom's Puppy Chow balanced on top of it.

Gidget, on the other hand, wanted to dissuade me from going to my room. She raced me to the stairs, got there first, and sat on the bottom step, where she meowed loudly.

Bending over and scratching behind her ear, I explained, "I know you're hungry, but we can't go into the kitchen now—Dad's in there. You'll have to wait a bit longer. Sorry, girl."

She uttered a "Meow" louder than the first and raised her paw to bat me.

"Aren't we in a sassy mood?" I paused and considered my options. "Okay. Maybe I can slip in there and not disturb him. I can take your food to my room and—"

Gidget squinted her eyes.

"Okay, our room."

After completing my mission, I went to my bedroom with the phone in one hand and a bag of cat food in the other.

While I dialed Craig's number, Gidget munched on her food, purring.

"Hi, this is Michelle. I've been thinking about this poisoning thing with Shelly."

"Okay. Go on."

I tugged on the telephone cord and pulled the window shade down. "Lawrence said that Shelly had different levels of arsenic in her system, which means someone gave her arsenic earlier in the day and then again later that night during the Open House. Since we know she had her water bottle when she used the treadmill, we need to find out who had access to it before and during her Jazzercise class. I'll ask Rick and Paul if they remember Shelly leaving it unattended any time that evening. Maybe we can figure out who added the poison to her drink."

"Why Paul?"

"Well, if she left it in the break room, he might have seen who was going in and out of there," I said.

"Don't you think you should let Detective Douglas do the investigating since it's a murder now and not strictly the sabotaging of Caroline's equipment? Perhaps we should sit low and let him do his job."

I let out a deep breath. "Are you kidding me and miss the story of a lifetime?"

"Don't be melodramatic," Craig said. "I sincerely doubt it's the story of a lifetime, and, besides, you're not qualified to—"

"Look, if you don't want to help. Fine—"

"Michelle, that's not what I said—"

I slammed the receiver down.

Who does he think he is? Of course, I plan to let Detective Douglas do his job, but I don't understand how my helping him a little can hurt.

I pulled my crime notebook out of the bottom drawer of my vanity and began skimming over my list of suspects. As I recalled the events of that fateful day, I drew a timeline and noted each one, no matter how trivial.

Somewhere in here is the answer. Shelly had her thermos when she left the break room after talking to Elaine and had it with her after the Jazzercise class. After I talk to Rick and Paul, I'll move on to Elaine and Meg. Maybe even that receptionist at Langford's gym? Perhaps then I can get a better idea of what Shelly did all day.

I dialed Rick's number.

Despite hoping he had new information, our conversation proved futile. Rick knew nothing about Shelly's thermos other than she had one. As far as her whereabouts that day, he wasn't any help there either. In the end, he suggested I stop by the fitness center in the morning and talk to Paul.

Before hanging up, I clutched my silver chain. I hated mentioning Elaine's name since I knew how much he disliked her, but I had to ask. "Do you know where I might find Elaine tomorrow? I have some questions for her, and I'd rather talk to her in person instead of on the phone."

"That's funny. I try not to talk to her at all." Rick laughed. "But, to answer your question, she should be at her office in the morning. My father's meeting her there around noon, so they can look at wedding venues or something. I don't know. I zoned out when he said the word *wedding*."

"Elaine has an office?"

"Yeah, it's at Langford's gym, of all places. Can you believe it? Elaine's paying rent to my mother's competitor when she knows my mom is struggling to get her business going."

"I don't mean to be catty, but that's probably exactly why she's doing it."

Thursday, December 19th

I grabbed one of my pillows and covered my eyes hoping to block the sunlight shining through my bedroom window. I desperately wanted to roll over and ignore the fact that it was morning, but I couldn't. I literally could not move. The weight on my chest was too intense. For a moment, I thought I was having heart trouble or a stroke or—

Then I heard it—a gentle purr. I opened my eyes, raised the blankets, and discovered a sleeping Gidget atop my chest and shoulders.

Why in the world is she under the covers? She never does that.

No sooner had the words crossed my mind than my icy cold nose and cheeks answered my question. My room was freezing.

I slid Gidget onto the bed, carefully keeping her nestled under the blankets, slipped my feet into my fuzzy pink slippers, pulled my robe tight, and shuffled downstairs into the kitchen.

My mom, snuggly wrapped in a bathrobe and wearing fluffy socks with her slippers—a far cry from her usual pristine house dress and flats—was frying eggs and bacon while sipping coffee from a Christmas mug.

The unhappy voices belonging to my father and brother drifted from the basement as I shivered and moved closer to the stove to get warm.

"Did the furnace quit working?" I asked my mom as I rubbed my hands together.

"Yes, and your father refuses to call a repair person. He's convinced he can fix it," she said, her arms crossed.

"Does he know anything about furnaces?"

"No." Mom shook her head as she flipped the eggs. "Thank goodness for some heat coming from the stove. I may cook all day." She chuckled. "I hope Mike can talk some sense into your father and convince him to call someone who knows what they're doing before he destroys the furnace."

"Why does he always insist on doing everything himself?"

Mom wrapped both hands around her coffee mug. "His father—your grandfather—did everything himself. He built the house your dad grew up in with his own two hands." She took a long sip from her mug. "Your father believes a real man should be able to fix everything."

"That's ridiculous! Especially now. When Dad was growing up, machines were simpler, and Grandpa didn't even have a furnace. He heated his house with a coal stove in the living room. I remember him getting up in the middle of the night to move the coals around to keep the fire going."

"Those nights sure could get cold, couldn't they?" Mom laughed. "But your father doesn't think about how things have changed, only that your grandfather fixed everything, and he wants to be like him. It never crosses his mind that his father would have to ask for help these days."

We looked at each other and immediately quit talking when we heard pounding footsteps coming up the stairs.

Dad and Mike opened the basement door and Dad went to the table, sat down, and poured himself a cup of coffee. Meanwhile, Mike went into the living room. Neither said a word.

"Did you get it working?" Mom asked.

"No, we tried everything. Mike is calling a friend who works on furnaces. I don't think it'll make any difference, but he's going to ask him if he has any ideas. I just need a few minutes to figure it all out."

"Maybe this guy can come over and look at it," I suggested.

Dad glared. "And maybe you should keep your ideas to yourself. I don't see you in the basement helping us."

"You never asked," I responded without thinking.

"Why would I? The last thing I need is some hifalutin college student telling me what to do." He grabbed his coffee mug and stomped back down to the basement.

I looked at my mother. "Is he always going to be mad at me because I went to college?"

She shrugged and said, "It's hard on your father and me. Our parents taught us to believe that family comes first, and we thought we taught you the same values. Mike and Crystal have always understood this is a family farm and that we need everyone's help to keep it going. But you don't seem to understand. It might be a good idea to take time off from school to reevaluate your priorities."

"That's not fair. I don't want to take time off from school. I love you and Dad, but I want more out of life than living here on the farm. I don't get what's wrong with wanting something different."

My mother shook her head. "What's so *wrong* is that we need your help."

Words escaped me. Things had been going so well at home the past week, and I didn't want to fight over Christmas break. I placed my bowl in the dishwasher and collected my thoughts as I looked out the window. "I never meant to hurt you. I just wish you understood." A tear ran down my cheek as I swallowed the lump in my throat.

"Your father and I love you, but we don't think what you're doing will make you happy."

"I love you, too. But don't you see, I've got to try? Otherwise, I'll never know."

***

The Petersburg Fitness Center felt eerie—a stark contrast to the festive atmosphere the night of the Open House. The lack of Christmas music playing over the speakers only emphasized that there were no patrons in the exercise room.

Rick sat on a stool behind the counter, reading the *Toledo Blade*. Without glancing up, he snapped, "I wasn't sure you'd make it in today."

"Why wouldn't I? I told you I'd stop by. I mean, it's okay that I'm here, right?" I froze in my tracks, unsure of what he would say next.

"Whatever." Rick continued perusing his newspaper.

"Is something wrong?"

He replied a curt "no," then threw the paper down and stared at me, his brown eyes shooting daggers. "Actually, yes. Why didn't you tell me? I thought we were friends, yet I have to learn about you and Craig through the likes of Elaine. Really? I didn't think you liked him."

"What are you talking about?" I leaned on the counter.

He looked at my glove-covered hand resting in front of him.

I sighed. "Oh, that? It's not what it seems. Honest, but you must promise me you won't tell anyone."

Rick narrowed his eyes. "What? More secrets besides being engaged?"

"Craig and I are NOT engaged. It's all part of our act—"

"Your act? Why would you tell people you're engaged? That's the most stupid thing I've ever heard."

"Will you let me explain? Craig thought he could get the financial information we wanted if he posed as a potential investor for Mr. Langford's gym. It sounded like a good plan, but I wanted to go with him to the meeting."

"And how does your engagement fit in all this?"

"I needed a reason for being with Craig when he met Mr. Langford, so I came up with the engagement idea. Don't look at me like that! I only did it to help your mom."

"Don't use my mom's problems as an excuse to lie. She'd never want you to do that. I mean, honestly, Michelle, what are you going to do when it gets out that you and Craig are *engaged*? What happens then? You tell the truth and blow your cover with Langford, or do you keep up the act and continue lying to your family and friends? Did you even think this through?"

I let out a deep sigh. "I guess not. It seemed like a good idea at the time."

"Well, it wasn't."

"Maybe not," I said.

Neither one of us spoke for a few moments. I looked around the empty room and took a few deep breaths. I had no idea what Rick was doing—I refused to look at him. Finally, I realized I had to be the bigger person and spoke up.

"I'm sorry about the engagement thing. You're right. I didn't think through all the consequences. So, I'm human, and I make mistakes. But what's done is done, and I have to move forward. I hope you can support me in that."

Rick shrugged and nodded. "Yeah, I know you're just

trying to help, but you gotta be more careful with your plans. You're not living in some movie script. People get hurt when the people they trust lie to them."

After taking another deep breath, I replied, "You're right. I'll work on that." Then I asked, "Did Elaine mention how she found out?"

Rick shook his head. "She didn't say, and I didn't ask."

Glancing out the front window, I felt a chill and instinctively put my hands in my pocket. "I don't guess it's a big mystery how Elaine found out. Craig and I only told Mr. Langford about our engagement, and he probably told Carl, and one of them must have told Elaine."

I paused for a moment, lost in thought. "Who knows who all they have told by now?" My voice trailed off as I turned away from the window, unsure of what to do next.

"Yeah, I have no idea about that one, but there's a good chance Langford told Elaine since she has an office at his gym. I doubt it was Carl. I don't think she has anything to do with him."

"Why do you say that?" I was intrigued.

"My mom introduced Elaine to Carl at the Open House, and they didn't seem to know each other. Maybe Carl doesn't hang out at his brother's gym much."

"That's odd," I muttered.

"Not really. Maybe he doesn't like his brother's gym."

"No, not that. It's just if Elaine and Carl first met at the Open House, they got chummy rather quickly."

Rick squinted his eyes. "Huh?"

His ears and cheeks turned red as I recounted seeing Elaine and Carl embracing outside Mr. Langford's fitness club.

"What do you think is going on between them?" Rick's brow furrowed as he tugged at the sleeve of his brown paisley shirt. "And when were you going to tell me this? My father has a right to know."

"And what exactly is she up to?"

"I have no idea, but she's up to something," Rick muttered.

"That's why we need to find out what that *something* is before telling your father. What if there's a logical explanation for Elaine and Carl's meeting? If we tell him what I saw and then discover nothing is going on, he'll blame us for trying to cause trouble."

"Great point. I just don't trust Elaine," Rick shrugged as he slid the newspaper to me, pointing to the leading headline. "Do they have to keep up with the bad publicity?"

"I'm sorry the paper is still covering the accident, but don't worry. We'll get to the bottom of it." I looked into his eyes and placed my hand on top of his. "And when we do, I'll write an article for the *Wildcats' Daily News* and clear your mom's name. Maybe the *Toledo Blade* would be interested in running it too."

I leaned over the counter. "Did you ever hear the rumor about Shelly dumping Paul for Carl?"

"No! Do you mean that dude's been seeing three women at the same time? Man, what's he got I don't have?"

Rick and I exchanged glances and, in unison, exclaimed, "A British accent."

After our laughter subsided, Rick's face grew serious. "I guess you want to talk to Paul, don't you?"

"Yeah, where's he at?"

"Cleaning the Jazzercise room, although I have no idea why. No one's been in there since...."

He didn't have to say anymore. I understood.

"Is it okay if I go on back?"

"Sure," Rick nodded. "You want me to go with you?"

"No, I'll be fine."

"Holler if you need me."

"Will do."

As I made my way towards the hallway door, I couldn't

help but steal a glance back at Rick. Our eyes met briefly, but as soon as he realized I had caught him looking, he quickly averted his gaze and pretended to be engrossed in the paper in front of him.

After not finding Paul in the Jazzercise room, I tried the break room and found him sitting on a metal chair eating a sandwich with his feet propped up on the table. As soon as he saw me, he sat up and rested his feet on the floor.

"Oh, sorry. I…I…was taking a break," he stammered.

"No big deal."

"Can I help you with anything?" Paul brushed his dark blond hair to the side.

"Actually, I was looking for you." I studied Paul, realizing how much he resembled Robert Redford in the movie *The Way We Were.*

His crystal blue eyes lit up.

"Yeah," I said. "I had a few questions if you don't mind."

"Shoot away." He pulled out the chair beside him, his muscles bulging beneath his t-shirt.

I placed my notebook on the table and got ready to take notes. "About Shelly—"

"Oh." Paul paused, his eyes narrowing. "I told the police everything I know. I don't think I have anything to add."

"Well, that may be true, but humor me. I could use the practice of interviewing people."

"Doing some investigative work on your own?"

Without directly answering his question, I said, "I'm going to write an article about Caroline's business and the accident. I don't mean to be insensitive, but I need to get all the information I can while things are still fresh in people's minds."

"What do you need to know?" He leaned back in his chair and clasped his hands behind his neck.

"Is it true you and Shelly broke up because she was seeing someone else?"

Paul's jaw muscles tightened as he sat up straight in his chair. "Yeah, that's about right."

"Rumor has it you didn't take it very well."

"How would you take it if someone dumped you so they could climb the social ladder?"

"I wouldn't like it." I stopped for a moment. "Did you and Shelly argue the day she died?"

He sighed. "Yeah, we had words."

"Before or after she left the fitness center that morning?"

Paul looked away. "I wish I could take back what I said to her that day. I had no idea—"

"None of us did," I said as I scribbled my notes using the shorthand I learned in high school.

"Yeah." He returned his gaze toward me, his eyes welling up. "But I said some hateful things to Shelly. When she came into the fitness center to meet with Elaine, I asked her to give us another chance. She said she wasn't interested. I told her I still loved her, and you know what she did? She laughed and called me a fool—said she never loved me and only dated me because of my connections."

"Your connections?"

"Yeah, Shelly thought my aunt would finance her pageant dreams. She believed that if she won a major pageant, she could use it as a springboard into modeling or acting. Shelly had big dreams. She wanted to be a star. But when my aunt wouldn't help her, Shelly found someone with more money."

"Is it true you told her that as long as she was alive, you couldn't go on without her?"

Paul leaned back in his chair and crossed his arms. "Where did you hear that?"

"Is that what you said?"

"Somethin' like that. I wanted her to realize how much I loved her—that I would never stop loving her."

"What happened when she left that morning? I saw the two of you fighting."

Paul crossed his arms and glared at me. "Yeah, what of it? We exchanged words. I wanted things resolved, and she didn't."

"What about her water bottle? Did Shelly always keep it with her?"

His jaw relaxed. "Funny thing about that water bottle. Shelly always had it with her—she said it made her look cool —but she rarely filled it with water. Usually, it had Gatorade or tea in it. Man, did she love her tea loaded with sugar!" he said with a smile.

After jotting *sweetened tea* and *Gatorade* in my notes, I asked, "When she was at the fitness center, did she leave her thermos in her locker or the break room?"

"You gotta remember she only started coming here a couple of weeks ago, and that was to help Caroline get ready for the Grand Opening. Of course, she liked to try out the new equipment as it got set up. She told Caroline she was making sure it all worked properly." Paul took a deep breath and chuckled. "Shelly had a bad habit of getting distracted and losing things, including her thermos. I'd find it and hunt her down to give it back to her."

"What about the day of the Open House? Did she get distracted that day?"

"Shelly got distracted every day, but she was upset when she came back for the Open House. I tried talking to her again, but she told me to back off, that everything was not about me." He looked away. "I found her thermos in the break room but didn't want to bother her anymore, so I took it to the Jazzercise room and left it there."

"You mentioned your aunt. Who's she?"

"Sarah. Sarah Bentley."

chapter fifteen

I was relieved when I didn't see Rick when I left the fitness center. My mind was a mess, and I needed time to process everything. Plus, now that Rick knew the truth about the fake engagement, I had to let T.J. know. *If only I could call him from work, but Mae would never allow that. When I get home, I'll phone him. At least then, I'll have more time to talk to him.*

In addition to my dilemma with T.J., I was perplexed about Caroline's friend Sarah being Paul's aunt. Did Rick or his mom know that Sarah and the gym's handyman were related?

And I couldn't stop thinking about Paul's creepy words to Shelly about not being able to go on as long as she was alive. How sinister was that?

Lost in my thoughts, I was oblivious to my surroundings until I drove into the parking lot behind Mae's Gift Shop.

As I walked around the corner to the shop's front door, the image of Shelly's thermos popped into my head. *Where was it? Has anyone tested it for arsenic?* If it had traces in it, I could turn it in to Detective Douglas as evidence, which would prove to him and Craig that I'm an asset to the investigation, not a hindrance. *They have no idea what a good investigative reporter I am.*

I ran back to my car, threw it into reverse, and drove to the gas station down the street. Thankfully, the phone booth was unoccupied.

"Rick, this is Michelle."

"Hey, what's up? You forget something?"

"No… yes…I need your help. Paul said Shelly had her thermos at the Open House, and I remember seeing her with it."

"Yeah, so?"

"Do you have any idea what happened to it the night of the accident?" Biting my lower lip, I waited for his reply.

"I put it in her locker like I always did when I found it lying around."

"Do you think it's still there?"

"Should be."

I leaned against the window in the phone booth. "Great. Could you get it for me?"

"Sure, but why?"

"There's something I want to check out."

Sounding puzzled, he said, "Okay. I don't see what good it will do, but I'll get it."

I twisted the black telephone cord around my hand and asked, "Can you make sure no one sees you getting it?"

Rick hesitated. "Yeah…but why all the secrecy?"

"Because I don't know who we can trust. Until we find out what happened, the fewer people who know what we're looking into, the better."

He let out a deep sigh. "Michelle, I think Craig's got you seeing demons where there aren't any. I think your theory that anyone here was involved in Shelly's death is wrong, but if it makes you feel better, I'll get you the thermos after Paul leaves at four o'clock. He's the only one here besides me, so that'll be easy enough."

"Thanks." I sighed. "After I get off at five, I'll swing by

and pick it up. One more thing—were you aware that Sarah is Paul's aunt?"

Silence.

"Uh...no, I didn't know that. Are you sure?" Rick asked.

"That's what Paul told me today."

"Wow...that's news to me. I wonder if my mom knows."

"That'd be interesting to find out."

I hung up and quickly dialed another number. "Mom, I have an errand after work, so I'll be late tonight."

***

Glancing at my watch, I saw it was three-thirty, only ninety more minutes, and then I could drive to the fitness center and pick up the thermos from Rick. Afterward, I could stop by the police station to see if Lawrence was working and if he had any ideas about how to get it analyzed without Detective Douglas's knowledge. *Shoot! I should have told Rick to wear gloves in case the killer's fingerprints were on it.*

The phone rang.

Mae scowled as she said, "Michelle, it's for you. Keep it short. You know the rules about personal calls when you're on the clock."

"Sorry, Mae. I'll make it fast." I took a deep breath and picked up the receiver. Since people rarely phoned me at work, I feared it was bad news. Haltingly, I said, "Hello?"

"Hey, Michelle, this is Rick. Listen, Detective Douglas came by and went through Shelly's locker. He took the thermos."

"Oh," I moaned.

"There was nothing I could do."

"No problem," I said. "Guess it means I was on the right track."

"What were you looking for?"

"Just following a hunch." Out of the corner of my eye, I

glimpsed Mae glaring. "Thanks for calling. I've got to get back to work, but I'll talk to you later."

"Mae giving you a dirty look?" Rick laughed.

"You got that right." I smiled. "Bye."

As soon as I hung up the phone, I grabbed a bottle of glass cleaner and cleaned the countertops in the cash wrap.

With arms crossed, Mae stood on the other side of the counter and went into a monologue about her policy regarding personal calls. I didn't have the patience to listen, so I looked around the store, hoping a customer might need help. Relief came when I spied a woman's reflection in the security mirror.

"It looks like someone needs help." I pointed to the mirror in the corner, shimmied past Mae, and made my way to the woman.

After helping my customer find the perfect birthday card for her granddaughter, I walked with her to the counter, where Mae was ringing up a purchase—three figurines from Germany. The $534.89 sale guaranteed Mae would be in a good mood for the next few hours, sparing me Mae's wrath.

No longer worrying about Mae being mad at me, I processed Rick's phone call and realized that since the police had the thermos, I didn't have to go to the fitness center or the police station after work. Lawrence would keep me posted on the findings.

The more I thought about it, the more I realized that Detective Douglas getting to the thermos before me was for the best. Did I really think I could get it tested without his knowledge or getting Lawrence in trouble? My pride in trying to prove to Detective Douglas that I knew what I was doing had clouded my judgment. Craig was right. I needed to learn to slow down and think things through.

***

Hanging my coat in the hallway closet, I was glad to be home. It had been a long day, and I was exhausted. I slipped out of my shoes and wiggled my toes. *Oh, that feels good! Is that warm air coming from the vent?* After setting my black loafers on the bottom step, I headed to the kitchen, where I found my parents.

"You got it fixed!" I said, smiling. "It's nice to have heat again!"

"It certainly makes the job easier when you have people—like your brother—you can depend on." Dad took a sip from his coffee cup and peered at me over its rim.

My mom laughed. "And it helps when he knows people who work on furnaces."

My father slammed his cup on the table and stood up. "I could have done it without his friend's help. I was on the right track."

"Yes, dear. Of course you were." Mom walked over and gave him a peck on the cheek. "Now, sit back down and finish your coffee. We're all grateful you got it fixed."

She turned toward me. "You got a call while you were at work. The number is by the phone."

"On top of everything your mother has to do to prepare for Christmas, she has to be your secretary, too? You're lucky she gives you the messages. Not me, no siree. They'd have to call back if they wanted to talk to you. I'm not your answering service."

"I'm sorry. I don't usually get so many calls. Do you remember who it was?"

"Yes…it was that Craig person. I hope he's not getting you involved in something dangerous again."

"I'm sure it's nothing like that."

"It better not be," my father growled.

Too tired for more drama, I turned around and, without saying a word, walked into the living room, unplugged the phone, and took it to my bedroom. Gidget was curled at the head of my bed and nestled between two pillows. Disregarding the fact she would not appreciate my overtures, I petted her head. The gesture was more for me than for her. I needed to destress.

She raised her chin and snarled but started purring within a few moments. All was forgiven.

I picked up the phone but hesitated to dial Craig's number. The last thing I wanted to hear was his lecture about not interfering with the police investigation. *Why is it all right for him to investigate Carl's life in London and Mr. Langford's finances, but it's wrong for me to question Paul and look for Shelly's thermos? Sometimes, Craig is just too much!*

"Okay, Gidget. Here goes nothin'. I can always hang up on him, right?"

She squinted her eyes in agreement.

When Craig answered the phone, he acted like nothing had happened the last time we talked. He never once acknowledged he had upset me by telling me to stay out of the investigation and to let Detective Douglas handle it. Instead, he told me the reason for his call. "Langford wants to meet us for a late dinner tonight so we can go over more details about the business." Craig laughed. "He must think more information will convince me to invest in his fitness center. I'll come by around seven o'clock to pick you up, and don't forget the ring. We have to be convincing."

He hung up before I had time to respond. "The audacity of that man! What makes him think I would want to go with him tonight? Oh, that's right, what girl in her right mind wouldn't want to go with him?" Gidget looked at me through slivered eyes as she listened to my rant. "But—" I sat down on the bed. "the only way I'm going to learn more about Mr. Langford's gym is if I keep up this charade and play Craig's game." I pulled the ring box out of my drawer and slipped it into my purse. I'd put the ring on in the car. There was no sense risking my parents seeing it and creating unnecessary drama.

Looking out my window, I saw T.J.'s car. *He's home! Hopefully, I can call and explain this whole mess to him, and he'll understand why I didn't tell him sooner.* But my hopes for a quick resolution to the fake engagement dilemma were crushed when no one answered the phone. I sank deep into my chair and wrung my hands. *Now what?*

On top of my potential problem with T.J., I had the immediate problem of telling my parents I wouldn't be eating supper with them tonight. I tried to think of a plausible explanation, but I couldn't think of one that wouldn't make my father angrier with me than he already was. Then it occurred to me there was no reason I couldn't eat with them. *Mom would have supper ready by six o'clock, and Craig wouldn't be here until seven. Why risk a fight when I could eat a little with them and then have a light meal with Craig and Mr. Langford?* Eating two suppers was the perfect way to avoid a confrontation with my father. Relieved to have a solution, I returned the phone to the living room and ventured into the kitchen.

"Did you call Craig?" my mother asked as she opened the oven door to check on the roast. The aroma made me regret my plan to only eat a little supper.

"Yes, he wants me to attend a meeting with him tonight. He'll pick me up around seven o'clock."

"What kind of meeting?" My father asked as he got up from the table and walked over to the coffee maker.

"Something to do about running a business." I shrugged.

My father poured himself another cup of coffee. "Are you starting your own business now?"

"No." I grinned. "But a little business know-how can't hurt."

He nodded. "I think that's a good idea. Helping with the farm from the business side might be more to your liking. I'd be interested to hear what you find out."

I smiled and exited without delay, happy to end the conversation before veering too far from the truth.

Back in my room, I sat on the edge of the bed, staring at the clothes hanging in my closet while Gidget moved from her spot by the pillows and crawled onto my lap.

"What am I going to wear? I have no idea where we're going. I should have asked but I didn't, and I refuse to call him back."

Gidget tilted her head, giving me a curious look. I sighed, surveying my options. "Not much to work with, is it, girl? Any ideas?"

I wanted to wear something that looked expensive. Craig most likely would never date a girl who didn't have money, let alone marry her. *How do I project class—something money can't buy but sets you apart from the riffraff?* I remembered a photo of Jackie Kennedy Onassis, my favorite style icon, wearing black slacks, a black blazer, and a white necktie blouse. Although my white blouse didn't have a necktie, maybe my Eiffel Tower necklace would add the right touch. If the ensemble was good enough for Jackie O, it was good enough for me!

Gidget, notorious for sleeping on anything black, maneuvered toward my pants lying on the bed while I sat at my vanity and freshened my makeup. I hopped up, moved my pants, and draped them over my chair. "Not tonight—tsk, tsk."

After getting dressed, I hurried downstairs and ate with my parents. To my surprise, dinner went relatively well. When Mom asked me why I wasn't eating much, I explained there would be food at the meeting, and I would have to eat so I wouldn't appear rude. The explanation seemed to work. *Now, if only my next dinner this evening goes as smoothly.*

chapter sixteen

Craig checked our coats at Grayson's Restaurant and told the hostess we were there to meet Mr. Langford. As she led us to his table, the pianist played a haunting rendition of "Silent Night" on the baby grand piano.

The view from Mr. Langford's table was beautiful—the tranquil Maumee River and Christmas-colored lights cascading down the hill to the riverbanks. The music, the view of the river, and a shower of snowflakes created an enchanting holiday atmosphere.

Tonight marked my third time dining at Grayson's, and to think I had never eaten there until a couple of months ago—first with Craig to celebrate the *New York Times* publishing our article about Professor Ladd's murder and then my lunch with Elaine the other day. I was starting to feel like I belonged.

Mr. Langford, wearing his charcoal gray suit, burgundy silk tie, and matching pocket square, looked the epitome of style as he stood and shook Craig's hand.

"It's nice to see you again, Michelle. I'm glad you could join us," he said, extending his hand toward me. The corners of his mouth barely turned upwards as he attempted to form a smile.

Completely unaware of the tension between Mr. Langford and me, Craig pulled out the chair next to our host for me. As I lowered myself onto the seat, Craig flashed a charming smile and took the chair beside me, positioning himself to face our host directly.

"Have you been here before, Craig?" Mr. Langford asked as he picked up his menu.

"Yes, I have. In fact, Michelle and I were here not too long ago." Craig reached over and gave me an affectionate hug. I breathed in the woodsy scent of his cologne, which reminded me of the outdoors in the fall when the leaves were changing colors.

"Then you are familiar with their menu. Their Prime Rib is first-rate—the best you'll find in this area." Mr. Langford stopped and looked at me. "And do you have a favorite?"

"Not really," I said as I scanned the menu. "Everything here is always good."

The server came for our drink orders, and Mr. Langford suggested we also order our meals because he was on a tight schedule. "A night filled with meetings, I fear," he muttered.

The server's attire immediately caught my attention, causing me to almost let out an audible gasp. He was dressed like me—black pants and a white shirt. The only difference was that he had a black tie, and I didn't. Despite my best efforts to dress to impress Mr. Langford, I couldn't shake the feeling that I looked more like a member of the waitstaff than Jackie O— not the impression I had hoped to make.

Craig nudged me. "Have you decided?"

I looked up. The server was staring at me. "Uh, yes. I'll have the Petite Filet Mignon, Medium Rare with a House Salad, a Baked Potato…and a glass of unsweetened iced tea."

After Craig ordered a Porterhouse Steak, Mr. Langford started his business pitch. "I haven't heard from you or your lawyer, so I wanted to get together and answer any additional questions you might have so you can make a decision."

Craig lifted his water glass, swirled its contents briefly, and then set the glass down. "My accountant has been reviewing the paperwork, and while I don't have more questions per se, I have reservations because of the current cash flow situation. I haven't closed the door to investing, but I'm not convinced you can stay afloat for the next year, even with my investment of capital. Your ideas are interesting, but I doubt their viability for a good return. I'm in this to make money, not be a philanthropist. Let's be honest. If I wanted to invest in a losing venture, I'd put my money in Caroline's gym."

As per our conversation on the way over, I assumed my role as Bad Cop to his Good Cop and, in an annoyed tone, said, "That's a little harsh."

Craig flashed a condescending smile in my direction and put his arm around me as he said, "I am well aware you and Caroline's son, Rick, are good friends, but with all the adverse publicity about Shelly's accident and the equipment malfunctioning, I don't see how her fitness center will survive. It's nothing personal." Craig shrugged. "It's just not where I think we should invest our money if we want to make a good return."

I leaned back in my chair and tried to discern if Craig was acting or expressing his true feelings. He was so believable. It was hard to tell if he was lying or telling the truth.

Staying in character, I pulled away, creating a visible divide between us. However, I have to admit, it wasn't difficult to be upset with him.

Craig, in turn, removed his arm from my shoulder and focused on Mr. Langford. "Convince me why I should risk my money on your fitness center, and I'll talk to my accountant and lawyer again."

Mr. Langford seized the opportunity to elaborate on his plans, projections, and whatnots. Meanwhile, I surveyed the room but stopped when I spotted T.J. and Meg at a table in the corner. I blinked, unsure if I was seeing correctly, but there was no doubt it was them. They were sitting across from each other, basking in the warm glow of candlelight and holding hands. *What are they doing here? Is it her birthday? What else could it be?*

T.J. must have sensed me staring at him. He looked my way, dropped Meg's hand, smiled, and gave a small wave. The next thing I knew, T.J. was walking toward our table.

"Michelle. What a surprise to see you here!" He glanced at Mr. Langford and Craig. "Sorry to interrupt, I wanted to say 'Hi.'"

"I'm glad you did." I smiled, happy to see him, until his eyes wandered to the ring on my finger. The color drained from his face.

Mr. Langford noticed T.J.'s reaction and said, "It's quite the ring, isn't it?"

T. J. swallowed hard before speaking. "Nice. I had no idea. When did all this happen?"

Craig spoke up. "It was all rather sudden. But the best decision I ever made." He put his arm around me and kissed my cheek. "I'm so glad she said 'Yes.'"

I couldn't move. I couldn't speak. The hurt was evident in T.J.'s eyes. Everything in me wanted to tell him the truth, yet I couldn't risk blowing our cover with Mr. Langford. It was a no-win situation, leaving me with the only option of riding out the storm of deception I had helped create. I reassured myself I would call T.J. in the morning and tell him the whole story. Hopefully, he'd understand. *What have I done? If only I had told him about this earlier, none of this would have happened!*

The server arrived at our table with our meals, and T.J. excused himself and returned to his table. He sat across from Meg and said something to her. She turned toward me and smiled.

"So, what do you think, Honey?" Craig's voice jarred me back to why we were at the restaurant.

"Oh, I'm sorry. I was just thinking—"

"Yes, I agree. This would make an excellent venue for the rehearsal dinner. Great minds think alike." He squeezed my hand.

I feigned a deep sigh and smiled. "Good. We've got that figured out. Now, what were you saying?" I cut into my Fillet Mignon, but I wasn't hungry anymore. I set my fork down.

Craig continued, "Sam has revised his marketing plan, which is more aggressive than the one he showed us the other day. Other investors would substantially minimize the risk. What do you think? Should we pursue investing in his business?"

"Who are your other investors?" I asked Mr. Langford as I glanced in T.J.'s direction.

I moved the broccoli florets from one side of my plate to the other as I listened to Mr. Langford's response. "I'm not at liberty to say. Once we finalize the paperwork, I can release their names, but until then...I'm sure you understand." He looked at my plate. "Is your meal okay? We can send it back if there's a problem."

"No." I shook my head. "It's fine. I'm just thinking." I took a sip of water and continued, "When do you think the paperwork will be completed?" I set my water glass down and noticed T.J. was now sitting next to Meg, his arm around her and deep in conversation. I clutched the silver charm around my neck.

"Within the next few days." Mr. Langford's answer caught me off-guard. While focusing on T.J. and Meg, I forgot what I had asked him.

I turned toward Craig. "I think we should wait and see if his other investors come through before making a final decision. Of course, it's up to you." I looked into Craig's blue eyes and shrugged. I wanted to look away, but his intense gaze wouldn't release me. He said nothing. I held my breath. Did I say something wrong?

"Perhaps a little over-cautious, but I think you're right. A few more days shouldn't hurt anything." Craig turned toward Mr. Langford. "That will give you time to close the other deals, and then I can talk to my financial advisor about the decreased risk to my investment. After that, my accountant and lawyer should be able to move on it, but with the holidays, realistically, it might not be until after the first of the year."

"I had hoped to have this finalized by the end of the month." Mr. Langford bit his bottom lip, clearly disappointed, and I wondered what he was holding back from saying.

For the rest of our meal, we engaged in polite, non-threatening conversation about the weather and holiday plans. My eyes often wandered to T.J.'s table. He and Meg looked like a couple in love, but were they? In the end, what did it matter? I had hurt my best friend, and I had to live with that.

Our conversation was interrupted when the server brought a message to Mr. Langford. "You have a phone call, sir."

After Mr. Langford left, Craig put his arm around me and whispered, "It's going to be okay. Trust me. By the way, you did great." He pulled me close.

The tender moment between us ended when a woman's laugh echoed through the restaurant. *I've heard that laugh before.* My eyes grew wide when I turned and saw Elaine and Sarah dining together on the other side of the restaurant. *What are they doing here? Since when did they become the best of friends?*

I elbowed Craig. "Elaine and Sarah are here. Did you know they knew each other?"

"Isn't Elaine engaged to Rick's father?" he asked, glancing over his shoulder.

I nodded. "Yeah, and Sarah is supposedly Caroline's friend. What gives?"

Craig looked puzzled. "I don't know."

"Should we go over and say 'Hello'?"

Craig thought for a moment. "No, I don't think so. Let's sit back and see what happens."

"Sounds good. I'd rather not have to explain our engagement to Sarah, even though she probably already knows. I've had enough *acting* for one night."

Mr. Langford soon returned, and although he seemed distracted, he insisted we order dessert. While I ate my cherry-covered cheesecake, Craig reiterated that he would discuss the improved business plan with his financial advisor. Amazed, I listened as he continued to lay the groundwork for moving ahead with his investment yet somehow managed not to commit himself to a firm date for a definitive answer. *He really is a smooth talker!*

Mr. Langford signed the credit card slip in the black leather folder and stood, signaling our dinner had come to an end. With a slight smile, he shook Craig's hand and nodded in my direction.

As we walked towards the exit, I couldn't resist turning back to look at T.J.'s table. However, to my disappointment, there was no sign of him or Meg, only two busboys clearing the table. The thought of T.J. misunderstanding my engagement and feeling hurt made my heart ache. I felt guilty that I had not explained the situation to him before he learned about it, but for now, I had to put my concern for T.J. in the back of my mind and carry on with the pretense of being a happy fiancé.

Craig and I walked cautiously behind Mr. Langford, trying to keep a low profile and pretending to be deeply engaged in conversation. As we approached Elaine and Sarah, my stomach began to knot in anxiety. Could we pass them without being noticed, or would Mr. Langford stop to chat with them? To my great relief, he either didn't see them or deliberately chose to ignore them. Either way, we were able to pass by without incident.

After tipping the girl at the coat check, Craig and I hurriedly slipped into our coats and headed out.

Mr. Langford held the door open. "In a hurry?" He laughed and added, "If your people have questions, have them call me. This is an excellent opportunity, and I'd hate for you to miss out on it. Together, we can make good things happen for Petersburg."

When we got to Craig's car, we sat silently while the defrosters worked their magic.

Finally, Craig spoke. "I'm sorry T.J. got so upset."

"I should have told him what we were doing…with the ring and all." I sighed. "I'll straighten it out with him tomorrow."

"If you tell him the truth, are you sure he won't tell anyone? If he does, our cover will be blown."

"Look, I already had to tell Rick, and I know he can be trusted. The same goes for T.J. I'll explain the situation, and I'm sure he'll understand. After all, that's what friends are for."

Craig stared at me and asked, "Are you sure it's only friendship between the two of you?"

"Of course, we've been friends forever. And you've seen how close he is with Meg."

"Is that what's bothering you—that he's with Meg?"

"No. Don't be ridiculous. I don't like hurting my friends, and I don't like people hurting them."

"What are you talking about?"

"What if he's dating a murderer? What if Meg poisoned Shelly?"

Craig furrowed his brows. "You don't seriously think Meg did it, do you?"

I sighed. "No…but I can't rule her out. She had the opportunity and motive."

"Killing over a dress?"

"T.J. said Meg was furious that she had to buy a new gown for the pageant," I said.

"True, but think about it logically. To add the arsenic to Shelly's thermos in the morning, Meg would have had to have the arsenic with her when she went to the gym…and that would have been *before* they fought over the dress. There's no way that could have happened." Craig paused. "So, out with it. What are you really upset about?"

"Nothing. I just want to straighten out the mess I created. I'm tired of lying."

Craig nodded. "I get that. Talk to T.J. Once we get all the info we need from Mr. Langford, we can end the charade and life can return to normal."

Neither of us said a word as he drove the rest of the way home. I was too upset to talk, and I suspected he was at a loss for how to console me.

When Craig pulled into my driveway, he placed his hand on mine. "Don't be so hard on yourself. You're a good person, Michelle Kilpatrick—a very good person. I'm sorry I let you get tangled up in this mess, and as soon as I can, I'll get you out of it."

For the first time, I looked into his eyes and saw such compassion that there was no doubt in my mind—he truly cared.

chapter seventeen

Friday, December 20th

With only five days before Christmas, I should have been filled with holiday cheer, but I was not. In fact, cheer was the furthest thing from my mind. Instead, the look on T.J.'s face when he saw the ring on my finger last night haunted my every waking moment. The sooner I told him the truth, the sooner I could put the lies behind me.

The only problem was finding the time to talk to him. Since I had to be at work by 8:30 this morning, it was too early to call him before I left the house. Even if he were up, his parents wouldn't appreciate an early morning phone call. The phone call would have to wait until after work.

I attempted to push thoughts of T.J. out of my mind by singing "Feliz Navidad" with Jose Feliciano, but I was unsuccessful. To paraphrase Ernest Lawrence Thayer's famous line in his poem "Casey at the Bat," "There would be no joy in Mudville" until I straightened everything out with T.J. Never again, I promised myself, would I create such a web of deception. Nothing was worth this stress.

After tying a white scarf with a candy cane motif around

my neck, I raised my window shade. It was snowing, a guarantee that Mae's Gift Shop would be busy with customers frantically shopping for gifts. On the plus side, that meant the day would go by quickly. I tucked my silver chain and its Eiffel Tower charm behind my scarf—unseen to others but a constant reminder of my dreams to see the world, especially Paris.

Gidget thumped her tail against the wall as she sat on my windowsill. She had no tolerance for things falling from above—snow, rain, hail, leaves. It didn't matter. After several minutes of observing snowflakes floating to the earth outside my...or her...window, her patience had run out. She wanted to be as far away from the falling sky as possible. She darted in front of me, letting out an angry meow.

"Just a minute." I walked over and patted her head, but she batted at me in disgust. "I just need to grab my purse and notebook, and then we can go, all right?"

Gidget's eyes followed me as I grabbed my things lying on the pink and white comforter, her tail swishing back and forth. When I turned the radio off, she bounded to the floor with a thud and bolted into the hallway as soon as I opened the door, only stopping when she reached the top of the landing.

"My, aren't we in a hurry today? Come on. Let's go get some food."

On my way to the kitchen, I paused and admired the beautiful Christmas decorations in the living room. For a moment, I forgot about my troubles as I imagined the Catalog House in the movie *Miracle on 32nd Street*. Garland hung on the fireplace and across the window valances. A wreath adorned with gold ornaments and red bows hung on the door. Every surface was home to a bit of Christmas—candles, a nativity scene, silk poinsettia floral arrangements. I wanted to breathe it all in and take its warmth and joy with me.

With the festive spirit of Christmas in the air, I opened the door to the kitchen. The candles and freshly baked cookies filled the room with delightful scents of vanilla, cinnamon, and nutmeg. My mother was singing "White Christmas" with Bing Crosby, and I wondered if I had somehow slipped into an episode of *The Twilight Zone*.

Except for when Crystal was over and insisted on having music to work by, my mother never played music. The noise, as my father called it, from the radio or Mom's cassette tapes got on his nerves. Yet, even without Crystal in the kitchen, my mom was gently swaying to the sounds of Christmas as she stood over the stove frying eggs. A platter of bacon sat by a pile of several cassette tapes stacked neatly on the counter. I pinched myself to see if I was dreaming, but no, I was wide awake.

"Where's Dad?" I asked as I got a milk container from the refrigerator.

"He and Mike are working on some mysterious project. They said they had to get an early start if they were going to finish it by Christmas."

"Sounds exciting! Any idea what they're working on?"

"Not the slightest." She smiled. "Ready for breakfast?"

"Sure am. Smells delicious!"

"I love it when you have time to sit and have a proper breakfast instead of grabbing a muffin and running out the door. Have you thought any more about taking time off from school?" Mom carried two plates to the table, each with two eggs over easy, three strips of bacon, and a biscuit. I placed her cup of coffee and my glass of iced tea on the table.

I looked down, avoiding her gaze, and shook my head.

Fortunately, my mom didn't press the issue. Instead, she said, "I'll never understand how you can drink something so cold first thing in the morning—especially when it's winter." She shook her head and held her steaming cup of coffee close to her face.

"I guess it's 'cause coffee's too bitter, and hot tea reminds me of being sick, so tea over ice it is…I need the caffeine fix." I laughed.

Gidget finished her milk and sat by her saucer, washing her face while Mom and I ate our eggs and bacon. We made small talk about the weather and our plans for the day. Without thinking, I let it slip that I needed to stop by the police station after work. A slip of the tongue that I soon regretted.

"Why in the world do you need to go there? You're not in trouble again, are you?" Mom set her cup down and stared at me, waiting for my answer.

"Oh, no, nothing like that." I leaned back in my chair. "I just need to talk to Lawrence, that's all." Even without meeting her gaze, I knew she was scowling, so I quickly finished my biscuit. If she intended to ask me more questions, she did not, and before she had time to change her mind, the phone rang. Mom darted into the living room to answer it.

From what I overheard, I deduced the caller was my sister, which meant it would be a long conversation. I walked past her, waved goodbye, and said, "Got to go to work." I escaped unscathed.

As I drove to work, images of T.J.'s expression when he saw my ring, the act of someone putting arsenic in Shelly's thermos during the Open House, and Elaine and Sarah dining together filled my mind. Then there was Paul telling me Sarah was his aunt. Did Caroline know? If she did, why hadn't she mentioned it? If not, why did Sarah keep it a secret?

My train of thought drifted to Shelly's thermos. Surely, that's where someone put the arsenic. That was the only plausible explanation. The question was, who had access to it? So many people were at the fitness center that night—it could have been anyone. Yet, if the killer gave Shelly arsenic that morning and then again that night, what had happened? Was the arsenic taking too long to kill Shelly, so they gave her more? Or did they not know what they were doing and gave her the wrong amount in the first place and had to correct their mistake?

Regardless of the killer's motivation, they had to have access to Shelly's thermos in the morning and at the Open House. That narrowed it down to Elaine, Paul, T.J., and Meg. And, of course, Rick, his mom, and...me. Well, I knew it wasn't me, and I doubted it was Rick or his mom. Thanks to Craig, Meg was no longer on the suspect list. But who then? I mentally added the names of Sarah, Carl, and Mr. Langford. Perhaps they had worked with Elaine or Paul.

The moment the doors opened at the gift shop, business was brisk. We were so busy that we had to eat our lunch while at the cash register, grabbing a bite or two between ringing up sales. Granted, it wasn't very professional, but no one seemed to mind—especially Mae's regular customers, who were thrilled to see her shop thriving. Stacy and Lilly, the new girl Mae had hired for the holidays, reported for their shifts at two o'clock, which meant I got to go home.

Poor Mae, despite already feeling drained, she had to work until closing. Without the financial help from her cousin Steve, finances had become tighter than ever. Still, her resolve to make her store a success was unfaltering. A profitable holiday season would make all the difference.

Most days, my Orange Bomb stood out in the sea of white, black, and red cars in the parking lot, but today, it blended in with all the other snow-covered vehicles. Thankfully, I had associated my parking spot with a memory clue—I was the third child, and alphabetically, my name came between Crystal's and Mike's...in the middle. So, my car was by the third lamppost near the middle of the row.

I brushed the snow off the door handle, climbed in, and turned on the defrosters. When the heat became visible on the windshield, I grabbed my snow scrapper and swept the white fluff off the roof. Long ago, I learned that if you don't remove the snow from the car's roof, it will come back to haunt you when you stop abruptly for a red light, causing a blanket of snow to slide from the roof and cover your windshield—not the best scenario for driving.

After I got back into my car, it took a few minutes for my fingers to thaw, even with the heat blasting. Once the feeling returned, I drove to a nearby gas station to use the payphone. I wanted to clear up the misunderstanding between T.J. and me and didn't want to wait until I got home. The lie had already gone on for too long.

I dialed his number as my heart pounded in my chest. I had never been nervous with T.J. before. This was an uncomfortable feeling, and I didn't like it.

T.J. answered, his voice reserved, lacking any hint of friendliness. "Listen, Michelle, I've got a lot going on at the moment, so unless it's important, now is not a good time."

I inhaled deeply. "Sorry to bother you, but I need to explain something, but you have to promise you won't tell anyone."

"Sure. Whatever."

I visualized him giving me a major eye roll as I explained the fake engagement with Craig and the necessity of keeping it quiet. I pleaded, "Please don't tell anyone. I haven't even told my family."

"I wish you would have talked it over with me. Hopefully, I could have talked you out of doing something so stupid."

"And when was I supposed to *talk this over* with you? You're always with Meg. I couldn't talk to you with her around."

"Is that what this is about? Meg? So because I'm seeing someone and you're not, you have to pretend like you're engaged?" he shouted.

"That's low. For your information, I tried to call you before Craig and I met with Mr. Langford, but you weren't home." I choked back the tears. "I knew you wouldn't understand. I'm sorry I'm not perfect like Meg. I just wanted to help Rick and his mother."

"Yes, but lying isn't the way to do it. Nobody wants that." T.J. paused. "And nobody, especially me, wants you to be Meg. Michelle Kilpatrick is exactly who you need to be… minus a few of the theatrics." He chuckled. "Friends?"

"Always."

***

After ending my call with T.J., I drove to the park and explored its winding roads. I stopped when I came across a desolate area at the back of the park. In my great attempt to help Rick and his mother, the only thing I had to show for it was hurting Rick and T.J.—my best friend. *What have I done?*

The more I thought about it, the more I realized the only way out of this mess was to end the fake engagement. I needed to tell Craig I couldn't pretend to be his fiancé any longer. Although I knew the sooner I talked to him, the better, I decided to wait until after I checked with Lawrence to see if he had any news about Shelly's case. At least then, perhaps, I could soften the blow of ending our plan by giving Craig information that we could use to find the killer.

As I rushed to the police station, each traffic light seemed to be intentionally working against me by turning red as soon as I grew near, and when traffic was moving, it did so slowly. What should have been a relatively quick ride became painfully slow.

Sitting behind the wheel, impatience began to consume me, so I tried to calm my nerves by thinking about my list of suspects and which one was most likely to be Shelly's killer. However, my mind soon drifted towards questioning my own abilities. I wondered whether I was competent enough to help Rick's mother save her business. The more I thought about it, the more I doubted myself. Maybe I had bitten off more than I could chew.

As I pulled into the station's parking lot, my doubts about my investigative abilities vanished when I witnessed Detective Douglas and Lt. Grogan rushing toward the detective's vehicle. Two more officers were following close behind, and in a matter of seconds, the two cars took off from the station, their sirens blaring loudly.

I dashed toward the building and, once inside, headed toward Lawrence, who was standing behind the reception desk, talking with a uniformed officer.

As I waited at the end of the counter, I nervously fiddled with the decorations on the small Christmas tree. Since my last visit, someone had rearranged its decorations by grouping all the same-colored ornaments together. To pass the time, I mixed up the colors by rearranging the tiny glass balls.

After redecorating the tree, I leaned against the counter and drummed my fingers across its surface. Lawrence briefly glanced in my direction and nodded, acknowledging my presence. When the officer he had been talking to turned and walked away, Lawrence moved down the counter, stopping in front of me, a curious expression on his face.

"How did you find out?" Lawrence asked.

"Find out what?"

"About the shooting?"

I shrugged.

His eyes widened in disbelief. "You don't know?"

"Know what?"

"I assumed with your nose for a good story, you had heard."

"Lawrence." I sighed in exasperation and shook my head.

"There was a report of a shooting. Someone tried to shoot Sarah Bentley and get this...she says it was Carl Westwood."

My mouth dropped open. "What? Why would Carl shoot Sarah?"

Lawrence barely started to answer my question before I asked him another one. "Had they been arguing?"

I caught my breath, and Lawrence, seizing a moment of my silence, said, "I have no idea what's happening. I only know what I heard from the dispatcher and the officer I was talking to. He was with Detective Douglas when the call came in."

Leaning over the counter, I lowered my voice. "You'll keep me posted on what you find out, won't you?"

Lawrence glanced over his shoulders and, seeing no one nearby, replied, "I'll do the best I can."

"Thanks!" I said, giving him a grateful smile.

"If you didn't know about the shooting, why *are* you here?"

His question caught me off-guard. With all the excitement, I had momentarily forgotten the reason for my visit.

"The thermos—did they find any arsenic in it?"

As Lawrence was about to answer, he noticed an officer walking behind the counter. Quickly, he pushed his glasses up his nose and followed the officer with his gaze.

"Hey, Lawrence, do you have any carbon paper? I can't find any in the back office," the officer asked.

Lawrence nodded as he walked to the other end of the counter and opened a drawer. "I think I've got some in here." He ruffled through some papers. "Yep, how many sheets do you need?"

"You got five?

"Sure. Here you go."

After the officer was out of earshot, Lawrence returned to our conversation. "This may not be for public knowledge, so not a word to anyone, but there were traces of arsenic in Shelly's thermos."

"Anything else?"

"Gatorade. Unlucky for her, arsenic has no flavor. Shelly never knew it was in her drink."

A guy wearing faded jeans and a weathered University of Petersburg varsity jacket stormed into the lobby and slammed his fist on the counter. "Excuse me, can I get some help here? I need to report a robbery. Somebody broke into my car and took all the presents I had in the back seat." He let out a sigh of frustration.

Lawrence looked at me with a sense of resignation and said, "Got to go. 'Tis the season."

After leaving the station, instead of going straight to my car, I walked around the corner to the payphone and called Craig. I told him about the shooting and the arsenic found in Shelly's thermos. "Do you think the person who poisoned Shelly knew she often left it unattended?"

"That's probably a good assumption," Craig replied.

"Maybe this info will help us narrow down the number of suspects." I took a deep breath. "Craig, we really need to wrap this up. I can't go on pretending to be engaged for much longer. It's tearing me apart."

"I know this has put you in a tough spot. Just don't do anything rash. We need to plan our next steps carefully and avoid making impulsive decisions. That's what started this whole engagement thing in the first place. Until then, promise me you won't take matters into your own hands. We don't know what or who we're dealing with." Craig paused. "At the very least, keep me informed about what you're doing."

"It's a deal," I said, crossing my fingers.

"And no crossing your fingers..." His voice trailed off as I hung up the phone.

*****

As I walked through the front door, my mother greeted me with an anxious expression and handed me a small piece of paper with Rick's phone number. "He sounded upset. You should probably call him right away."

Rick must have really sounded upset for Mom not to object to me phoning some guy she doesn't know. I headed for the phone in the living room, and my mom went into the kitchen.

Rick answered on the first ring.

"Hi, my mom said you called. What's up? Everything okay?" I asked.

"No, things are crazy around here. I can't talk. Can you come over?"

"Sure, I'll be right there."

Mom stood in the kitchen doorway. Her green housedress was the same color as the holly on the dishtowel she was holding.

How does she do that? I shrugged. *I do well in getting things to coordinate, let alone match.*

Mom's voice snapped me back to reality. "Is everything all right?"

"I don't think so. Rick wants me to come over."

"Any idea what it's all about?"

"No." I shrugged. "Guess I'll find out."

"I suppose that means you won't be here for supper," she said with pursed lips.

"Sorry. I'll swing by Yancy's on my way to Rick's and pick up a hamburger, so don't worry."

"You'd think he could at least wait until you've had supper."

"He's so upset; he's probably not even aware of the time."

She narrowed her eyes. "Maybe."

Whatever concern my mom had for Rick was of little consequence now that it interfered with me being home for supper. Ignoring her curt remark, I ran upstairs to my room, grabbed my notebook, and went to the kitchen, where I kissed her goodbye. "This might take a while, so don't worry if I'm out late. Bye."

chapter eighteen

Rick swung open the front door as I neared his porch. "Hey, thanks for coming over. Sarah's in the other room with my mom. Wait till you hear what she's got to say."

"Yeah, what's all this about a shooting?"

"Crazy, huh?" Rick extended his hand toward me. "Here, let me take that."

After hanging my coat in the closet, Rick and I made our way to the kitchen, where we found Caroline and Sarah sitting at the table, engrossed in conversation. In fact, they were so preoccupied that they didn't even notice we were in the room until Rick pulled out the two chairs across from them.

Caroline looked up, startled. "Michelle, I had no idea you were coming over."

Rick sat straight up. "I asked her to stop by 'cause I thought Sarah could tell her what happened. Maybe it'll help us figure out what caused Shelly's accident and put an end to all the bad publicity for the fitness center."

"I don't see how what's happened to Sarah has anything to do with Shelly's accident or our bad publicity. I appreciate you wanting to help, Rick, but you should have talked to me first." Caroline glanced at Sarah and then back at Rick. "Sarah may not want everyone to know what's happening with her and Carl. It's a private matter."

Sarah set her coffee cup down, and the porcelain made a muffled thud as it hit the Christmas-themed linen placemat. "It's okay, Caroline. Word is going to get out soon enough, and I'd rather it be the truth and not conjectured theories," she said with a forced smile as a trail of black mascara ran from her red, swollen eyes down her cheek. "One minute, Carl and I were having a nice breakfast, and the next minute, he was like a madman." Sarah reached into her purse, pulled out a tissue, and dabbed her eyes.

I leaned over the table and asked, "What do you think caused the change?"

"I confronted him about the rumor that he had been seeing Shelly."

"What'd he say?"

"Carl denied it—said it wasn't true. I wanted to believe him, but he just kept going on and on with his denial. That line from Shakespeare's *Hamlet*, 'The lady doth protest too much, methinks,' kept going through my mind."

I leaned in closer. "What happened then?"

"I was confused. He was angry. He left."

Sarah glanced around the kitchen, and I wondered what she was looking for, but I didn't want to pry. As I watched her, I noticed how tidy Caroline's kitchen was. Not a dish was out of place, and the marble countertops gleamed under the light fixtures.

When Sarah returned her attention to Rick and me, she narrowed her eyes and bit her bottom lip as if carefully choosing her words. "The night of the Open House, I saw Carl tinkering with the treadmill in the far corner of the gym —the same one Shelly got on."

"Did you ask him why?"

"He said he found some screws lying on the floor and was trying to figure out if they were from the treadmill."

"Did you tell the police?" I asked.

"No. I didn't even think about it when the police questioned me. It wasn't until this morning that I connected Carl's actions with Shelly's accident."

Propping my arm on the table, I cupped my chin. "What happened?"

"When I got his coat out of the closet, two screws fell out. Something clicked, and I asked him about them. He became fidgety and said he meant to give the screws to Paul, the handyman at the fitness center, but he forgot with all the commotion surrounding Shelly. He grabbed his coat out of my hands."

Rick tugged at the sleeve of his brown paisley shirt. "Wait until you hear this. Sarah, tell Michelle about the rat poisoning."

Sarah took a deep breath before responding. "Carl bought some rat poisoning and took it to Caroline's gym."

Overcome with a sudden desire to respond logically, I took a page from Craig's playbook. "That's hardly a crime. A lot of people buy rat poisoning this time of year."

Sarah spoke up. "Yes, but why take it to the fitness center? Carl claimed Elaine asked him to bring it, but why would she, of all people, do that? Besides, neither Caroline nor I ever mentioned a rat problem at the gym to anyone. If there were rats, I would have called an exterminator right then and there."

I squinted my eyes. "Interesting. Rat poisoning contains arsenic, doesn't it?"

Rick ran his hand through his disheveled brown hair. "Remember what Paul said when we went into the break room that morning—that someone had spilled something, and he had to clean it up? And Elaine complained about getting something on her hands."

"Yeah," I nodded. "I remember her wiping her hands with a tissue."

Sarah got up from the table and walked over to the kitchen sink, where she gazed out the window for a few moments. Without warning, she slumped over, crying. "I never thought Carl capable of hurting anyone. He's always been so kind and thoughtful, but after today, I don't know what he is capable of."

Caroline joined Sarah by the sink and threw her arms around her. "There, there. It's all going to be okay."

Sarah returned to her chair, still shaken. "As if our fight wasn't bad enough, this afternoon, Carl tried to shoot me. I shudder to think what would have happened if he had not missed."

"I don't understand. He left, and then he came back?" I asked.

"Yes, I looked out my picture window, and he was standing by my oak tree with a gun pointed in my direction. I don't know what possessed me to act so quickly, but I fell to the ground just as a bullet whizzed by my head."

"You are so lucky." Caroline patted Sarah on the back.

"I immediately called the police, and that nice Detective Douglas and three other officers were at my door within minutes. They searched the neighborhood, but there was no sign of Carl. The police are still trying to find the bullet, so they know what kind of gun he used. Apparently, from the angle of the tree and the hole in the glass, they think it may have struck the brick fireplace and ricocheted off. The detective told me I was lucky it didn't hit me."

Rick walked to the refrigerator and pulled out a can of pop. He looked over his shoulder. "Do you want something to drink, Michelle? Sorry, I should have asked sooner. Guess I'm not a very good host tonight."

I shook my head. "No, don't worry about it. I'm fine."

As Rick returned to the table, he said, "Sarah's spending the night here. Her son is out of town, and we're all concerned Carl might try to kill Sarah again. The police will patrol the area and post an officer in front of our house."

"Sounds like a good idea. We don't need anyone else getting hurt." I paused and addressed Sarah. "Paul mentioned you're his aunt. What a small world!"

Sarah's eyes flickered to Caroline, her expression indicating a hint of hesitation before she responded. "Imagine my surprise when I saw my nephew at the Open House. I had no idea Caroline hired him, and he had no idea Caroline and I were friends. Paul was just as shocked to see me as I was to see him."

Caroline's reassuring smile faded as a knock at the door interrupted our conversation. The four of us exchanged uncertain glances, our attention now directed towards the entrance.

Caroline turned to Rick. "Were you expecting anyone?"

"No," he said as he got up but stopped when Caroline motioned for him to sit back down.

We waited silently as she went to the door and listened for any signs of danger. We collectively breathed a sigh of relief when she returned with Detective Douglas.

"Ms. Kilpatrick," he said. "Why am I not surprised to find you here? Investigating for another story, are we?"

"No, just catching up with Rick."

He looked at Rick and then back at me. "I certainly hope the two of you aren't doing your own sleuthing."

I spoke before Rick could answer. "Wouldn't dream of interfering. I just need more information for an article I'm going to submit to the newspaper about Caroline's fitness center—something to bring her good publicity, but I've got to get going. My parents will be expecting me soon."

"Are your parents ever not expecting you soon, Ms. Kilpatrick?"

"No, sir, they keep me on a tight leash." I shrugged.

Rick gave me a hug. "Thanks for coming over."

"Anytime." I smiled and told everyone goodbye.

As Rick opened the front door, Detective Douglas' voice boomed down the hallway.

"Ms. Kilpatrick, go home and enjoy the holidays. Let us do our job. Your life could depend on it."

"I'll remember that. Merry Christmas, Detective Douglas!"

***

Yancy's parking lot provided me with the perfect place to stop and gather my thoughts. After retrieving my notebook from the back seat, I opened it to my notes on Shelly's accident and wrote that the police lab had detected arsenic in her thermos. I also added the new information regarding Carl—his affair with Shelly, shooting at Sarah, and taking rat poisoning to the fitness center. It took several minutes to jot down all the details.

Despite my attention to detail, as I reread my notes, I became convinced I was missing something—the same nagging feeling I had while trying to solve Professor Ladd's murder. The evidence against Carl was piling up. He had both motive and opportunity, but would he really murder Shelly to save his relationship with Sarah? I let out a heavy sigh. Something about Sarah's story didn't make sense, although she seemed sincere when recounting the events and was visibly upset. *No one could fake their emotions that well...* and then I remembered Craig. Could I discern when someone was being honest? I wasn't sure.

One thing was obvious—I had too many unanswered questions. First on my list: What time was Sarah at the fitness center? *Rick said Sarah and Carl were at the gym the morning of the Open House, but Sarah said she never saw Paul until that night. Does that mean they were at the gym before Paul arrived? Yet Shelly came in with Elaine while Paul was getting things ready. If my timetable is correct, Carl was at the gym before Shelly arrived. So, how did he add arsenic to her thermos?*

I replayed the events of that fateful morning in my head. *That's it! Someone other than Carl tampered with Shelly's thermos. He must have brought in the arsenic and had an accomplice to carry out his devious plan. His brother was a likely suspect, but what about Paul or Elaine?* Paul was the jilted boyfriend. Elaine was Shelly's blackmail victim. At least, I thought she was a blackmail victim. Every piece of information resulted in more questions. My head was hurting. I needed to get home.

While writing in the warmth of my car, snow had covered the passenger side windows thanks to the westerly wind. Armed with my trusty snow scrapper, I cleared my windows before starting the drive home, but as I finished the last window, I felt a tight grip on my arm from behind. Something hard, which felt like a gun, pushed against the small of my back. I turned my head. It was Carl Westwood.

chapter nineteen

"I'll take that!" Carl snatched the snow scrapper from my hand. "Now, do what I say, and you won't get hurt." He pressed the gun harder into my back. "Do you understand?"

I nodded.

"Okay, we're going to walk to my car, and you're going to stand by the passenger side. I'll tell you when to get in. Don't try anything funny. I'll have this on you the whole time." He pushed the gun further into my back.

"I...I don't understand. What are you doing?"

"Just shut up and walk." His voice quavered, revealing he was about to break.

Despite my jelly-like legs, I managed to match his pace. Thoughts of how to escape ran through my mind, but every scenario I envisioned ended with my broken body lying lifeless on the pavement in a pool of my own blood.

Following his instructions, I stood by the passenger door of a shiny red Pontiac GTO, my eyes glued to Carl's every movement as he walked to the driver's side. Likewise, he never took his eyes off me. In a cat-like motion, he bent down, unlocked the car door, and signaled for me to climb in. Despite knowing that I shouldn't get into his car, the loud thumping in my chest prevented me from taking any proactive measures. I felt trapped with no way out.

"Where are you taking me?" I pleaded.

"Someplace where we can talk." Carl paused. "I didn't do it. I didn't shoot at Sarah, and I have no idea who she saw, but it wasn't me."

"Then go to the police. Talk to Detective Douglas. I'm sure he'll believe you."

He turned and looked at me sternly. "You don't believe that, do you?"

I shook my head. "No, I suppose not. But if you're innocent, kidnaping me at gunpoint isn't going to help."

"You're not really kidnapped. I'll let you go, but I need you to tell me what Sarah is telling everyone."

"How do you know I talked to Sarah? Have you been following me?"

"No, not you. Sarah. My brother got a call from one of his friends who works at the police station who told him Sarah reported I shot at her. I tried calling her, but there was no answer, so I guessed she had gone to Caroline's house. When I saw her car in the driveway, I parked down the street, thinking I could talk to her when she came out."

"Weren't you afraid the police would see you?"

"Yes, and no. This is my friend's car. The police won't be looking for me in it…at least not for a while. Sam promised he wouldn't tell them, but when that detective went to Caroline's house, I got nervous and started to rethink my plan of waiting for Sarah. That's when I saw you leave the house."

"And you followed me?"

"Yes. I wasn't sure how to get your attention, but when you got out of your car to clean the windows, I knew that was my chance."

"A bit dramatic for needing to talk to someone, don't you think?"

Carl nodded. "I didn't think you'd come if I asked you. I have to clear my name, but I need to know what Sarah is telling everyone."

"Why, so you can come up with an alibi?"

"No, so I can set the record straight. You helped solve that professor's murder, so I'm hoping you can help me."

"You could have just asked instead of kidnapping me at gunpoint." I turned and stared out my window. Carl's actions didn't align with his words, and my uneasiness grew as we drove down an unfamiliar road, farther away from town.

He nervously glanced into his rearview mirror and said, "I'm at a loss for where to turn or who I can trust. I don't even know if I can trust you, but I had to take a chance."

How long will it take the police to track Carl down? Sarah said they were looking for him. Then it occurred to me it would be several hours before anyone missed me. My parents weren't expecting me until late, and they might not even realize I wasn't home until I didn't come down for breakfast in the morning. I needed to convince Carl I was an ally if I hoped to survive this ordeal.

"Where are we going?" I asked, my voice shaking. I stared out the window, trying to look for landmarks along the way —a barn, a sign advertising fireworks, and a picket fence decorated with wreaths and garland. If I made it out alive, the police would want information about where Carl was hiding.

"I've been watching a friend's cabin while he's in Florida for the winter. No one will look for us there, so we can talk. But first, tell me what Sarah has been saying."

I recounted Sarah's version of events—the fight over him dating Shelly, the screws falling out of his pocket, the rat poisoning he took to the fitness center, and seeing him standing by the tree and shooting at her through the front window.

As I finished, slush filled with loose gravel bounced off the vehicle as he drove down a one-lane road.

Carl shook his head and muttered, "I didn't shoot at her. That's not what happened."

"Then tell me what did happen."

"Let's go inside," Carl said as he parked the car in front of the cabin. He opened my door with his key and grabbed my arm as if to remind me not to run away. His grip was firm but nowhere near as tight as it had been at Yancy's parking lot.

When we stepped into the living room, his demeanor shifted from threatening to welcoming. "Why don't you sit down, and I'll see what there is to eat. Do you want some hot tea?"

I shook my head in disbelief as he turned to go into the kitchen. *He is either a naïve villain or trusts me a great deal to offer me a cup of hot tea. I could throw it at him and make a run for it. Of course, that gun he has could be a game-changer.*

During his absence, I grabbed a multi-colored afghan hanging over the back of the brown leather sofa—perfect for throwing over his head after splashing him with the tea. But when I glanced out the window, I realized that escaping into the cold in the middle of nowhere was probably not my best option. Perhaps he was smarter than I had given him credit.

Laying the crocheted blanket across my lap, I hollered, "How long do you intend to keep me here?"

Carl looked contemplative as he entered the room. "Long enough to tell you what really happened. Then I'll take you back to your car," he said.

"And what makes you think I won't tell anyone where you're staying?"

He paced back and forth on the bear rug in front of the fireplace, processing my question. "If you don't believe me, I may as well turn myself in. If you do, you'll keep my secret."

"You're aware my parents will be expecting me, right? They'll call the police when they realize something's wrong, so if you're going to convince me you're innocent, you better start telling me now."

Carl plopped into an oversized brown leather chair, pushing the hair off his forehead. His face was pale. "It is true, Sarah and I discussed Shelly. She told me about the rumor that I was seeing Shelly, and I told her it wasn't true. Sarah said she didn't believe me, and then she accused me of poisoning Shelly. I wasn't even aware that someone had poisoned Shelly, but Sarah threatened to call the police and tell them it was me. I admit I got mad, and we exchanged words."

"What happened next?"

"I left, and I went to my brother's gym."

"What about the screws? Did you remove them from the treadmill Shelly used?"

"I did no such thing. I noticed a couple of screws on the floor under the treadmill that night, and I put them in my pocket. I was going to give them to Caroline, but then everything happened with Shelly, and, well, I forgot I even had them until they fell out of my pocket at Sarah's."

I looked around the room at the pictures of deer and geese hanging on the log walls. I compared the account I had just heard with Sarah's version of events. The eyes on the deer's head mounted above the fireplace glared down at me as if questioning my powers of deductive reasoning.

"And what about the rat poisoning?" I asked. "Why did you take it to the fitness center?"

"Now that's the strange thing. Elaine called and asked me to bring it. She said Caroline was having a rodent problem. I thought it was out of character for Elaine to be concerned about Caroline, but with the Open House, I thought perhaps she was trying to be helpful and mend fences before she married Dr. McGuire." He rose from his seat and stirred the logs. "Believe me. I didn't try to shoot Sarah. I couldn't have. According to what Sam was told, at the time of the shooting, I was with him at his gym."

I threw my hands up in the air. "Well, there you go. You've got an alibi."

"Except, I don't think the police will take my brother's word for my whereabouts. They'd think he was covering for me."

"Did anyone else see you at the gym?"

"No, that's the problem. It was only the two of us. Business was slow, so Sam sent the receptionist home early." Carl paused. "The police would say he did that to set up my alibi."

I leaned into the cushion and shook my head. "I think you might be giving them too much credit to come to that conclusion. But...let's assume you're right...for now." I set my mug of tea on the wooden stump converted into a coffee table. "Regardless, it was wrong of you to scare me like you did. And what if someone saw you kidnapping me?"

Despite the flames roaring fiercely, Carl kept stoking the logs. Regret filled his words. "Not my best moment. I acted without thinking."

"You seem to have a history of that," I mumbled.

He spun around. "What was that?"

With a boldness I didn't know I had, I repeated my comment, adding, "This isn't the first time you've been in trouble with the law, is it?"

Carl's eyes narrowed. "What exactly do you mean?"

"You got into a fight with your financial advisor, didn't you? What was that all about?"

"How did you find out about that?"

I waved my hand. "That doesn't matter. I want you to tell me the whole story."

Carl turned away.

A wave of frustration washed over me, and I leaned forward, pressing my point further. "Look, if you want me to help you, I need the truth about *everything*."

Carl swallowed and shifted his weight, avoiding making eye contact with me as he searched for an explanation.

"Well, are you going to tell me?" I demanded.

Carl muttered, "It's a long story."

"It seems I've got the time."

He inhaled sharply. "I'm not proud of everything I've done. It began when I was an economist in London. On a whim, I ventured into the world of writing, which turned out to be quite lucrative. My financial advisor suggested I invest all my profits from writing into the stock market, and for a time, I made quite a fortune, so I invested all my savings. But then the market crashed, and I lost almost everything in one night. That's when George Terrell, my financial advisor, offered me a way to regain my money through some high-stakes gambling. I was desperate, so I tried it, and at first, I won."

Carl paused for a moment as if methodically recalling the events. He sat in a chair by the fireplace. "It didn't take long before my luck turned, and I was losing more money than I could pay back. I kept thinking if I played one more hand, I could turn things around, but I never did." Sorrow crept into his voice. "My father bailed me out several times so I could cover my gambling debts, but before he died, he cut me off financially. Desperation consumed me, and I firmly believed that Terrell was rigging the games against me. I couldn't take it anymore, so I went after him."

"What happened then?"

Carl sat straight, crossing his arms. "The police arrested me, but Terrell agreed to drop charges if I signed a promissory note specifying a repayment plan *and* that I would leave London. That's when I came back here."

"And when your father died, did you inherit enough money to pay off your debts?"

Carl's gaze lowered as he spoke. "In my father's will, he stated that because of my gambling addiction, Sam, the estate executor, was to invest my share in his fitness center. If the gym was profitable, Sam would begin to pay me back. If not, I was out of luck. Plus, if I died or went to prison before the repayment was complete, my share would go to Sam regardless of whether I had any heirs."

We both sat silently for a few minutes, the only sound being the sharp snaps and pops of the fire. Although the warmth of the flames should have been comforting, I felt uneasy as I wondered what was going through Carl's mind.

He looked at me. "Not a pretty story, is it? Like I said, I'm not proud of my life's choices."

"I don't suppose you're alone in that," I said. "Do you have a good relationship with your brother?"

"It's fine," he said. "Sam helped me get established in Petersburg again. In fact, he introduced me to Sarah."

A sudden gust of wind shook the bushes against the cabin's windowpane. I pulled the afghan tighter around my shoulders.

"So, where did they meet?"

"At the Petersburg Country Club. They play golf together."

"Wow, that's convenient," I said, my thumb tracing the chain around my neck. As I leaned back in my seat, my brow furrowed in thought. "I'm confused. Why would Sarah accuse you of shooting at her?"

"I have no idea. The only thing I'm certain of is that it wasn't me."

"Who do you think told Sarah about you and Shelly?"

"If I had to venture a guess, I would say Elaine, but I'm not sure why she would tell Sarah a lie like that."

"Speaking of Elaine—the two of you shared an intense hug outside your brother's gym the other day. Is there something going on between the two of you?"

Carl's eyes grew wide. "What? Have you been spying on me?"

I took a deep breath. "No, not you. I followed Elaine one

day. But that's not the point. Are you seeing Elaine? I need the truth if you want me to help you."

Without a moment of hesitation, he shook his head. "No. Nothing is going on between Elaine and me. We're friends, or maybe *acquaintances* is a better term...and that's the truth."

I rested my arm on the throw pillow adorned with a cross-stitched brown bear. "What do you know about Elaine? I had no idea she and Sarah were so close."

"I got the impression they've known each other for a long time. They seem to have some shared history. Sarah's always been evasive about how she and Elaine met, but I know they confide in each other. When I first met Sarah, the three of us did a lot of things together, but after Elaine's engagement to Dr. McGuire, I haven't seen much of her. She and Sarah often meet for lunch, though."

"Is it true that Elaine has an office at your brother's gym?"

"Yes. She rented some space there. Sam says she's inquired about investing in the gym, so he's been giving her the royal treatment, trying to secure the deal."

"Speaking of investing...I heard you've been trying to talk Sarah out of investing in Caroline's business."

Carl strode toward the window, taking a fleeting glance outside before turning toward me and answering. "Of course, investing in any new venture is risky. I cautioned Sarah against making such an investment, but stressed that it was her money and her decision."

"So, you didn't pressure her to invest in your brother's gym?"

"I wouldn't say pressure. I told her if she was determined to invest in Caroline's gym, why not invest in both business-es...to even out the risk?

"But you stood to profit if Sarah invested in Sam's gym, right?" I bore into him with a piercing gaze.

"Yes, but that wasn't my motivation. I'm an economist, remember? I think about the big picture, about the future."

"Your future?"

"No, I was only concerned about Sarah's financial well-being," he said as he crossed his arms.

As I took another sip of tea, the bulge in his coat pocket reminded me of the importance of lowering the tension in the room. I tried to pretend we were old friends just having a conversation and asked, "What did Sarah say about investing in both gyms?"

"She said she'd think about it. We left it at that."

A loud knock shook the front door. Carl whipped around to look out the window as a voice boomed from the other side, "Michelle! Are you in there? Are you okay?"

It was Craig. Summoning all the courage I had, I moved toward the door, unsure how Carl would react. I kept my eyes on his hands and the gun.

Carl shouted, "What are you doing?"

Looking Carl in the eye, I spoke firmly. "Craig knows I'm here, and he will not go away until he's seen with his own eyes that I'm safe."

The pounding grew louder as Craig twisted the knob and kicked the door.

Before letting Craig in, I said, "I believe you didn't try to shoot Sarah, but we'll need help to prove it. If you trust me, believe me when I say Craig can help us. I'm going to open the door, okay?"

With dread and resignation, Carl nodded and stepped away from the window.

No sooner had I twisted the deadbolt than Craig crashed through the door. With his arms raised, he went toward Carl, ready to attack.

I grabbed Craig from behind. "Stop! He has a gun."

Craig's eyes darted around the room. He grabbed the fire poker and charged toward Carl, who shouted, "Stop! It's not loaded." He fished the gun from his pocket and slid it across the wooden floor, saying, "See for yourself."

Craig checked the gun and, finding no bullets, dropped it in his pocket. "That was a stupid stunt, Carl. You could have gotten yourself killed."

Carl stood motionless with a blank expression, not uttering a single word.

"But I still ought to punch you for kidnapping Michelle." Craig raised a fist.

I tugged on Craig's arm. "I'm okay. Carl didn't hurt me. He just wanted to talk. It's a long story. We need to stay calm and sort out this mess. Let's sit down."

When neither man moved, I raised my voice and shouted at them like they were two naughty children. "Sit down! Both of you!"

To my surprise, they obeyed, although neither seemed very happy about it. I returned to my spot on the couch, and Craig scooted closer to me. Both men sat rigidly in their seats, their bodies tense and their eyes darting back and forth, ready to pounce at the slightest provocation.

I turned to Craig. "Thanks for finding me, but how in the world did you know where I was? I don't even know where I am."

As Craig answered, his eyes never wandered away from Carl. "I had gone by Langford's gym, and Langford told me Carl was with him at the time of the shooting, but he took off because he didn't think the police would believe him."

I tilted my head. "But that still doesn't explain—"

"How did I figure out where you were?"

"Yeah, nobody knows I'm missing. My parents won't even worry until I'm not home later tonight."

"Mr. Langford mentioned his brother was watching a friend's cabin and where it was. I assumed that's where he went. I was on my way to find him when I saw your car parked at Yancy's."

Through narrowed eyes, I looked at him. "You recognized my car?"

"It's kind of hard to miss your Orange Bomb."

"I suppose you have a point." I chuckled.

"I went inside to find you, and when you weren't there, I asked the cashiers. A girl said that when she was coming to work, she saw you getting into a car with an older guy, and you appeared upset." He stopped and pointed at Carl. "There was no doubt in my mind who you were with—"

"I would never hurt her," Carl said.

Craig glared at Carl. "You expect me to believe that? You took her against her will to a cabin in the middle of nowhere."

"Craig," I said, touching his shoulder, "it's okay. You're here now."

Craig's eyes moved from Carl to me. "Okay," he sighed as he slipped out of his coat. "Tell me what's going on."

Carl walked to the fireplace and aimlessly moved the burning logs. Meanwhile, Craig nodded as I relayed the events leading up to his arrival at the cabin—his eyes focused on Carl.

When I finished, Craig muttered, "If Carl is telling the truth—"

"Which I am." Carl turned around, pointing the black iron-wrought poker at Craig.

Craig jumped up from his seat, and for a moment, I thought he might dive toward Carl.

Still wrapped in the afghan, I moved between the two men, removed the poker from Carl's hand, and carried it back to the sofa.

"Okay, everybody cool?"

Both men nodded.

"Okay. Let's work on the assumption Carl is innocent, shall we?"

Craig nodded. "Then what? The police are looking for him. Technically, we'll both be guilty of withholding information from the police if we don't tell them where he is."

I smiled. "Well, it wouldn't be the first time, would it?"

"No, I guess not. What's your plan?"

"First, we need to find out what's going on with Elaine. Is she behind the rumor that Carl was seeing Shelly? And if so, why was she trying to ruin Sarah and Carl's relationship? Also, has Elaine invested in Mr. Langford's gym? Not sure it matters, but I am curious." I walked back and forth across the room, holding the poker firmly in my hand and wearing the afghan like a cape, which made me feel like Sherlock Holmes. Perhaps subconsciously, I thought the cape would help me think like the famous detective or at least be a source of inspiration.

"If only I had my notebook, but maybe I can remember my notes." After thinking for a few moments, but only visualizing a blank page, I shook my head. "It's useless. I can't think of a thing except that I have to figure out who shot at Sarah. She said it was Carl, meaning it was a man or…could it have been a woman dressed like Carl?"

Craig interjected, "We need to find out where Elaine was this afternoon."

"I think that's a good place to start."

"Anything else, Sherlock?" Craig asked.

"Yeah, Shelly had something on Elaine…something she was holding over her. It would be helpful if we could figure out what that was."

I stopped by the fireplace and stoked the fire for a few minutes before turning toward Craig. "Do you think there's a connection between the shooting and Shelly's death? The timing seems a little suspicious."

Craig looked pensive. "It's possible, but then again, maybe not. I don't think we can rule out the possibility, but the shooting might have more to do with a lover's triangle than anything else."

Carl protested. "But I wasn't seeing anyone besides Sarah."

I shook my head. "That doesn't matter, Carl. A lie is as good as the truth if someone believes it."

Craig tugged at the cuff of his light blue oxford shirt until it peaked under his navy pullover sweater. "I have the name of the private detective Anne hired while investigating the finances at the Petersburg Lumber Company. Let me see what he can find out about Elaine."

I sat back on the couch and twisted my Eiffel Tower charm between my fingers. "I'll stop by Elaine's office in the morning and see if I can find out where she was this afternoon."

Craig smiled. "Anything else?"

I thought momentarily and then remembered Paul's name in my notebook. "Were you aware that Paul, the handyman at Caroline's gym, is Sarah's nephew?"

Craig's eyes grew wide. "I didn't know that. Are you sure?"

"That's what Paul told me yesterday. Did you know, Carl?"

"Sarah has never spoken of any family to me apart from her son," Carl said, furrowing his brow in confusion.

Crossing my arms, I said, "That's strange, don't you think? Rick had no idea until I told him." I paused for a moment before continuing, "Sarah insists that she didn't know that Paul worked at the gym until the Open House. But what I can't wrap my head around is, when she saw him there, why didn't she say anything about it? Especially since she and Caroline are supposedly best friends. I mean, if I had just discovered that my nephew worked at the gym my friend owns, I would have mentioned it to her. Wouldn't you?"

"Maybe—" Craig speculated "she didn't think it was worth mentioning?"

"Or," I said, "she didn't want anyone to find out. Perhaps it's no big deal, but it bothers me that she kept being Paul's aunt a secret."

I ran my fingers through my hair. "Carl, tell me again why you took rat poisoning to the fitness center the morning of the Open House."

"Elaine said Caroline needed some and asked me to pick some up on my way to the gym."

"Why would Elaine call you and not Sarah?"

"I don't know. I was trying to be helpful."

"Perhaps a little too helpful," I muttered.

chapter twenty

After leaving the cabin, Craig dropped me off at Yancy's, where I picked up my car. Driving home, the dread of facing my parents' wrath weighed on me. There was no way I could tell them Carl had *kidnapped* me. They'd insist I call the police. If I didn't, they would probably make the call themselves. The only glimmer of hope I had was if they had gone to bed believing I was still at Rick's house. Then I wouldn't have to explain anything.

However, my hope for an easy way out was quickly dashed.

As soon as I closed my car door, the front door to the house opened, and I could see my father standing behind it. Steeling myself, I took a deep breath and headed into battle.

"Where have you been, young lady? It's two o'clock in the morning!" my father scolded. His words sent a chill down my spine and my heart racing.

"Rick called hours ago. He said you left one of your gloves at his house," my mother said, puzzled. "Where did you go after you left Rick? Your father and I have been worried sick."

I slipped off my coat. "I'm sorry. Some things came up. Someone tried to shoot—"

My father's face contorted with rage as he yelled, "You've

been off playing investigative reporter again—never considering you might give your mother a heart attack. What have I told you about calling us if you're going to be out late?"

"There wasn't a phone." I moved toward the stairs, but my father blocked my way.

"No phone. You expect us to believe that?"

"It's the truth. It's not my fault there wasn't a phone. I got home as soon as I could." I stepped to the side and brushed past my mother. "I'm an adult. I shouldn't have to tell you my every move."

As I went up the stairs, my father's voice trailed behind me. "As long as you live under my roof…"

Slamming my bedroom door, I threw my purse and coat onto the vanity chair and plopped on the edge of my bed with a thud. Gidget, curled in the pillows, stirred from her sleep and moved close, purring and rubbing against my arm. I scooped her up, held her to my chest, and whispered, "What are we going to do? I can't tell them what happened."

Out of nowhere, I heard a rhythmic tapping sound against my window. Curious, I got up and looked outside and determined it was a tree branch blowing in the wind. As I gazed out my window, I saw T.J.'s car parked in his driveway, illuminated by a bright security light. The multi-colored Christmas lights twinkling across his front porch danced in the breeze while the moon cast a silvery glow on the snow. It was a breathtaking scene, but its beauty failed to console me as tears streamed down my face.

I was about to pull down the shade when a limousine pulled into our driveway. A solitary figure jumped out from the back and ran towards the front of my vehicle.

What in the world?

The person left something on my windshield and quickly returned to the backseat of the limousine, which sped back to the road.

I ran downstairs and threw on my coat.

"You're not going out again, are you?" My mother snarled as she emerged from the kitchen.

Catching my breath, I said, "Someone was in the driveway. They put something on my car."

Her voice softened. "Be careful. Do you want me to get your father?"

"No, I'll be okay. I'll be right back."

"I'll watch you from the door." Mom stood behind the glass storm door as I ran to my car.

My heart raced as I unfolded the paper and read it. Although my mom's figure was barely visible through the frosted storm door, her presence made me aware that my actions had put not just me in danger but my parents as well.

Mom opened the door and yelled into the night, "What did you find?

I held the note in the air.

She tilted her head and pushed open the door as I came closer. I rushed inside, thankful my father didn't see her holding the door open and letting all the cold air in the house.

"Well, what does it say? Who's it from?" She grasped her hands.

I shook my head as I slipped off my coat and hung it in the closet. "I don't know who wrote it. Don't freak out. It's a warning to back off."

"What do you mean? Let me see that note." My mom grabbed it out of my hand. Her eyes grew wide as she read the ominous warning: "Stop. Back off. You have been warned." She looked at me. "What are they talking about? What are you involved in?"

I bit my bottom lip and breathed deeply to steady my nerves. So far, I had avoided telling my mom the full extent of my involvement in investigating Shelly's death. Despite not wanting to tell her about Carl and my adventures this evening, the note changed everything.

"Can we go into the kitchen and talk?" I said. "I don't want to wake Dad."

As we sat at the table, I told her about the meeting at Craig's house, lunch with Elaine, talking with Mr. Langford, going to Rick's house, and, finally, being abducted by Carl—everything, minus the ring. I wasn't ready to deal with that drama.

My mom's response to my *adventures* was as I expected.

"You have to go to the police...Carl...this note...it's too dangerous."

"That's exactly why I didn't tell you earlier. Like it or not, I'm in the middle of it. The problem is I have no idea what I'm in the middle of—am I close to finding Shelly's killer, or is someone afraid I'll learn a disturbing secret about Elaine or —" I paused and looked around the kitchen. "Is there something else I don't know about?"

My mom's eyes narrowed, looking at me like Gidget does when she wants me to do something. "That is why you *must* go to the police. Who knows what you've gotten yourself mixed up in this time? I blame that Craig Mason or McNutt...or whatever his name is. Nothing like this ever happened when you and T.J. hung out together."

"It's not Craig's fault, but I can't go to the police. If Carl is innocent and I turn him in, I'm convinced the police will arrest him, and then they won't investigate Sarah's shooting any further. They will think they have the shooter, and the real person who tried to shoot her will be on the loose." I shook my head. "The next time, he...or she...might not miss, and I could never forgive myself. I can't let that happen. I just can't."

Mom stood up and pushed her chair under the table. "I think you're making a big mistake." She slammed her finger on the note lying on the table. "It's one thing for you to put yourself in danger, but what if this person comes after your father or me? Can you live with that?"

"I don't want anything to happen to you or Dad, but—"

"If you don't call the police, I'm going to. The choice is yours." Her tone left no doubt she was serious.

My heart pounded in my chest. "Fine, I'll go tomorrow."

"Good. I'm going to bed. It's been a late night." She headed for the kitchen door and looked over her shoulder. "Are you coming?"

"No, I'm going to sit here for a few minutes."

Consumed by panic, I buried my head in my hands and cried. *What am I going to do? I can't betray Carl's trust, but I can't risk my family getting hurt.*

The door creaked, and I glanced up, expecting to see my mom in the doorway. When I did not, my eyes darted to the floor. Gidget wandered to my chair, stopped, stretched her front paws onto my lap, and let out a soft "Meow." The brief interchange between our kindred spirits telegraphed her concern. She understood.

I picked Gidget up and squeezed her gently, her purr calming me. She looked up at me with her big green eyes as if to say everything would be okay. I whispered into her fur, "Tomorrow, I'll figure it out. I'm too tired tonight," and carried her toward the door. A flip of the switch and the room went dark.

Saturday, December 21

Whatever hopes I had that the morning light would give me wisdom on how to solve my problems, I was sorely disappointed.

Gidget sat by the window, batting at a string hanging from the frayed hem of the shade. As I slowly got out of bed, my head throbbed from the lack of sleep. I dreaded the thought of facing my parents, knowing that they would have discussed my involvement in the investigation into Shelly's death and the note left on my car last night. To say my father would not be pleased would be putting it mildly, and I could feel a knot forming in my stomach as I thought of his reaction.

I grabbed my white shirt and black pants from the closet and, after getting dressed, slipped into my black cardigan, taking care to ensure it wasn't bunched up in the back. No holiday accessories today—I didn't feel festive and I didn't have the energy to fake it. Although unsure what I would tell the police, I knew I had to go to the station when I got off work at two o'clock.

Standing at the top of the stairs, I remembered the engagement ring. I had no intention of wearing it, but perhaps I should put it in my purse. *Never know what a day might bring.*

I grabbed a muffin off the kitchen counter as my parents drank their coffee at the table. Hoping to get out before either one brought up the subject of the note, I headed for the door and said, "Gotta run. Have to get to work. See you tonight."

I thought perhaps I would escape unscathed, but as I reached for the doorknob, my father's stern voice bellowed, "Make sure you go to the police. No excuses."

"Okay."

As the words left my mouth, my mom looked up at my father and placed her hand on his. His countenance became less stern. "Michelle," he said, "your mother and I talked last night. We're concerned about your safety. We don't want anything to happen to you."

Mom added, "We love you. We're just trying to protect you."

As I shut the kitchen door, I took a deep breath. *Here's hoping the worst is behind me.*

While driving to Mae's, I rehearsed what I would tell the police, but nothing seemed right. It wasn't until I heard Andy Williams singing "It's the Most Wonderful Time of the Year" on the radio that I thought of a solution. Technically, I only had to tell the police what they needed to know, not every little detail. What a revelation! I could tell them about the note and as little about everything else as possible.

When I arrived at Mae's Gift Shop, I saw a crowd huddled and waiting outside the door, ready to charge into the store the moment the doors opened. In my perfect world, Saturday mornings were for sleeping in late, but these shoppers didn't share my viewpoint.

Knowing Mae needed my help getting the store ready to open, I hastily unlocked the door and positioned myself in front of it, blocking the crowd as they pushed, trying to rush past me. Despite their attempts to enter, I stood my ground and said, "We'll be open in a few minutes. I'll tell Mae you guys are waiting."

Once inside, I locked the door behind me and spotted a woman with dark hair wearing a fur coat walking behind the crowd of shoppers. She bore an uncanny resemblance to Elaine. *Shoot! I forgot to call Elaine this morning and make an appointment with her so I can check on her whereabouts at the time of the shooting. Note to self: Police station and then call Elaine.*

I pushed the cash drawer in the antique register while Mae unlocked the front door. The horde of frantic Christmas shoppers stormed into the shop, and the scene soon became chaotic as customers needed everything from help to locate a particular card to wanting figurines in the locked showcases. Within thirty minutes, a line ran from the register to the back wall. My head was spinning, but the last Saturday before Christmas was shaping up to be a retailer's delight.

Mae worked the floor while I feverishly tapped away at the register's keys. The pressure to keep the line moving provided a much-needed adrenaline rush to reinvigorate me. As I rang up a sale of Christmas partyware, I glanced at the line of waiting faces and saw Mrs. Winterfield and her daughter, Elizabeth—smiling.

When Mrs. Winterfield handed me her stack of Christmas

money envelopes, her smile widened as she looked past my shoulder toward the front door. "Well, if it isn't Craig Miller!"

"Mrs. Winterfield, how nice to see you." Craig gave her a friendly hug. "I see you're out doing some Christmas shopping."

She laughed, regaining her footing after teetering from his hug, and leaned on her cane. Showing him her stack of money enclosure cards, she replied, "With so many grandchildren and great-grandchildren, giving them money is the easiest thing to do. They can buy whatever they want, and I don't have to keep up with all the new-fangled stuff they're into these days."

Mrs. Winterfield dug into her purse and laid her money on the counter. "And how are you, Craig? Gracious me, it's been a while since I last saw you. How is that new book of yours coming?"

Elizabeth glanced over her shoulder, apparently sensing the people in line were growing impatient as her mother tied up the line by talking to Craig. She placed her hand on her mother's shoulder and guided Mrs. Winterfield to a spot away from the register where they could talk without being in anyone's way. I desperately wanted to hear what they were saying, but the sound of the cash register dashed any hope of that.

After Mrs. Winterfield and Elizabeth left the store, Craig strolled behind the counter.

"Would you mind bagging for me?" I asked.

He grinned. "No, happy to help. I had no idea you'd be this busy." In an instant, he whipped out a bag from underneath the counter and got to work.

I handed him a rose gold necklace. "The jewelry boxes are to your left, on the top shelf…thanks, you're a lifesaver."

As Craig packed the necklace, the customer wrote a check. I requested her driver's license and a credit card, noted them on the back of the check, and then placed it under the register tray.

I exhaled a deep breath. "It's been like this ever since Mae opened this morning. Crazy."

Anticipating the next sale, Craig reached for a large bag, popped it open, and said, "I'm surprised you're here this morning...after last night."

The next customer's eyes grew wide.

"Trust me, nothing that exciting." I laughed as she handed me twelve evergreen taper candles. I turned to Craig. "You'll need to wrap each of those in tissue paper so they won't break."

After he finished wrapping the candles, he handed the woman her package. Grinning, I patted Craig on the shoulder. "Nice work. You know, if that writing gig of yours doesn't work out, maybe your mom will let you work here."

No sooner had I said the words than the customer's mouth dropped open in shock. "Oh my gosh! You're Craig Miller! I thought I recognized you. I've read all your books!"

Caught off guard, Craig stammered, "Uh... well...thank you. I'm glad you like them."

She rummaged through her purse for a small notepad. Only momentarily taking her eyes off Craig to ask me, "Do you have a pen?"

I nodded and handed her one, which she gave to Craig along with the notepad. "Can I have your autograph, please?"

The customers following in line all asked for his autograph, their voices filled with excitement. Clearly enjoying his time in the limelight, a smiling Craig obliged each request. By one thirty, everyone had gotten what they wanted—a personalized note from Craig—and the long line of autograph seekers faded away.

Leaning my back against the cash register, I asked, "I didn't have time to ask earlier, but did Mrs. Winterfield or her daughter have anything interesting to say?"

"No, just the usual chit-chat—the weather, her grandkids, my book...and, oh, yeah, a trip she took a few months back."

"Oh, where did she go? I don't remember Mrs. Winterfield talking about a trip."

Craig glanced sideways, momentarily staring into space. "I don't think she said. I remember asking, but somehow the subject got changed."

With a smirk, I replied, "You don't suppose she had anything to do with the illegal domestic spying by the CIA that the *New York Times* reported today, do you?"

Mae wandered to the cash wrap after everyone was gone and hugged Craig, oblivious to the excitement she had missed while wrapping gifts in the back room. "What are you two laughing about?"

"Nothing, just glad we survived the morning rush," Craig said.

"Well, I'm glad you came by. I'm going to grab a bite in the back. Do you want to join me?" Mae asked.

"Thanks, but I think I'll pass. I need to get going in a few minutes."

After she was out of earshot, I whirled around to Craig and confessed that I had forgotten to call Elaine this morning. My shoulders slumped like I'd broken a sacred vow by not following through on my word.

"It's not that big of a deal," he said.

Still, I couldn't shake the feeling that something was very wrong. "But what if she turns out to be our killer?"

Craig's emerald green eyes glazed over as he paused to think. After a few moments of silence, he asked, "Do you have any plans for after work?"

"I promised my mom I'd go to the police station as soon as possible and tell them about the note."

"The note? What note?" he asked, his brows furrowing in confusion.

With trembling hands, I dug into my pocket, unfolded the paper, and handed it to him.

Craig pulled his dark-rimmed glasses out of his blazer pocket. As he read it, I told him about the limo, the shadowy person who put the note on my car, and my mother's insistence that I tell the police.

"Are you going to tell them about Carl?"

"My mother wants me to, but I don't think I should. That would betray his trust. I don't know what to do."

"I'm not convinced you should trust Carl, but I'll follow your instincts on this one...for now." He slipped his glasses back into his pocket. "Why don't I go with you to the station, and then we can go to Langford's gym and see if we can learn anything about Elaine's whereabouts yesterday afternoon?"

"That'd be great, but I better call my parents so they don't worry. I'm in enough trouble as it is."

Craig handed me the phone.

"Mae doesn't let us use the phone for personal calls. She gets *really* mad."

"If she says anything, I'll tell her I made you do it." He smiled and looked down at my hand. "Don't suppose you have the ring with you—for when we go to Langford's?"

"It's in my purse. Let's just say being prepared is my middle name."

chapter twenty-one

When Craig and I arrived at Langford's fitness center, no one was there except for the receptionist sitting behind the counter. The college-aged girl's long brunette ponytail swayed to Jim Croce's "It Doesn't Have to Be That Way" as it played through the speakers. She was so engrossed in reading the latest issue of *Rolling Stone* that she didn't even notice us until Craig greeted her with a "Hi, Mindy. How's it going?"

At the sound of his voice, she jumped, and the magazine slipped from her hands onto the counter. "Craig, I'm sorry. I didn't hear you come in." Regaining her composure, she pulled her ponytail to the front of her shoulder and gave him a coy grin.

"That's okay." Craig tilted his head and raised an eyebrow, attempting to read the article upside down. "Is it good?"

"Yeah, it's about George Harrison. He's the best, I mean, as far musicians go."

Craig nodded. "Yes, he is one of a kind. Have you heard his latest album, *Dark Horse*, yet?"

"Nope, but I'm hoping it finds its way under my Christmas tree," she giggled.

Craig returned a smile as he held one hand in the air and

crossed his fingers in agreement before glancing down the hall. "Is Elaine in?"

"Nope," Mindy said.

"Was she here yesterday?"

She shook her head.

"Any idea when she'll be back?"

"No. Sorry." Mindy gazed into Craig's eyes. "Is there something I can help you with?"

Craig flashed his Hollywood white smile and said, "Thanks, but I need to talk to Elaine. When was the last time you saw her?"

Mindy's eyes lit up. "She was here this morning…had a meeting with some lady."

"Do you remember the lady's name?" I asked, running my fingers through my hair.

Mindy acknowledged my presence for the first time since we walked into Langford's gym. Her eyes darted to the sparkling diamond ring on my finger, and her expression soured as she uttered a frosty response. "No. I don't keep track of Elaine's appointments. She just rents office space here." Mindy then turned her attention back to Craig, making it clear she was not interested in talking to me.

Craig leaned over the counter, narrowing the space between him and Mindy, and asked, "Can you describe the woman?"

Mindy's face softened. "Older than Elaine, closer to Mr. Langford's age, I guess. She has short blonde hair, is always nicely dressed, and wears some large rocks on her fingers."

"Does she come here often?" Craig pressed.

"Yeah. She drops by a lot."

Craig stared into Mindy's eyes, "Come to think of it, I do have a favor to ask of you. In fact, you might be the only one who can help. Do you think you could find any information on Elaine in your files? I'd really appreciate it, if you could."

Mesmerized by Craig's gaze, Mindy said nothing as she stared back at him.

I cleared my throat. "Uh, Mindy. Info on Elaine?"

Mindy snapped back to reality with a disgruntled sigh. "Yeah, give me a minute. Her file's over there." She briskly went to the cabinet at the end of the counter and pulled open a drawer. After thumbing through the files, she pulled one out, closed the drawer and placed Elaine's file in front of Craig.

Mindy cupped her head on the counter and asked, "Is there anything else you need me to do?"

"Not yet, but thanks." Craig smiled as he flipped through the papers until he came to Elaine's rental agreement. He laid it on the counter so I could read it too.

I scanned the page for anything interesting, but nothing stood out until Craig pointed to the bottom. His eyes were alight with excitement as he asked, "Well, what do we have here?"

I gasped when I saw the words "Emergency Contact: Sarah Bentley."

Craig closed the file and slid it back to Mindy. "Thank you, Mindy. You've been a great help." He paused. "It'd probably be a good idea not to mention we were here this afternoon. I don't want to get you in trouble for showing us the file."

She gave Craig a sly wink and smiled. "You were never here."

As we left Langford's gym, I glanced over my shoulder. Mindy was once again reading her copy of *Rolling Stone*, except this time, she was wearing a huge smile.

"You made her day." I teased Craig.

"What can I say?" He grinned as I gave him an eye roll.

Leaving a trail of footprints in the freshly fallen snow, we made our way to his silver Jaguar. Always the gentleman, he unlocked the passenger door and held it open as I slid onto the red leather seat. "I need to grab my ice scrapper out of the trunk, but first, let me turn on the car and get some heat going. No sense both of us freezing."

While Craig brushed away the accumulation of white flakes, I mulled over Elaine's connection to Sarah. *This is just too weird! First, Sarah and Paul are related, and now Sarah is Elaine's emergency contact.*

Craig climbed into the car and placed his hands in front of the vent. He let out a contented sigh as the warmth spread through his fingers.

I shook my head. "Don't you have any gloves?"

"Forgot them. I didn't realize it was going to snow today."

"To paraphrase a friend, 'Rule Number One for anyone living in the Midwest during the winter: Always have a pair of gloves with you.'"

"I wasn't very nice that day, was I?" Craig chuckled, remembering how my pen had rolled under his seat in our journalism class. Instead of simply handing it back to me, he lectured me on the necessity of a good reporter never being without an extra pen.

"No...no, you weren't." I shook my head, amazed at how far we had come since that day and my first impression of him being a snob. *Well,* I smirked. *Maybe I wasn't so far off on that one.*

"You've taught me a lot since that day," Craig grinned as he backed out of the parking spot and headed for the exit. "So...what do you think about Sarah's name on Elaine's contract?"

"Sarah and Elaine are definitely friends. But why list Sarah as an emergency contact and not Dr. McGuire?" I crossed my arms and leaned back in my seat. "And why try to drive a wedge between Carl and Sarah? I'm going to say it again. Elaine sounds like a troublemaker."

Craig waited for an opening in the traffic before pulling out onto the street. "But why? What's her end game?"

"Maybe she has a thing for Carl?"

"But she's engaged to Dr. McGuire?"

"Perhaps his British accent swayed her? When I spotted them the other day, Elaine looked pretty smitten with him." I sat straight up. "What if Carl rejected her advances, and she wanted to get back at him? What better way than to disguise herself as Carl and shoot at Sarah?"

"Oh, two for the price of one, huh?"

"Exactly! By framing Carl, Sarah loses the man she loves, and Carl loses his freedom by ending up in prison. It's the old *if I can't have him, then nobody can* scenario."

"You're way too much of a romantic with that explanation. However, I do like the possibility of Elaine disguising herself as Carl. I could use that in my next book."

"Well, if it's not my love triangle theory, what else could it be?"

"Let's think...what if Elaine doesn't actually like Sarah...or it could be Elaine has doubts about Carl's sincerity toward Sarah and wants to save her friend from getting hurt?"

I looked out the window as I considered his ideas. "I like my version better, but you may have a point," I said.

He beamed.

"What?"

"Nothing," he said. "I just love it when you admit I might be right."

"Sometimes, sir, you are insufferable. You know that?"

Craig raised an eyebrow in response, and his grin grew even wider.

"Okay, Mr. Know-It-All, before we get too sidetracked with Elaine's motivation, we need to figure out who tried to shoot Sarah. Was it Carl or someone else?

Craig cocked his head. "Any ideas?"

I frowned and shook my head. "No. How 'bout you? You're the great mystery writer."

With a smirk, he asked, "Do I detect a hint of sarcasm, Ms. Kilpatrick?"

"No...it's just that—"

"Have you ever read any of my books?"

I slumped in my seat. "Uh...n...no...I haven't had time with finals and all."

"Sure." Craig's green eyes twinkled. "So, you really have no idea how I would write my way out of this, do you?"

"No, but I assume—"

"Never assume," he said as he turned toward me, his voice stern and his eyebrow arched. "Haven't I taught you that yet?"

As Craig spoke, the rumbling sound of my father scolding me echoed in my head, bringing up memories of past mistakes and disappointments. I felt a knot form in my stomach as I clenched my fists, trying to control the surge of emotions threatening to overwhelm me. Taking a deep breath, I turned my attention back to my window. The view outside was a blur as I tried to push back against the turmoil Craig's words had inadvertently ignited.

After a few moments of strained silence, Craig rested his hand on my shoulder, his voice apologetic. "I'm sorry," he said. "But sometimes I worry because you get an idea in your head and then you act on it without thinking it through first."

I shrugged. "You're right. But sometimes, I don't have time to wait."

Craig sighed heavily. "True, but it can be a dangerous game if you don't think first. If you're going to be a reporter chasing stories, remember to think before you act, or else it could cost you your life." He paused and smiled. "Okay, enough of my lecture...now, back to my book. Tell you what? Next time I see you, I'll give you a copy of each of my books."

"Thanks. That'd be nice."

"I'll even autograph them. They'll be worth a fortune someday!" He laughed.

I couldn't help but laugh too. "You are sooo conceited!"

"I know. Isn't it wonderful!"

I shook my head, still laughing.

Once our laughter faded, I proposed an idea. "We need to talk to Sarah again. Hopefully, she can tell us more about the shooter and what she knows about Elaine…and how well they know each other." I paused. "It's possible Elaine killed Shelly because she was threatening to expose something in Elaine's past that would jeopardize her marriage to Dr. McGuire. Hopefully, Sarah knows something about that."

Craig said, "I think it's quite possible that Elaine killed Shelly. After all, she had the means and motive to murder her. On top of that, I think she'd be quite happy to cause problems for Caroline's business."

"Yeah, but like you said, we've got to think this thing through. After all, we are working on the assumption that Carl is telling the truth. What if he's not? What if he killed Shelly, and Elaine was only trying to protect Sarah from Carl by breaking them up? I don't know who killed Shelly, but someone thinks I'm getting close to the truth, and they want me to back off. But how can I back off when I don't even know what I'm backing away from?" I nervously twisted my hands together.

"Calm down, Sherlock. It's going to be okay. We'll talk to Sarah and see what she says, and then we'll go to the police station and tell them about the note you got last night."

"That sounds like a plan, but let's not tell her we talked to Carl. We don't want to lay all our cards on the table until we know who's telling the truth."

chapter twenty-two

Since neither Craig nor I had Sarah's address, I suggested we call Lawrence at the police station and get it from him. Granted, I knew Rick probably had her address or could get it from his mom, but I didn't want to bother him. They had enough on their minds without wondering why Craig and I wanted to talk to Sarah.

Craig stopped at a nearby gas station and pulled beside the pay phone, getting close enough for me to reach the receiver from inside his car. At least, that was his reasoning.

As he searched for Lawrence's business card in his wallet, I leaned out the window to reach the receiver and deposit my dime. Craig's laughter behind me confirmed how silly I looked hanging—or more precisely, falling—out of his car. Somehow, he managed to contain his amusement long enough to read me the phone number. Thankfully, Lawrence answered on the second ring, and within a few minutes, I had Sarah's address.

6251 Orchard Lane was on the other side of town in one of Petersburg's few upscale neighborhoods. As we drove down the street looking for Sarah's house, I noted that the homes sat on what I guessed to be two-acre lots, giving the homeowners more privacy than most neighborhoods in town. While the architecture was impressive, what caught my attention was the size of the front yards—they were massive.

Upon arriving at Sarah's house, Craig knocked on the door. We waited on the porch for her to answer, shivering in the cold. I wasn't sure she would open the door, but she did.

"Hi, I'm Michelle. We met yesterday at Caroline's house. I'm a friend of Rick's. This is Craig Miller. Mae's son."

"I'm sorry we didn't call first, but may we come in?" Craig asked.

Sarah looked puzzled and said nothing for a moment, then, with a shrug, opened the storm door. "I, uh, I guess so. Won't you please come in?"

We followed Sarah into the living room, and I could only imagine the wheels turning in her head as she contemplated why two virtual strangers had stopped for a visit. Not wanting to give her time to question our motives for coming to her house, I immediately expressed concern for her well-being—a ruse to hide our true mission of finding information on Elaine.

"We were in the neighborhood and saw your car. I thought you were staying with Caroline. Is everything all right?" I tried my best to sound sincere, crossing my fingers that she wouldn't ask why we were driving through her neighborhood or how we knew where she lived.

Sarah smiled. "Yes, thank you. That's very sweet of you. I needed some things from the house, so I came to get them. Other than that, I'm managing as well as I can." She motioned to the red floral sofa. "Please, sit down."

As Craig and I settled on the couch, Sarah began speaking —her voice trembling. "I'll feel much better when the police catch Carl. I can't believe he tried to kill me!"

Leaning forward, I asked, "Are you sure it was Carl? Did you get a good look at him?"

"I think I can recognize the man I've been dating, don't you?"

The tension in the room swelled. The visit was not going as smoothly as I had hoped, but since she mentioned Carl, I went with it while trying to diffuse the situation. "Oh, no, I'm not doubting you. It's just so hard to believe he would try to hurt you. I've only met him a few times, but he seemed nice. I guess I was hoping there was another explanation, that's all. At Caroline's, you said you were in the living room when it happened. Any chance you recognized the clothes but didn't see the face clearly?"

"What exactly are you getting at?" Sarah uncrossed her legs and planted her feet on the gold shag carpet.

"Would it have been possible for the shooter to have dressed like Carl? Maybe someone who disapproved of you seeing him?"

Sarah's posture relaxed, and she leaned back in her chair. "I...I suppose. I never considered that possibility, but who would have such a vendetta against Carl and me?"

"I'm not sure. Was there anyone who wanted to break you and Carl up?"

"There might be a few women. He is a rather fine catch." She smiled, but it faded when she added, "At least that's what I thought."

Craig spoke up. "Forgive me for being blunt, but how well do you know Elaine?"

Sarah's eyes widened as she jolted upright and crossed her arms. "She...she's an acquaintance of mine."

"A good acquaintance, apparently, considering the two of you get together quite often," I said, my voice sounding sterner than I intended.

Sarah snapped, "What of it?"

"Nothing, but why be so mysterious about it?" I asked.

Sarah shook her head, and her gaze shifted. "It must seem strange since I'm Caroline's friend. Yet here I am, friends with her nemesis, Elaine. The truth is, Elaine and I were friends before I met Caroline. When I found out Elaine was seeing Caroline's ex, well, I couldn't bring myself to tell Caroline about my friendship with Elaine. I wasn't sure she'd understand."

"That makes sense," I said as I glanced around the room, gathering my thoughts.

Sarah's living room was impeccably arranged as if straight out of an *Architectural Digest* photo spread. From the Capodimonte nativity scene on the coffee table to the Christmas tree decorated with golden angels and glittery gold bows to the gold garland strung over the mantel, everything was perfectly placed.

As my eyes wandered over to the mantel, I noticed a picture of Elaine, and I immediately asked, "How long have you known Elaine?"

Sarah sat back in her chair and began reminiscing. "Let me think...I knew Elaine's mother before I moved to Boston. We had been friends for years, so when Elaine's mother passed away, she came to live with me for a few months. My husband had recently passed away, so we bonded over our shared grief and helped each other through a difficult time. When Elaine went back to Indiana, we kept in touch. Later, my son got a job with a law firm in Petersburg, and around the same time, Elaine decided to move here too."

Sarah chuckled as she continued, "Josh and Elaine loved Petersburg so much that they convinced me to move here too. And why not? I had nothing keeping me in Boston. Josh was here, and Elaine is like the daughter I never had.

I leaned forward, not sure it was the right time to ask, but I asked anyway—no sense waiting. "Was Elaine supportive of your relationship with Carl? Did she like him?"

Sarah glanced to the side and then back at me. "I see where you're going with this. You've undoubtedly heard the rumors that Elaine and Carl were seeing each other. Well, they weren't. Those were only vicious rumors."

Craig diverted our attention as he strolled to the large

picture window with its cardboard bandage covering the hole left by the bullet. He looked down the street in both directions before turning and addressing Sarah. "Is it true Carl didn't want you to invest in Caroline's gym but suggested you put the money in his brother's business?"

"My, but the rumor mill has been busy, hasn't it?" Sarah smiled as she adjusted the armrest cover on her velvet chair. "The truth is Carl thought Sam's gym would be less of a financial risk. Elaine agreed and told me she was going to invest in his gym herself. She suggested I do the same. She was only trying to help me."

His eyes narrowed. "Are you sure?"

"Why would I doubt her?"

Craig threw his hands in the air. "Maybe because she and Caroline don't get along."

"Elaine would never let her emotions cloud her judgment when it comes to money," she said, her eyes narrowing slightly.

"Whatever." Craig sighed in disbelief as he returned to his seat on the sofa. "Do you know what information Shelly had on Elaine—something Elaine wanted to keep from Dr. McGuire?"

"No! That's preposterous! Where on earth did you hear that?"

"From me," I said. "I was at Caroline's fitness center when I overheard them arguing. Elaine had received some sort of note and accused Shelly of sending it, but Shelly denied it. She said if Elaine wanted to keep the secret hidden, she'd have to ensure Shelly won the Miss States of America pageant. Do you have any idea what they were talking about?"

Sarah tilted her head and gazed into the distance. After clearing her throat, she explained, "When Elaine was in college, she worked part-time for an elderly woman in Bicknell, Indiana, as a maid or companion, I'm not sure. Elaine did whatever the woman needed—running errands, doing her laundry, reading to her…that sort of thing. The woman was quite wealthy and had amassed a large collection of artwork from her travels around the world. She had also inherited several expensive jewelry pieces from her mother and grandmother and, of course, had some very exquisite pieces from her husband."

Sarah brushed her hair behind her ear, revealing a diamond drop earring. "To make a long story short, several valuable pieces of jewelry and collectible items went missing. The police arrested Elaine, and she served two years in prison for her crime. Her mother died during that time, so when she got out, she came to stay with me. Elaine was determined to make a new life for herself and eventually became a pageant coach."

"How did Shelly learn about the theft and Elaine's time in prison?" I asked.

"The woman Elaine worked for was Shelly's grandmother."

My mouth dropped open. "Why in the world then would Shelly want anything to do with Elaine?"

"Shelly was as conniving as she was beautiful. Elaine had become a successful pageant coach, and Shelly knew she could hold Elaine's past over her to pressure Elaine to use all her resources to guarantee Shelly did well in the pageant circuit."

"Use her resources?" I asked, confused.

Sarah shook her head. "When it comes to money and fame, you have no idea how many people make backroom deals."

Craig settled back into his spot on the couch next to me. "So, what you're telling me is that Elaine had a strong motive to want Shelly dead?"

With a long-suffering sigh, Sarah conceded, "Yes, I guess I

am. Even so, I refuse to believe she could be capable of taking such drastic measures. That isn't who she is."

"If she killed Shelly, it's not like she was acting rationally. Life happens. People change. Sometimes, we don't know them as well as we think we do." Clasping my hands, I leaned forward. "Let me ask you this. Could she have been the one who fired the gun?Perhaps she dressed like Carl to make you think it was him."

Sarah squinted her eyes as she wrung her hands. "But why? Why would she do that?"

"Perhaps she believed Carl posed a threat to her relationship with you, and she wanted him out of your life."

Sarah's face telegraphed her doubt.

"Think about it this way—what if she was terrified that if you and Carl became serious, you wouldn't have time for her? If you were like a mother to her, perhaps the possibility of losing you was unbearable."

Sarah dropped her head into her hands and uttered a despairing groan. "Until now, I would never have thought Elaine capable of such an act. Never in a million years." She shook her head slowly, repeating, "Elaine... Elaine..."

With tears in her eyes, Sarah raised her head and said, "I guess I better tell the police about the connection between Shelly and Elaine." She stroked the arm of the chair. "You're right. I didn't see the face of the person with the gun, only the clothes. It could have been Elaine dressed like Carl."

Craig shook his head. "Let's not jump to conclusions. There isn't enough proof to blame Elaine. It's only a theory at this point."

"That's right." Sarah sounded relieved. "We don't know that it was Elaine, only that it might not have been Carl. Oh, I hope neither of them was involved! You will look into it, won't you?"

"We'll do what we can, but don't worry. The police will

find the person responsible for trying to shoot you." I stood to my feet. "Just update them so they have all the facts."

Sarah nodded. "I will. As soon as I get back to Caroline's house, I'll call Detective Douglas."

"When are you going back?" I asked as I buttoned my coat.

"Actually, I was getting ready to leave when you arrived."

"If you don't mind," Craig said as Sarah led us to the door, "we'll wait in the car and then follow you to Caroline's house to make sure you get there safely."

"Oh, thank you. That would be so kind."

Before leaving, I glanced over my shoulder at the brick fireplace and remembered the missing bullet.

"Sarah, have the police found the bullet yet?

"No, they swept the room but concluded my dog may have moved it. Detective Douglas told me to watch for it and to call him if I found it."

"I didn't know you had a dog," I said.

Sarah proudly smiled as she went to the fireplace and took down a family picture of her with her son and a Teacup poodle. "My baby's at the kennel for a few days until all this excitement dies down. I couldn't ask Caroline to take both of us in." She kissed the dog in the photograph and returned it to the mantle.

Craig and I waited in his car while Sarah loaded her things into her trunk.

Craig glanced at me. "So, what are your thoughts?"

I took a deep breath. "I'd say Elaine has moved to the top of our list of suspects in Shelly's murder. Now, if we can just prove she did it."

As we continued to discuss the new information, Craig drove closely behind Sarah's car. Suddenly, she stopped, and Craig hit the brakes hard. Despite wearing my seatbelt, I grabbed the door handle to prevent myself from flying through the window.

"That was a little close," I muttered.

"I didn't realize she was going to stop for the yellow light. I thought for sure she was going to keep going." He glanced at my white knuckles and chuckled. "You okay?"

"Yeah." I nodded. "Never a dull moment with you."

"I'll take that as a compliment." He grinned. "Now, where were we? Ah, yes…the shooting. You were saying?"

"I think Elaine's involved in that too. But how are we going to prove it?" My shoulders sank. I was running out of ideas.

Craig placed his hand on mine. "It's a lot to process—trying to solve Shelly's murder and the tampering of the treadmill all at the same time. Let's focus on Shelly's poisoning first. That one might be easier to figure out."

"Yeah, you're right. I'll ask Lawrence if they found fingerprints on Shelly's thermos and, if so, if they found a match. Elaine should be in the system since she was in prison." I pointed to the traffic light and smiled. "It's green. Sarah's on the move again."

Craig chuckled. "Thanks. Guess I should focus on driving, huh?"

"Just a little." I laughed and then paused. "Even if Elaine's prints are on the thermos, that still doesn't prove she poisoned Shelly, does it?"

"No. What we need is a witness who saw somebody with Shelly's thermos. Better yet, if they saw somebody put something in it."

My mind raced as I imagined someone planning Shelly's murder."That might prove difficult. I can't imagine anyone would do such a thing with witnesses. But I could ask Paul if he saw anyone near Shelly's thermos that day." I shrugged. "But what if the killer is Paul? We can't ignore that possibility. He might be the one who poisoned Shelly." The complexity of the situation was overwhelming. I rubbed my forehead.

"Speaking of Paul," Craig said, "I wonder if he's ever

mentioned anything to Amy's brother? Maybe he's confided in him."

"That's a good idea. I need to call Amy and find out if she's heard anything. Man, this is so confusing. It's not a wonder my head hurts."

"Remember, one thing at a time. After Sarah safely arrives at Caroline's house, we'll see if Paul is working at the fitness center. Maybe we can get a few answers. And then we need to stop by the police station."

I pulled my coat sleeve up and glanced at my watch.

"Do you have time, or do you need to get home?" Craig asked.

"I've got the time. It's my parents." I sighed, frustration creeping into my voice. "I wish I had a portable phone or a walkie-talkie to call them. It's a drag trying to find a phone all the time."

"You can probably use the one at the fitness center."

"That'll work." I paused. "Sometimes it's good to have you around."

Craig said nothing as he looked straight ahead, but he was smiling.

chapter twenty-three

Despite the festive sounds of Bobby Helms' "Jingle Bell Rock" playing in the background, holiday joy was nowhere to be found at the fitness center. Only two patrons were present. One furiously pedaled away on a stationary bike while the other struggled on the incline machine. The soft hum of their machines only added to the somber mood—a far cry from the bustling activity during the Open House before Shelly's tragic death.

Rick, wearing a red and green paisley shirt, stood behind the front desk and casually flipped through the pages of the *National Lampoon*. Had it not been for the bell above the door ringing when Craig and I walked in, I'm not sure he would have noticed us.

He looked up as the door closed behind us. "What brings you guys here?"

Craig glanced around the room and wasted no time getting right to the point. "Is Paul here?"

"Yeah, he's in the break room probably eating supper."

I wiped the condensation off my glasses and stepped closer to the counter, determined to soften Craig's blunt tone. "How's it goin'? Everything okay?"

Rick nodded and gave me a slight smile. "Yeah, everything's cool—as much as it can be." His eyes drifted to Craig and then back to me and his smile faded. "What are you guys up to? Still engaged?"

"You know we're just pretending so we can get some information. Which is why we're here. We need to talk to Paul. Is it okay if we go back and find him?"

"Sure. Still drilling him about Shelly?" Rick looked straight into my eyes.

"Just a few questions, that's all. Would it be all right if I used your phone to call my parents?"

As I dialed my number, I overheard Rick talking to Craig. "Dude, I'll be glad when this whole thing is behind us. The newspaper is killing us with its headlines about the Petersburg Fitness Center murder. I'm not even sure people realize Shelly died from being poisoned and not from being thrown from the treadmill." He took a deep breath. "It's hard to change people's first impressions even when proven wrong."

My heart ached for Rick and his mother. The paper had been quick to jump on the assumption that the malfunctioning treadmill caused Shelly's death. Even with all the subsequent articles focusing on the poison, they still couldn't resist mentioning the treadmill not working properly.

Craig's words echoed in my head: "Don't jump to conclusions!" I made a mental note to never let assumptions color my investigating or reporting. Stick with the facts—just the facts.

After my phone call, Craig and I found Paul in the break room eating a sandwich while reclining on a chair, his feet propped on the table. Startled, his body jerked upright, causing a loud thud as his feet hit the floor.

"Sorry," I said, "Didn't mean to scare you."

"No problem," Paul said in a low voice. "I wasn't expecting anyone to come through the door, that's all." He ran his hands through his tousled dark blond hair.

Craig smirked. "Don't let us interrupt your supper."

Paul narrowed his eyes and took a sip from his can of orange pop. "What do you need?"

Craig and I exchanged a knowing glance. We walked over to the table and pulled out two chairs across from Paul. My heart was pounding. The next few minutes were crucial. We needed the truth.

I started, "How well do you know Elaine?"

Paul grew more rigid. "Elaine Anderson?"

"Yeah, have your paths crossed much?" I leaned forward, resting my clasped hands on the table.

"Not really. Rick introduced us. During the remodeling, she would meet Dr. McGuire here, and a couple of times the three of us had lunch back here."

Craig put his hands behind his head and tipped his chair back, balancing it on its back legs. "Did you ever try to get her to introduce you to some of her pageant girls?"

"No, I probably should have." Paul laughed. "Instead, I made a fool of myself chasing after Shelly. Now I've heard she was dating Carl. No way could I compete with that dude and his *European* charm."

"There's a rumor Elaine had eyes for him, too. Quite the ladies' man." Craig grinned.

"I don't think there's any truth to that story. Elaine's just the flirtatious type. She's harmless. Besides, she's engaged to that hot-shot doctor. She'd do anything to keep him."

"With her good looks, I doubt she has to do much to keep his attention." Craig chuckled.

"You'd think, right? But, get this, a while back, she asked me if she could borrow my pass for the Chemistry Lab. Dr. McGuire was doing a gig as a guest lecturer for the section on chemical reactions within the human body. Elaine said the doc was going to the lab after work to set up for the next day's demonstration. She wanted to get there before he did and surprise him with a romantic dinner—candles, flowers, the whole nine yards. She seemed intent on impressing him.

So, I called my lab professor and asked if that would be all right. He said 'sure'. He didn't see a problem."

"Wow," I uttered. "I didn't realize she was such a romantic."

"Elaine certainly thought of everything." Craig plopped the front legs of his chair on the floor, stood up, and placed his hands on the back of my chair. "Well, we better be on our way and let Paul finish his supper in peace."

"That's all right—" Paul said as he lifted his can of pop to his lips.

"No. We've kept you long enough. Thanks for your help," Craig said.

As we walked through the front room, my eyes scanned the area for any sign of Rick, but he was nowhere to be seen. I knew he would return shortly because he'd never leave the front room unattended for long, so I pulled on Craig's arm and suggested we wait. He said nothing but shook his head and picked up his pace toward the door.

"What's up?" I asked as we walked to the car. "You seem a bit antsy."

"I want to go see Dr. McGuire and ask him a few questions."

"Don't you think it would be less confrontational if Rick talked to him?" I rubbed the silver chain around my neck, not sure how Craig would respond to my suggestion that Rick, not him, should question the doctor.

Craig chewed his bottom lip. "You might be right. We could go back and ask Rick if he'd be comfortable getting some information from his father."

When we turned to go back, a gust of wind threatened to knock me off my feet. Craig grabbed onto my arm and pulled me close. His breath brushed against my skin, and the woody scent of his cologne was intoxicating.

I wanted to stay in his embrace forever, feeling secure and content, but my heart raced with fear and safety as he held me tight. Uncomfortably aware of my inner battle, I abruptly pulled away.

"Don't forget, we're engaged, Sherlock. It's okay if we look like a couple." He winked.

"I almost forgot." I laughed. "Guess I'm not used to being an engaged woman."

Craig grinned as he held open the door to the fitness center.

This time, I was relieved Rick was away from the front counter. I was saved from the embarrassment of him witnessing me falling into Craig's arms. Although Rick knew the truth about my engagement to Craig, my intuition told me he would not have appreciated watching the tender moment unfold between Craig and me.

As we waited for Rick to return, I used the time to compose myself. I took a few deep breaths and tried to calm my racing heart. When I heard the hallway door open, I put on my best smile and pretended to be calm and collected.

Rick hollered, "Did you forget something?"

"Sort of." I waited for him to draw nearer before continuing. "I was wondering if you could help us. If you don't want to, it's okay."

"What gives?" Rick cocked his head, glancing between me and Craig. "Okay, what are you two up to?"

Craig started. "We need to know if Elaine—"

"Had a romantic dinner for my dad at the chemistry lab?" Rick interjected.

"How did you know about that?" I asked.

"Paul just asked me. He wondered if my dad ever mentioned it to me."

"And had he?"

"No." Rick shrugged. "He never said anything about it, but that doesn't mean much. My dad rarely talks to me about Elaine." He paused. "Let me guess. You think she got the arsenic from the chemistry lab."

"It's just a hunch," I said. "It doesn't mean she did."

"I'm no detective, but I'm guessing you might need to talk to Todd's dad, Professor Spratt. He's the head of the chemistry department."

"How did I not know that?" I asked.

"You forget Todd and I went to grade school and high school together. There's not much I don't know about that dude."

"I'll remember that," I said with raised eyebrows. "Do you have Todd's number?"

Rick noticed a stack of 3x5 index cards lying beside the telephone. He quickly grabbed one and wrote down Todd's phone number.

Puzzled, he asked, "Why would Elaine resort to stealing from the chemistry lab when she could easily buy arsenic from a store? After all, isn't arsenic used in rat poisoning?"

"Interesting fact," Craig explained, "but rat poisoning has had norbormide in it for the past few years, not arsenic. However, when it comes to medicine, several use arsenic or one of its compounds to treat diabetes, psoriasis, syphilis, skin ulcers, and joint diseases."

"And how exactly do you know all this?" I asked, shaking my head.

"I was curious, so I went to the library and did some research." He grinned.

After leaving the fitness center, we drove to the police station. I wasn't sure if having Craig with me made the task any easier or simply impossible for me to put off doing. In the end, it didn't matter. I had to keep my word to my parents and tell the police about the note.

Much to our surprise, neither Lawrence nor Detective Douglas were in, so I asked the officer on duty to make a copy of my note and give it to the detective when he returned. What a relief! Not only did I not have to talk to Detective

Douglas, but I didn't have to say anything about Carl—time was on my side, at least for the moment.

Next stop: the parking lot behind Mae's Gift Shop so I could get my car.

"See you tomorrow, about one thirty—your place?" Craig asked.

"Sounds good. Hopefully, we can get some answers from talking to Dr. Spratt instead of getting more questions. Wouldn't that be something different? See you then."

As I slid into the driver's seat of my car, my stomach grumbled, reminding me I hadn't eaten anything since breakfast. I felt queasy. Was it because I was hungry or because I feared someone might not be pleased with me continuing my investigation? A chill ran down my spine.

chapter twenty-four

Sunday, December 22nd

With only three shopping days before Christmas, Mae's cozy gift shop was alive with activity. Customers bustled through the aisles, and when they left, their hands were full of brightly wrapped gifts and ornate gift bags of all shapes and sizes.

As I rang up purchase after purchase, my thoughts were consumed by unanswered questions that tormented me. *Who killed Shelly? Why? Who shot at Sarah, and what was their motive? Did someone intentionally tamper with the treadmill?* I couldn't shake the feeling that the threads of these mysteries were intertwined, yet I had no proof.

"Michelle. Michelle, anybody home?"

"Todd, you startled me."

"Yeah, man, you looked like you were a million miles away."

Seeing Todd immediately lifted my spirits. I was not alone in my quest to solve Shelly's murder. He and my other friends from the Commuter Lounge wanted Shelly's murder solved and Rick's mother's name cleared as much as I did.

A heavy sigh escaped my lips. "I guess there's too much on my brain these days. Sometimes, I feel like it's going to explode."

"This Shelly thing is crazy, isn't it?" Todd rubbed his scruffy chin.

"You got that right. Everything about Shelly's death and the treadmill gets more complicated by the minute," I said, shaking my head and mustering a broader smile. "So, what brings you by?"

"Rick called last night and said you wanted to talk to me. I thought I'd drop by since I hadn't heard from you. He said you need some info from my dad?"

Todd stepped to the side while I rang up a customer's purchase. His eyes grew large as the elderly woman counted out her change, sliding one coin at a time toward me until she reached $4.49. Glancing at Todd, I chuckled as he tried to stifle his laughter.

After I handed the woman her bag of Christmas cards and dropped all the coins into the cash register tray, Todd returned to his spot at the counter. With his dark hair and baby-faced good looks, he resembled the drawing of Paul McCartney on the Beatles t-shirt he wore under his unzipped black leather jacket.

Although Mae was helping a customer select a milk glass vase, she kept looking in my direction while I spoke with Todd. I could tell from the expression on her face that she was not happy.

Despite Mae becoming more cheerful after taking some time off from the store, she still adhered to her strict policy of no personal conversations while on the floor.

I could risk Mae's displeasure by continuing to talk to Todd or avoid her wrath by asking him to leave, which might delay my meeting with his father to get some much-needed answers. The solution to my dilemma came when Stacy and her customer approached the register.

"Stacy," I said. "I need to help him find something. Could you work the register for a few minutes?"

"Sure." She nodded.

I exited the cash wrap and turned toward Todd. "I'll show you where they are."

He looked confused but played along as I led him to the card racks by the side wall.

"Sorry 'bout that. Mae doesn't like us talking to friends while we're working."

His shoulders drooped. "I didn't even think about that."

"No problem. Just look like we're trying to find the perfect birthday card for your—" I glanced at the rack to see where we had stopped, "your sister, mother, or grandmother. Take your pick." I laughed.

"Um... let's go with Mother."

As I handed him a few cards, I said, "Craig and I were wondering if the university keeps arsenic in the lab. If they do, do they keep it under lock and key, or is it easily accessible? I wanted to ask your dad stuff like that."

"Rick said Elaine borrowed Paul's pass to the lab." Todd replaced a card in the rack, picked up another one, and pretended to read It.

Meanwhile, I picked one and held it in my hand, ready to hand it to him once he finished reading the card he had.

"It might mean nothing, but Craig and I need to check a few things out...just in case."

"Makes sense." He nodded and handed the card back to me. "My dad is at the lab this afternoon doing inventory so he can order supplies for the next quarter. If you have time, you might catch him there. He goes in through the back entrance. It should be unlocked. And if you don't get there this afternoon, he should be home tonight. You can call him then."

"Thanks. Hopefully, Craig and I can swing by after I finish work today."

As my gaze shifted away from Todd, I caught sight of Mae storming toward us. Her purposeful strides echoed through the air. Despite being dressed in a striking red silk wrap dress and a scarf adorned with Christmas motifs, her stern expression made it clear that she was not in a festive mood.

"I think Mae found us out," I muttered.

Todd glanced over his shoulder and saw her too. He whispered, "Guess I better go before I get you in too much trouble." Speaking loudly for Mae's benefit, he said, "Thanks for your help. I'll be back later," and bolted for the front door.

Mae stopped next to me and crossed her arms. "What was that all about? A friend of yours?"

"Yeah, he goes to U.P."

"And he stopped by to get a card but couldn't find one?"

I knew she was on to me. "Our friend's mother owns the Petersburg Health & Fitness Center—"

"The one where that girl died?"

"Yeah," I took a deep breath. "That's the one. His dad might have some information to help solve what happened."

Her eyes bore into mine. "Just remember, I pay you to do your job here, not to do your investigative work. Understand?"

"Yes. I won't let it happen again—" I paused. "But would it be okay if I call Craig? I'll keep it short. It's important."

She breathed a deep sigh and narrowed her eyes. "Just this once."

I made my way to the cash register, but when I saw Detective Douglas coming through the door, my day went from bad to worse. If I could have turned around and hid, I would have, but since he was looking straight at me, I could not. He saw me as clearly as I saw him.

"Detective Douglas, is there anything I can help you with?" I asked, hoping he was here on Christmas shopping duty but fearing he was not.

"No, Ms. Kilpatrick. This is official business. Is there a place we can talk?" He brushed the snowflakes from his short brown hair and pulled his coat back to reveal his badge.

Scowling, Mae said, "Detective Douglas, this is not a good time. We are quite busy, and I need Michelle at the register."

"Ms. Emerson, I understand that, but you need to understand that I am here on official business. Ms. Kilpatrick and I can either talk in the back room with or without your permission. Which do you prefer?"

Mae let out a groan and shrugged. "Just make it fast."

Both responses surprised me—Detective Douglas's stance against compromise and Mae's letting him have his way without an argument.

As soon as the back room door closed behind us, Detective Douglas drilled me about the note left on my car.

I sat down at a small table, and he followed suit, scribbling in his notepad as I rattled off as many details as I could remember about the night the limo appeared in my driveway —the time on the clock, the color of the car's exterior, the build of the person with the note. Occasionally, he would glance at me, shake his head, and then return to writing his notes.

After I finished my account, I mentioned I had seen a limo twice on previous occasions at Caroline's fitness center. Surprisingly, he did not belittle me for being paranoid. Instead, his face grew more serious as he continued writing. Then, without warning, he snapped the cover over the notepad, returned it and his pen to his pocket, and looked me in the eye.

"Ms. Kilpatrick, I assume you've been playing investigative reporter again. Is writing an article for the newspaper how you justify interfering with my investigation?"

"I'm only trying to clear Rick's mother's name so she can start her business. I don't think that is interfering. I've done nothing to stand in the way of your police work." I crossed my arms.

He took a deep breath, and I could almost hear him counting to ten to calm himself. "Judging from the words on this note: 'Stop. Back off. You have been warned,' I'd say you've been doing more than checking out a malfunctioning treadmill." His voice was measured but with an unmistakable hint of anger.

"Okay, so I've been looking into Shelly's. poisoning and—"

"And?" His eyes grew wide.

I looked down and shuffled my feet. "And Sarah's shooting."

The detective gave a sideways glance and said, "Sounds like you've been up to more than gathering information for a story in the paper. When will you learn to stay out of police business? I have no idea who you've upset, but I must ask you to stay out of this investigation for your own protection. Do I make myself clear?"

"Yes, sir," I muttered. "Is that all? I need to get back to work."

"Yes, I'm done." He stood and pushed his chair under the table. "But keep me informed if you get any more notes or anything suspicious happens. The best I can do is have an officer drive by your house for several days to check on things. I can't protect you every minute of every day, so take this threat seriously and stop with the investigating. I can do my job without your help."

Detective Douglas left the store by way of the aisle on the far left. I, on the other hand, wanted to be as far away from him as possible, so I used the aisle on the opposite side to get to the cash register.

Mae was helping a young man by the front showcase and flashed me a look that left no doubt she wanted to know what had transpired between me and the detective. Thankfully, she had to go into the back room to wrap the man's gift, giving me ample time to destress and call Craig before she returned.

Replaying the detective's warning in my mind, I convinced myself that tying up a few loose ends didn't technically amount to interfering with the investigation. Besides, I would be careful. I didn't want to risk me or my family getting hurt or worse, but I needed answers so I knew how to proceed with the Carl-in-hiding fiasco. The clock was ticking, and I knew I had to act fast.

***

Craig pulled into my driveway at precisely four-thirty. I rushed outside to meet him before he got out of his car. Although I appreciated Craig's chivalry in coming to my door, I had already experienced enough drama in my day. I didn't want my parents asking Craig a bunch of questions before we left. I just wanted to get going.

"In a hurry?" he asked.

"I don't want to miss Dr. Spratt at the lab, that's all." I snapped my seatbelt buckle, nestled in my seat, and took in the sights as Craig drove to campus. The tranquility of the snow-laden fields was contagious. The longer I looked at them, the calmer I felt. Soon, I told myself, we would have answers, and the mystery of Shelly's death would be behind us.

Craig and I chatted about our plans for Christmas. He would spend the day with his mother for the first time in many years. I sensed he was both excited and nervous. "I have no idea what we're going to do all day. There's only so much eating the two of us can do," he laughed. "What do you and your family do for Christmas?"

"Well, my brother and sister and their spouses come over in the morning, and we open presents. Then, after lunch, Mike and his wife go to her parents' house, and Crystal and her husband go to his mother's house. It's always a mad dash because someone has to be somewhere by a certain time, and somebody is taking too long to say goodbye. But it's okay. It's all part of the family tradition." I chuckled.

After quickly finding a parking spot in the empty lot by Overman Hall, we entered the brick building, went upstairs, and walked down the hallway until we spotted an open door. I raised my hand and crossed my fingers. "Hopefully, he's still here. "

When we stepped into the lab, Dr. Spratt and a young man, whom I assumed to be a student, were indeed there—both wearing white lab coats and blue jeans. Gripping the clipboard, the student made notations as Dr. Spratt listed off several chemical compositions: "Acetic Acid. Acetone. Ammonium Hydroxide."

Sensing our presence, the assistant spun around in surprise and faced us. "Uh...Dr. Spratt...I think you have visitors."

The professor turned our way and brushed a few wisps of hair that had fallen across his eyes to one side. "Can I help you?"

Dr. Spratt and his son Todd shared a striking resemblance. They both had a medium build, brown eyes, and dark hair. However, there was one notable difference, the professor had silver hair strands on his temples. For a moment, it felt like I had been transported to the future, standing in the presence of a mature Paul McCartney.

"Dr. Spratt," Craig said, jarring me back to the present. "Todd told us we might find you here. We had some questions we wanted to ask you."

"Yes. Come in. You must be the friends he mentioned.

"Yes, sir," Craig replied. "Is now a good time?"

The professor nodded as he pulled his wallet from his trousers pocket and handed his assistant a ten-dollar bill. "Steve, could you run to the student union and pick me up a corned beef sandwich? And get something for yourself, too? In fact, why don't you take a break, sit down, and eat? Relax for a few minutes. It's been a long day."

After shedding his white lab coat, the skinny student exited, and from the smile on his face, I assumed he welcomed both the break from doing inventory and the chance to get food. Meanwhile, Dr. Spratt sat on a stool by the counter and pointed to the others. "Why don't you sit down and tell me what's on your mind?"

"Do you know Rick McGuire?" I asked.

"Yes, he's a friend of Todd's. Why?"

"You know about the girl who died at his mother's gym?"

"Yes, Todd told me about that. What a shame!"

"Yes, sir, it is," Craig said as he slipped out of his leather jacket and laid it across his lap. "Someone poisoned Shelly, and we believe the poison may have come from your lab."

Dr. Spratt jumped to his feet. "You're not implying I had anything to do with that girl's death, are you?"

"Oh, no, sir," I said. "We believe someone took the poison from your lab."

"That's impossible. We keep all toxic substances under lock and key." The long white sleeves of Dr. Spratt's lab coat swayed as he pointed to the cabinets lining the walls. "Tell me, what are you looking for?"

"Arsenic," I replied.

"I see." The professor exhaled deeply.

As I looked at the cabinets, a question crossed my mind, and I asked, "Are you the only one with a key?"

Without the slightest hesitation, Dr. Spratt replied, "No. Each professor has their own, and the same goes for graduate assistants."

"Anyone else?" Craig asked.

Dr. Spratt thought for a moment. "No. Not to my knowledge."

Craig hopped off his stool and strode across the room, his

eyes scanning each cabinet. "Where does everyone keep their keys?"

"I lock mine in my desk drawer. As for the others, I have no idea."

The three of us exchanged glances, and at that moment, I began to wonder about the whereabouts of all the keys and the number of people who had access to them.

The mere thought of tracking down each person who might have borrowed a key made me anxious, and I rubbed my forehead in frustration. At that moment, it dawned on me that instead of focusing on the key, we first needed to find out if any arsenic was missing from the lab. If not, then the list of individuals who could have used the keys was a moot point.

When I shared my insights with Dr. Spratt and Craig, the professor told us that determining whether arsenic was missing would be easy.

"I just need a minute," he said as he grabbed the clipboard his assistant had left on the counter. "We were taking inventory when you arrived. Let's see what we have." He scoured the page, then shook his head. "Hmmm...that's what I thought. We haven't checked the arsenic yet." Retrieving the key from his lab coat pocket, he made for the cabinet on the other side of the room and unlocked it.

He moved several bottles around on the shelf and became more animated the more bottles he moved. "That's strange. There should be a full bottle here, and it's gone."

He strolled to his desk and opened his notebook, flipping through its pages. "No. No one noted using all the arsenic." He looked up, perplexed.

Remembering what Paul told us, I asked, "Were you aware one of your professors permitted a student to loan his chemistry pass to Elaine Anderson so she could set up a surprise dinner for Dr. McGuire the night before he lectured here?

Dr. Spratt shook his head. "Sorry, but I haven't heard about a pass being loaned to her. Normally, we do not permit that, but I suppose someone could make an exception considering her connection to Dr. McGuire. She's his fiancé, right?"

"Yes." Craig nodded.

"It's possible that someone didn't see any harm in doing Elaine a favor, considering Dr. McGuire is held in high esteem by the teaching staff. Even so, that doesn't mean she had access to the arsenic or that anyone took it, for that matter. It could simply be a case of the arsenic being used in class and someone forgetting to write it down."

Craig leaned on the counter. "You're right. We don't want to jump to conclusions. The only thing we know for sure is that the arsenic is missing. What we don't know is who used it and why?"

***

As Craig and I walked from Overman Hall to his car, the sound of Craig's hand tapping against the fabric of his pants was the only noise between us. As much as I wanted to ask him what he was thinking, I stayed quiet and didn't press him. He would tell me when he was ready.

Craig put his key in the passenger door lock but stopped before turning it and said, "We know Elaine borrowed Paul's lab pass, but we don't know if she went to the lab. We're still working on a rumor that gives us circumstantial evidence at best. I'm at a loss about what to do next."

Placing my hand on his arm, I suggested we swing by the gym on our way back to my house to ask Rick if he talked to his dad about that *romantic dinner.*

"But whether or not she did still proves nothing." Craig shook his head.

"True, but if there was no dinner, we'll know she lied to Paul. At least that's something."

"I suppose." He shrugged.

***

Craig and I walked toward the fitness center, where we noticed Rick standing behind the front window, staring into space. A woman dressed in baggy clothes powered through her treadmill workout nearby. Paul was in the back, spotting a teenage boy deadlifting weights.

When we stepped inside, Rick greeted us but shifted his gaze from me to Paul as if to let me know Paul was in the room.

"Can we talk?" I asked Rick.

"Let's go to the break room," Rick said as he turned and led us toward the hallway door. He shouted, "Paul, we're going to the break room! If anyone comes in, tell them I'll be right back."

Paul nodded, gave a slight wave, and then returned his attention to the young man with the weights.

The door had barely closed before Rick said, "My dad was adamant that Elaine never set up a surprise dinner for him at the lab."

I narrowed my eyes in confusion. "Why would she make up such a story?"

"My dad said Paul probably made the whole thing up to cover his tracks. Who knows? Maybe he did. We don't know which one is lying, do we?"

"No, I guess not. I hoped we were getting closer to who poisoned Shelly, and Elaine seemed like such a viable suspect." Craig said.

Rick ran his hand through the back of his mullet. "If Elaine had anything to do with Shelly's death, I hope we find out before she and my dad get married. Did you know she's talked him into a New Year's Day wedding?"

"Wow," I gasped. "When did this happen? Last I heard, they didn't have a date."

"Right? I don't know how she did it, but she convinced him today that they needed to get married ASAP."

Craig pulled his gloves out of his coat pocket and smirked. "Interesting. I wonder if the fact that a husband can't testify against his wife has anything to do with it?"

chapter twenty-five

"Looks like you've got company," Craig said as he pulled into a parking spot my father had cleared from the snow drifts on our front lawn. Four cars were in the driveway, including T.J.'s green Chevy Nova.

"Oh, my goodness! Tonight's the night of our party with T.J.'s family. We always do it on the Sunday night before Christmas."

"Every year, huh?"

"Yeah, my mom reminded me when I called her this afternoon, but I got so wrapped up in all that Elaine-arsenic stuff at Rick's that I totally forgot. I'm going to be in so much trouble." I twisted the chain around my neck as panic welled up inside of me. My parents were going to be super angry that I forgot about tonight's plans. What waited for me behind the front door would not be good.

Craig, sensing my anxiety, laid his hand on my shoulder. "Would it help any if I went in with you? Maybe I could take some of the heat off you."

As much as I appreciated his offer to rescue me from my parents' wrath, I knew it wasn't wise to put him in the middle of a difficult situation. "I can't ask you to spend your evening with my family. Not sure how fun it will be with my parents mad at me, but thanks."

Craig unbuckled his seat belt. "No problem. Besides, you're not asking. I'm inviting myself. Let's go give everybody something to talk about."

I cocked my head. "Are you sure?"

A smirk crossed his face as he touched my hand and chuckled. "First, you might want to hide that rock on your finger. We don't want to give them too much to talk about tonight."

As I put the ring in my purse, Craig sprinted to my side of the car and pulled the door open with a mischievous grin. "Come on. Let's not keep them waiting."

He grabbed my hand and hurried toward the house. I wasn't sure if his quick pace was because of the icy wind or his undeniable curiosity about the inner workings of the Kilpatrick family. Craig had no idea what he was getting himself into. I only hoped he...and I...wouldn't regret his decision.

The chatter coming from living room drifted onto the front porch, but the room went silent when Craig and I entered the house. All eyes were locked on us.

Mom raced to the entryway. Despite her forced smile, the intensity of her gaze left no doubt she was on the verge of unleashing her anger. "I thought perhaps you had forgotten about tonight. We had almost given up on you."

Craig intervened. "Mrs. Kilpatrick, it's all my fault. We were following up on some leads for a story, and we lost track of time." He extended his hand. "I'm Craig Miller. Michelle has told me so much about you, but—" he glanced at me, "Michelle, you neglected to mention your mother looks more like your sister than your mom." Turning back to my mother, he added, "But I'm sure you hear that all the time."

My mom's cheeks went from light pink to a bright rose. "Well, no, but thank you, Mr. Miller—"

"No, please call me Craig. You've graciously shared your daughter with me over the holidays so we can work on story ideas."

Mom raised her eyebrow. "I trust the two of you haven't been getting into trouble."

"No, Mrs. Kilpatrick. Keeping Michelle safe is a top priority."

"Well, I'm glad to hear that," she said, her face softening. "Now, Michelle, why don't you introduce Craig to everyone, and I'll put his coat in the office. Make sure you both get something to eat. There's plenty of food in the kitchen."

Craig and I strode into the living room as my mom scurried down the hall. As I glanced around the room, I saw my father lounging in his comfortable recliner, engrossed in a conversation with Mr. Wilson, T.J.'s father, who was sitting on the couch. Near the Christmas tree, Crystal and her husband Mel listened as Mrs. Wilson *oohed* and *aahed* over the antique ornaments like she does every year.

The only people seemingly not enjoying themselves were T.J. and Meg. Despite sitting side by side in front of the roaring fire, their rigid posture and stoic faces made the tension between them palpable.

Crystal left Mrs. Wilson admiring another ornament and came to hug me. "Hey, sis, glad you brought Craig." After she gave me an exaggerated wink, she spun around and announced, "Everybody, this is Michelle's friend, Craig Miller."

The kitchen door swung open as if on cue, and Mike and his wife, Suzie, emerged. Mike made a beeline for Craig, his hand outstretched. "Hi. I'm Mike, Michelle's brother, and this is my wife, Suzie. Michelle told me she knew you, but I never expected to meet you."

Mike, who is not usually emotional, was almost giddy at meeting Craig Miller. "I've read all your books. They're awesome."

Craig's eyes sparkled with delight. "Thank you. I'm glad you like them. Hopefully, you'll like the next one too."

Mike continued. "Can't wait! When will it be out?"

Craig glanced at me. "With your sister's help, by October."

As Craig, Mike, and Suzie chatted, Mrs. Wilson joined her husband on the couch, where she focused her attention on the charismatic Craig Miller—a man visibly enjoying hobnobbing with his fans.

Mike bombarded Craig with question after question about the publishing industry, how to secure an agent, and if he would have the time to read the manuscript of his book-in-progress. For every question Craig answered, my brother had three more. I shot a frantic glance in Crystal's direction. Never one to fail me when in need, she motioned to Mel to join our group. Seizing the moment when Mike took a breath, Crystal hijacked the conversation by introducing her husband to Craig.

Back from coat duty, my mom acted like she had known Craig for years. She grabbed his arm, dragged him across the room, and introduced him to my father and Mr. and Mrs. Wilson.

Meg and T.J. made their way toward us, yet despite their attempt at being sociable, I could sense an underlying tension in their every move and word. Meg's smile was stretched too wide, and her eyes seemed to avoid meeting mine. T.J.'s laughter was strained and forced, lacking its usual warmth and ease. The whole exchange seemed awkward.

Not counting Meg and T.J.'s ill mood, things were going smoothly. And then it happened.

Meg asked, "Where is your ring?" My mouth dropped open, my heart stopped, and for a moment, my legs grew weak.

"What?" Crystal exclaimed in shock. "A ring? Are you engaged?"

My mind raced as I tried to think of an explanation. I couldn't blow my *engaged* cover, not yet, not until we solved the case. I started to speak, but all that came out was "I...I... um..." as I desperately searched for Craig who had stepped away with Mike.

He rushed to my side. "We've got a lot of things to sort out, but not tonight. Did you say there was food in the kitchen? I'm starving."

However, Meg wasn't about to let it drop. Undeterred by Craig's explanation, she continued pressing for answers, "But when is the..."

T.J. shot Meg a stern glare, sending her a message to keep quiet. He steered her back to the hearth, where they became involved in an intense conversation.

My mom and Crystal followed Craig and me into the kitchen. Mom stood between me and the table, her arms crossed and her eyes not wavering from mine. "What's going on?"

I glanced at Craig. He put his arm around me and tipped his head toward mine. "You need to tell her."

Craig and I had never discussed what to do if my family learned about our engagement. To tell my mom the truth might jeopardize our search for Shelly's killer, but there was no way I was going to lie to her. My only recourse was to stand there, speechless.

"This isn't how we wanted you to find out," Craig said. "But I guess the cat is out of the bag."

I held my breath, waiting for his confession.

"Your daughter is very special, Mrs. Kilpatrick, and I want nothing more than for her to be happy, and if I'm the man who can do that, I am lucky indeed."

Crystal hugged me, exclaiming, "This is so exciting!" She turned toward Craig. "I knew you were the one when you came by the house the other day!"

Amazed, I watched the master wordsmith at work. Craig

never once confirmed we were engaged, nor did he deny it. He skirted around the entire issue, and no one noticed.

Crystal gushed about how wonderful Craig was as I prepared myself for my mother's disapproving words. After all, Craig was not T.J., the guy she had picked out for me years ago.

To my surprise and bewilderment, she threw her arms around me and said, "My little girl is going to marry a hot-shot author. Wait till I tell the ladies at church. They will be so—"

"Mom," I interjected, "I think you should wait."

"Why? Mrs. Hilton just announced her daughter Becky is engaged. The women from the quilting group are already planning her shower. Wait till I tell them the news. Oh my, do you have a date?"

"This has all happened recently," Craig explained. "I think it best if we wait until after the holidays before making plans."

"Yes, yes, you are absolutely right! People are too busy with the holidays now to appreciate such good news."

"Could I ask you both to be so kind as to keep our engagement in the family for the time being? My mother doesn't know yet, and I don't want her to find out through the grapevine," Craig said.

"Yes, by all means. I will tell everyone in the other room mum's the word." Mom strolled toward the door and then pivoted back to Craig. "In all the excitement, I forgot to ask, how did Meg know, and we didn't?"

I spoke up. "I talked to T.J. earlier when he saw the ring. He must have told Meg."

"The ring!" cried Crystal. "I want to see it."

I took a deep breath. "It's in my purse. I didn't want to wear it before telling you about it." That much was true, I told myself.

Mom shook her head. "Your father will never believe this." A huge smile crossed her face as she left the room.

Like a mother duck leading her ducklings, the three of us followed her into the living room. Mom asked everyone to keep our engagement a secret until Craig told his mother. They all nodded and smiled, happy to be included in such top-secret information. Everyone, that was, except T.J. The blank look on his face spoke volumes.

Crystal demanded I show her my ring, and once it was on my finger, she paraded me around the room so everyone could see it. My mom was most impressed, saying it was the largest diamond she had ever seen. "You'll never go hungry." She laughed. "A ring that size would buy enough food for an entire year, I bet." Mom paused as her eyes grew wider. "Oh, my, you'll be living at the Peterson Estate. You'll never want for anything. Wait until I tell Ida Jo!" She chuckled all the way to Dad's chair.

Crystal, always one for music, played one of Mom's favorite Christmas albums—Elvis Presley's *It's Christmas Time*. Laughter soon ensued as Mike entertained us with his impersonation of Elvis singing "Blue Christmas." Mr. Swivel-hips had us laughing so hard the engagement news faded into the background.

During Mike's impromptu performance, my mother leaned over and whispered something into my dad's ear, making him smirk and nod in agreement.

I leaned on Craig and asked, "What are we going to do? My family thinks we're engaged. I don't like lying to them."

"I'm sorry, but it's only for a little while longer."

"That doesn't help," I said through gritted teeth.

"How 'bout this? I ask you to marry me. You say, 'Yes,' and we call it off after the holidays. Technically, you won't be lying."

"I think that's a rather grey area."

Craig's eyes sparkled with mischief. "What about it? Wanna be my wife?"

Before I had a chance to respond, my mom invited everyone to help themselves to more eggnog and cookies before we opened presents.

"Don't be shy. Get yourself a plateful," she said as she gestured towards the platters of Christmas cookies, peanut brittle, and fudge.

After everyone made a trip to the dessert table, Mom and Crystal gathered the wrapped boxes under the tree and passed them out.

I edged closer to Craig and whispered, "Every year, we exchange gifts between our two families." Although perturbed with him for his part in this engagement mess, I regretted there would be no present for him. I didn't want him to be excluded, but I also had no idea how to improve the situation.

To my surprise, my mom placed a wrapped box in Craig's lap. His face lit up with amazement and disbelief.

"But, Mrs. Kilpatrick, I don't have anything for you."

"Oh, don't be silly. It's just a little something. Can't have my future son-in-law going home empty-handed," she laughed.

Craig ripped open his package and, with wide eyes, lifted the snow globe and gave it a good shake. A flurry of sparkling glitter blanketed the miniature plastic evergreen trees inside. Grinning from ear to ear, he nudged me and shook it again, proudly showing me the winter scene in his hand. He looked like a child on Christmas morning, completely caught up in the magic of the moment.

I mouthed a "thank you" to my mother, who had been watching Craig's reaction. Never again would I think having a few extra gifts under the tree was a silly idea.

This Christmas, our gift-giving was characterized by practicality and warmth. Mrs. Wilson knitted gloves for the women and hats for the men, while my mother gifted the women-folk, as she called us, handmade aprons embroidered with delicate flowers. The men received high-powered flashlights complete with batteries. All very useful gifts.

As Crystal collected the wrapping paper lying on the floor, Mom shut off the record player and sat at the piano. She began playing "Jingle Bells" and, with a wave, encouraged everyone to join her and sing.

Two voices were noticeably missing as I sang with the chorus of off-key singers—T.J.'s and Meg's. They sat in front of the hearth, but Meg had her back facing T.J. despite his attempts to talk to her. With a sigh, T.J. rose from his spot and headed for the table with the eggnog and cookies. Seeing an opportunity to talk to T.J. alone, I told Craig I would get something for us to drink.

I caught up with T.J. by the cookie trays and leaned close to him. "Is Meg okay? She looks upset."

T.J. glanced over his shoulder at Meg. "She's mad because I told her to drop it about your engagement. I couldn't tell her why, and then she accused me of keeping secrets. I guess it doesn't matter now since it sounds like your engagement is official, or is it? It's getting hard to know what's true with you anymore."

"I know. I'm sorry. I'm just trying to find Shelly's killer. At the time, I thought pretending to be engaged was a good idea, but now it's blowing up in my face. The last thing I ever meant to do was to have my ruse cause trouble between you and Meg."

"It's all right." T.J. shook his head as he surveyed the selection of cookies. "I like her, but sometimes she can be so unreasonable."

I bit my bottom lip and thought about telling him Meg wasn't his type, but realized now was not the time. Instead, I said, "Hopefully, this charade will be over soon, and then you can tell her the whole story. Blame me. After all, I'm the one who made you promise not to tell anyone."

"I'm not sure the two of us having a secret will make her feel better." The corners of his mouth turned up slightly.

"Why would that bother her? I mean, we're just friends, right?" I held my breath as I grasped my Eiffel Tower charm. At that moment, I realized I wanted him to disagree with me, but the faint smile faded from his face, and he stared at his feet.

"Yeah, that's it. We're just friends." His gaze flicked over to Craig's direction. "After all, you've got bigger fish to catch now."

"What are you talking about? Bigger fish? Craig? No. We're friends. Maybe more like—" I hunted for the words, "colleagues."

T.J. filled his plate with cookies and muttered, "I don't believe that." He paused. "Forget it. It doesn't matter."

"T.J., don't be like that." I nudged him, but he turned away.

I stood by the table, watching T.J. walk back to Meg and sit beside her. He said something and then wrapped his arm around her, pulling her close. Meg coyly smiled at me as she took his hand and rested her head on his shoulder.

I listened to my mom sing "Hark, the Herald Angels Sing," and something jarred my memory—I told Craig I would get us something to drink. I quickly grabbed two glasses of eggnog and made my way back to him.

Craig looked up as I handed him his glass. "Something wrong with T.J.?"

"Yeah, I think he's mad at me."

"Why?"

My shoulders dropped. "Because when I told him the truth about our engagement, I asked him not to tell anyone. Now it's caused problems between him and Meg because she thinks he's keeping something from her."

"Are you sure that's all?" Craig raised an eyebrow.

"Yeah, he said that's why she's upset." I swallowed hard, avoiding his gaze.

"I wasn't talking about T.J. and Meg." His voice dropped in a low rumble. "I thought perhaps there was something between you and—"

"No. No, there's not." I snapped louder than I intended. Glancing around the room, I was relieved the singing had muffled my words.

Craig looked me in the eye. "Are you sure?"

"Yes," I whispered.

"As long as you're sure." He reached over and took my hand.

I looked at T.J., but when our eyes met, he turned away.

As the clock struck eleven, my father rose from his chair, walked over to the end table, and clicked the lamp off. With no further fanfare, he announced he was going to bed and left the room. My father's straightforwardness was well known to my family and the Wilsons, but I was unsure how Craig would react.

"No need to worry about it," Craig laughed as we walked to his car. "I've never seen anyone end a party like that before. Your father doesn't leave any doubt about when it's time to go home, does he?"

"No doubt at all. My father doesn't beat around the bush, does he?" I chuckled.

We stepped off the driveway into the snow as Mr. and Mrs. Wilson backed their car out, and I watched as T.J.'s car followed his parents to their house across the street.

Mike climbed into his vehicle and shouted, pointing at Craig's Jag, "Cool set of wheels, man."

"Thanks. She gets me where I'm going."

Mike glanced at the front porch. "Well, guess I better warm this thing up while Suzie says goodbye to Mom. Nice meeting you, Craig, or should I say, brother? You guys have a good night, and congratulations on your engagement! It'll be great to have another guy in the family."

I smiled and waved, but I felt awful. I knew I had to tell Mike the truth, but I had a gut feeling he would be more upset about not having Craig as a brother-in-law than not knowing about the secret engagement.

"Well," I sighed, "I guess you've met the family now."

"It was fun. Thanks for letting me stay."

"My mom has taken a real shine to you. You obviously have a way with women." I grinned.

"I hope so." Craig hugged me, but I took a step back. He looked toward the porch and laughed. "Not much privacy around here, is there?"

I looked over my shoulder and saw my mom and Suzie watching. I shrugged. "What can I say? The joy of living at home."

Craig leaned against his car. "What's next on your sleuthing list?"

"I'd like to go back to Sarah's house and look around the front yard. Something's not right."

Craig nodded, thinking momentarily, and then stepped back from his car. "Okay. I can swing by in the morning."

"I have to work until two o'clock. Can we go after that?"

Craig leaned over and gave me a quick peck on the cheek. Smiling, he said, "We are engaged, you know. Gotta make it look believable. Tomorrow at two-thirty?"

"Yeah, sure. It's a date. I...I mean, see ya," I stammered.

chapter twenty-six

Monday, December 23rd

I rushed to my bedroom and let out a deep sigh as I sank into my bed, exhausted from working another chaotic shift. I kicked off my shoes and wiggled my toes, aching from standing on the hard floor by the cash register. If only there was a way to "wiggle" my frayed nerves after an uneasy night dealing with my *engagement,* that would be perfect.

Last night's events continued to haunt my waking hours —my mother's excitement over my impending nuptials, my brother welcoming Craig into the family, and the image of T.J. and Meg sitting together in *my* living room. For more Christmases than I could remember, he and I sat at that very spot by the fireplace during our annual family Christmas party. Why did he have to bring her?

I wished things between T.J. and me could return to how they used to be when everything was so easy. Being the best of friends, there was a time when we could talk for hours and share our deepest thoughts and dreams, but now, that seemed lost. And then there's Craig. Last night, was he trying to figure out how I felt about T.J.? About him? Why? Did he care about me, or was it all part of his act? I just don't know anymore.

"Michelle!" my mom hollered from the bottom of the stairs. "Craig's here."

I chuckled as I overheard her motherly advice. "Now, promise me you'll be careful. That ice can sneak up on you."

"No problem, Mrs. Kilpatrick. I won't let anything happen to Michelle," he answered as he held my coat so I could slip my arms into it.

I looked over my shoulder in time to see her placing a firm hand on his arm.

Smiling, she said, "And take care of yourself too. You're part of this family now."

The way they interacted was funny and heartbreaking at the same time. Craig, a successful mystery writer, had been on his own for so long that I was sure he wasn't used to someone telling him to be careful when driving. And although I was glad my mother approved of Craig, I now had the added pressure of knowing she would be devastated when she found out the truth.

As I debated the pros and cons of Craig's acceptance into our family, he clasped my arm. "Let me help you to the car. There's a lot of ice out here. I don't want you falling...not after promising your mother I wouldn't let any harm come to you. She'd never forgive me."

I grinned. "You got that right. You know she's going to hold you to that promise?"

"She left no doubt." He laughed. "Sarah's place?"

"That's the plan." My smile faded as I mentally rehashed the events of last night.

Craig backed the car out of the driveway and glanced in my direction. "Are you okay? You seem tense?"

"It's been a long day already."

"My mother?"

I smiled, glad to have an excuse for my mood, even if it wasn't the whole story. "How'd you guess?"

"Just a lucky hunch." He chuckled.

As Craig drove toward the expressway, the snowy countryside helped me unwind. The fences and trees, covered in white with heavy clumps of snow scattered about them, created a beautiful scene. For a moment, I imagined myself back in a simpler time when life was slower, and Christmas was not as commercialized. I found the stress of the season, Shelly's murder, and trying to help Rick and his mom exhausting.

Leaning back in my seat, I turned toward Craig. "I'm starting to doubt myself. I believed Paul when he told us about the dinner at the lab, but what if he was lying? And what if my instincts about Carl are wrong too? I couldn't sleep at all last night. Maybe I'm not as good at reading people as I thought. To be honest, sometimes I have trouble telling when you're being honest with me."

Craig said, "I will always be honest with you."

I shrugged. "I hope so, but I can't deal with that now. The point is it's getting harder and harder to separate fact from fiction. What if Carl tried to kill Sarah?" I shook my head. "What if I'm guilty of harboring a criminal?"

Craig's eyes narrowed. "You're not harboring a criminal. He's not hiding in your house."

"He may as well be. I know his whereabouts, and I haven't told the police. If Detective Douglas finds out, he won't hesitate to throw me in jail."

"*Us.*" He corrected me. "He'll throw us in jail."

"Yeah, sorry 'bout that. Carl had me convinced he was telling the truth." I sighed heavily. "Now I'm not so sure."

"I don't know what to tell you," Craig said with a hint of exasperation. "Sometimes you have to follow your instinct—"

"But what if I'm wrong and somebody else dies?"

Craig sighed, his shoulders slumping. "Hopefully, it won't

come to that. I admit, I can't shake the feeling Carl's lying, but we decided not to tell the police where he's staying, and no matter what happens, we'll have to live with it."

"That doesn't make me feel any better," I muttered.

"Sorry, but that's the way it is, Michelle. We can't undo our decision," he said, leaving no room for disagreement.

I returned to gazing out the window, longing to escape this mess.

For the next few minutes, the only sound inside Craig's car was the quiet purring of its engine. I avoided looking at Craig. All I wanted was to go home and hide in my room, pretending that no one poisoned Shelly, tampered with the treadmill or fired a gun at Sarah. None of these incidents should have ever become *my* problem.

Even as fear and doubt consumed me, a glimmer of hope flickered in the back of my mind. Perhaps Carl was telling the truth. There was no evidence to the contrary yet. I desperately clung to the idea my intuition would not lead me astray. Besides, I was in too deep to start second-guessing myself now.

Craig spoke up, putting an end to the silence. "Listen, forget about Paul and Carl for the moment. What does your instinct say about the shooting at Sarah's house?"

"That something is off with her story," I stated.

"Okay. Let's start with that," Craig said matter-of-factly.

"But—"

Craig interrupted. "No. One thing at a time. When we get to her house, do you have any idea what you're looking for?"

I shook my head. "No, but I think I'll know when I see it." I reached for the silver charm around my neck and twisted it between my fingers.

"That's good enough for me, Sherlock. Let's go find some answers." He tapped my hand, letting me know everything would be all right.

Within a few minutes, we arrived at Sarah's, and a chill

ran through me when I stepped outside Craig's car and gazed at the festive decor up and down the street.

Christmas lights adorned the large brick houses and the trees in their front lawns, while an undisturbed blanket of snow covered the ground, as far as I could see.

Not to be deterred by the icy wind, I pulled my scarf over my mouth, marched toward Sarah's house, surveyed it from various vantage points, and examined the new front window. Craig followed close behind, shielding me from the bitter chill as I walked up and down the street searching for clues.

"What do you think? Anything suspicious catch your eye?" He turned his head as a gust of wind blew snow in our faces.

Once the wind stopped, I asked, "Why would anyone stand outside, in front of Sarah's house, for all the world to see and start shooting? Seems way too risky to me."

"A crime of passion, maybe? People don't think clearly."

"Maybe, but it still doesn't make sense. Why not move closer to the house so you have a better shot?" I crossed my arms, perplexed.

"Maybe they didn't want to walk through all the snow and leave footprints. It's a big front yard. Your feet would get cold." Craig's eyes twinkled.

"Be serious." I nudged his well-padded shoulder. "What all are you wearing? Like ten sweaters?" I laughed.

"Well, I wasn't going to freeze out here. I never know where you're going to drag me."

I trudged toward the garage, pausing to glance back at Craig. "Why didn't the shooter stand in the driveway?"

Craig caught up with me. "Probably because you can't get a clear view of the entire window from here."

"Right. It would be awkward to shoot from this angle. It's all wrong." I marched toward the tree Carl was supposedly standing by when he shot at Sarah. My heart skipped a beat when my eyes landed on something glistening in the tree. I wheeled around. "Come over here. What does this look like to you?"

Craig stepped into the snow, grimacing as his feet sank. He inched closer, squinting at the bark. "It looks like a bullet."

"That's what I think, too. Now, why would a bullet be in the tree unless—"

"Unless what?" Craig pressed.

"Unless the bullet came from inside the house."

"But that would mean—" he started.

"Exactly!" I exclaimed as I searched through my purse for something to dig out the bullet.

"What are you doing?" Craig asked, his eyes widening in confusion.

"I'm looking for something so I can get the bullet out."

"No, don't do that. Let's call Detective Douglas. How else will we prove the bullet was in the tree unless he sees it with his own eyes?"

I cocked my head. "I suppose you're right."

"Music to my ears."

"Oh, get over yourself." I grinned.

We found a pay phone at a nearby gas station, and I had Craig call the police. Despite not knowing much about the detective, I surmised he might be a bit of a male chauvinist and would take our discovery more seriously if a *man* told him about it.

Detective Douglas answered, and within minutes, he and Lt. Grogan arrived at Sarah's house. Craig and I met them on the sidewalk.

The detective's eyes narrowed as he asked Craig, "Where is this bullet you were talking about?"

Craig and I led the way to the giant white oak, and I pointed to the silver nugget lodged in its trunk. We fought back our laughter when Detective Douglas announced there was a bullet in the tree as if he was the one to make the discovery.

"Grogan," Douglas barked, "remove it and bag it for evidence."

Craig spoke up. "Don't you need a warrant?"

"Unlike your world of fiction, Mr. Miller, we don't need a warrant for everything. As you may or may not realize, this tree is between the street and the sidewalk, which means it is on public property. May we proceed?"

Craig nodded.

I, however, stepped forward, determined to get the answers I needed. "Detective Douglas, did you find any bullets or casings by the tree on the day of the shooting? Or in Sarah's house?" I asked, articulating each word to keep my voice steady.

He gazed at Sarah's large picture window. "No, Ms. Kilpatrick, we did not. For your information, we thoroughly searched the house and the front yard, but we found nothing. Although, with all this snow, we might have missed something."

"Could the bullet have been fired from inside Sarah's house toward the tree?"

He shifted his attention toward me. "That's a big assumption. For one thing, Ms. Kilpatrick, we have no idea how long the bullet has been in the tree or if the bullet came from a gun that, say, Sarah owns. That's what you're implying, right?"

The detective's eyes darted to Craig and then back to me. "Once again, I must ask you two to leave the investigation to us. That note should make it clear that you are treading in dangerous waters."

I let out an exasperated breath. "But if it wasn't for—"

Craig yanked my arm. "Yes, Detective Douglas. We don't want to interfere with your work."

"But—" I protested.

"We're going now," Craig stated. "You know how to reach us, if you have any questions."

With his arm linked to mine, Craig pulled me to his car,

and I slid into my seat as he held the passenger door open. I wanted to yell at him for dragging me away and stopping me from talking to Detective Douglas, but his eyes were wide with terror. Without pausing, he slammed my door shut, rushed toward the driver's side, climbed in, and started the car without buckling his seatbelt.

"Don't forget your seatbelt."

"In a second, but we have to leave right now."

"Why, what's wrong?" I turned toward my window.

"Don't look back," he yelled. "Look straight ahead. Don't turn around."

"You're scaring me!"

Craig said nothing as he drove to the next street, where he parked the car. Staring into the rearview mirror, he said, "Sarah. Sarah was there." His voice was laced with tension. "She parked halfway down the street while we were talking to Douglas. She didn't get out of her car, but I'm sure she was watching us. I just hope she didn't realize I saw her."

"What if she did? Would that be so bad?"

Craig shook his head. "That's the problem. I don't know."

"So, what do we do now?"

With his eyes on the road and hands clasping the steering wheel, he said, "Let's find someplace where we won't be so visible."

He drove to Yancy's and pulled into the parking lot, where he found a spot in the back.

Sensing that Craig needed some alone time to think, I asked, "Would it be okay if I run inside and call Amy? I meant to do it last night, but with the party—"

"No, go ahead. That's a good idea. That'll give me time to—"

I didn't wait for him to finish before hurrying inside Yancy's and depositing my dime in the payphone on the back wall. "Hey, Amy. Listen, I've only got a few minutes, but did your brother have anything to say about Paul and Shelly?"

"Yeah, sorry, I was going to call you earlier today, but I worked a late shift last night and slept until noon—"

"No problem. The holidays are crazy, aren't they? So, what did you find out?" I asked.

"Well, Daryl, that's my brother, and Paul got together this morning to study. I think I told you they were both pre-med students, right?"

"Yeah. So, what did Paul say?" I asked, my voice tinged with impatience as I struggled to keep Amy on topic.

"Dr. Spratt called Paul last night, and it really rattled him. Did you know Dr. Spratt is Todd's father? I didn't—"

"Yes, I just found that out too. Now, what did Dr. Spratt want?"

"He read Paul the riot act for loaning his hall pass."

"But I thought he had permission."

"He did, but now the professor who gave him permission is in trouble too, and Paul's worried this dude will take it out on him in class next quarter."

"Oh no, that's terrible," I muttered. "Did he say anything else about it?"

Amy sighed. "He wished he'd listened to Shelly when she warned him to stay away from Elaine." She took another deep breath. "Did you know someone put boxes of rat poisoning in Paul's locker?"

"No."

"Yeah...Paul found it there the night Shelly died, and he put it in the storage closet. However, when he heard someone poisoned Shelly with arsenic, he panicked and threw it away 'cause he didn't want the police to find his fingerprints on it. After thinking about it, he realized the rat poison may not have had arsenic in it. He didn't read the label, and now he doesn't know if he destroyed evidence. Poor guy, my brother said he's scared he'll get kicked out of school between the rat poisoning and the lab pass."

I startled Craig when I knocked on the passenger window,

so he would unlock the door. As I buckled in, he said, "When you said something wasn't right about the shooting, I have to admit I thought you were way off base, but I'm beginning to see what you mean...there's something off about Sarah's explanation."

"And," I added, "after talking to Amy, we have proof Paul got permission to loan his lab pass out."

"Really?"

"Yeah, Dr. Spratt reprimanded him for doing it, but that's not all." I continued to tell Craig about the rat poisoning in Paul's locker.

Craig thought for a moment. "Sounds to me like Elaine was covering her tracks."

"Not so fast—to quote you, 'Let's not jump to conclusions.'" I grinned as I grabbed my notebook from my tote. Flipping through the pages, I said, "Let's look at our suspects: Elaine, Sarah, Paul, Carl, and Sam Langford. What if we think of Shelly's death, the malfunctioning treadmill, and the attempted shooting of Sarah as three elements of one crime?"

"Why?" Craig asked.

"Because dealing with them as three separate crimes isn't getting us anywhere. We keep going in circles. Now, hear me out, and let's put the first two incidents together for starters. The sabotaged equipment and Shelly's murder both threatened the future of Caroline's fitness center—agree?"

"Agree." He relaxed his grip on the steering wheel and leaned back into his seat. "So, with your theory, who do you think moves to the top of our suspect list?"

"Carl and his brother benefit from the fitness center's bad publicity, but there was no reason to murder Shelly. That seems a little excessive to get rid of the competition. Of course, if Carl was seeing Shelly and she threatened to tell Sarah, that would give him a reason to kill her. So, I guess between Mr. Langford and Carl, Carl should move to the top." I thought for a moment.

"What about Paul?" Craig asked. "He could have wanted to murder Shelly—the old if I can't have her, nobody else can kind of motive, but again—"

I shrugged. "But I don't think he had a motive to destroy Caroline's gym unless—"

"Unless, what?"

"Unless he was working with Elaine. Think about it. Paul was the jilted lover, and Elaine was upset because Shelly knew about her criminal record. As long as Shelly was alive, Elaine lived in fear that Shelly would tell Dr. McGuire about her stint in prison. Add to that the fact that Elaine has no love for her fiancé's ex-wife, and voilà, you've got a motive. Elaine and Paul had the means to get the arsenic and the opportunity to put it in Shelly's thermos."

"Okay, so Elaine and Paul move to the top of our list too. The only one we've ruled out is Langford. What about Sarah?"

"I would have ruled her out until we found the bullet in the tree." I paused. "Of course, we don't know how long it's been there or if Sarah even owns a gun." I took a deep breath. "I'd feel better about her story being true if the police could find some shell casings by the tree. And it's still possible someone dressed up like Carl, or he could be the shooter."

Craig looked confused. "Let's assume for the moment Sarah is lying. I understand jealousy as a motive to get rid of Shelly, but why ruin Caroline's business? Aren't they friends?"

"Are they? I'm not so sure anymore." I shook my head and glanced out my window.

Craig rubbed his chin. "Don't you think it's weird that Sarah sat in her car and watched us with the police while we were at her house? If you went home and found a squad car in your driveway, wouldn't you want to know what was happening?"

"Definitely."

"Exactly my point! At the very least, I'm convinced she's covering for someone—Elaine or Paul, or maybe both of them."

"No offense, but I think we moved everyone to the top of our list except Sam Langford." I bit my bottom lip. "Yeah, I guess you're right. We need a new plan. I think it's time for the old Poirot ploy.

Craig eyed me. "Huh?"

A grin spread across my face. "I've got an idea."

"Care to share it with me?" he asked.

I shook my head and chuckled. "Not really. You got time to swing by Mr. Langford's gym? Maybe the elusive Elaine is in today?"

"Fine with me. Should you call your parents?"

"Not tonight. They're going out with friends and won't be home until late. I'm as free as a bird."

"Okay. Let's go. Perhaps afterward, we can catch a bite to eat if that won't interfere with your *mysterious* plan."

Still grinning, I looked out the window.

chapter twenty-seven

The strands of blinking Christmas lights outlining the windows at Langford's Fitness Center seemed brighter and more festive than when I had been there before. Perhaps it was because hope was building up within me that meeting up with Elaine would give Craig and me the proof we needed to solve Shelly's murder.

I walked into the gym expecting to see Mindy behind the front desk, but was taken aback to see Mr. Langford dressed casually in a burgundy warm-up suit.

"Craig, how nice of you and Michelle to stop by. Have you come to tell me you've decided to invest in my fitness center? You won't be sorry."

Craig smiled and extended his hand toward Mr. Langford. "No, not yet. I haven't had time to talk to my team…finishing my book…the holidays and all."

A glint of annoyance flashed in Mr. Langford's eyes, but he quickly masked it with a charming smile. "Well, don't wait too long. This is a once-in-a-lifetime opportunity. Elaine was just here, and she has some investors lined up."

Craig raised an eyebrow as he surveyed the fitness area. "Really? Is she still here?"

Mr. Langford shook his head. "No, she had to go…something about needing Carl to sign some papers so she can proceed with—"

"You told her where he was?" I cried.

"Yes, as I said, she needed—"

I whipped around toward Craig. "We need to go now!"

Mr. Langford furrowed his brows. "What's wrong?"

Neither of us answered him as we ran to the car.

"What do you think she wants with Carl?" Craig asked as he fastened his seat belt.

I wrung my hands. "I don't know. Hopefully, just to sign papers. But I've got a bad feeling."

"Me, too." Craig whipped out of the parking lot and sped to the cabin.

***

At first, I was relieved not to see Elaine's car at the cabin. Perhaps we had gotten to Carl before she did, but I thought otherwise when I saw two sets of tire tracks and several footprints going to and from the cabin.

"Do you think Elaine's already been here?"

Craig shrugged.

After pausing for a moment, I suggested he park behind the cabin.

"Why?"

"If she's still on her way, we don't want her to see your car when she gets here."

"Does it matter if she does?"

Everything in me wanted to scream that we didn't have time to debate whether he should hide his vehicle—he needed to trust me and move his car out of view. Instead of yelling at him, which would have only led to a longer discussion, I took a deep breath and explained, "Because I don't want to scare her off. We need to find out what she's up to."

Craig shook his head. "Gotcha, but I think I'll get stuck in the snow once I'm off the driveway."

"Umm...that won't work. Do you think you could pull closer to the shed? Maybe there's a tarp inside."

Craig narrowed his eyes. "Why would there be a—"

I barked, "Because sometimes when you don't have a garage, people have a cover for their cars to protect them from the snow."

"Huh? Doesn't the snow still cover—" he asked, questioning my logic.

"Craig, I know what I'm talking about. People use them to cover their cars, and I would think someone staying at a cabin might have one, okay?"

"Sure. Let's go ask Carl. Perhaps he knows." Craig parked next to the shed and unbuckled his seatbelt.

I threw my door open and looked over my shoulder at Craig as I dashed to the cabin. "You look in the shed. I'll talk to Carl and warn him Elaine is coming."

As Craig sloshed through the snowdrift in front of the shed, he shouted, "We should have had Mr. Langford call Detective Douglas. See if there's a phone in the cabin."

When I knocked on the cabin door, it swung open. "Carl? Carl, it's Michelle. Are you here?"

There was no answer.

I ran from room to room searching for Carl, but he was nowhere to be found. Flinging open the back door, I spied a set of footprints leading away from the porch into the woods. Fear and dread took over as I scoured the landscape. *Where are you, Carl?*

An enormous crash erupted from the shed. I flew toward it and yanked open the door to find Carl gripping Craig in a chokehold.

"Carl! Stop! Let him go!"

Carl relaxed his grip on Craig's neck. "Michelle?"

I rushed to Craig's side as he leaned over and took several deep breaths, his hands on his knees.

Carl stepped back, shaking. "Craig, I'm sorry. I didn't know it was you. I thought you were one of Elaine's goons." He went to the doorway, studied the landscape in all directions, and then pulled the door shut.

It took a few minutes for my eyes to adjust to the dark with the only source of light coming from a window covered with a vinyl shade. Once the room came into view, I spied various yard tools on the far wall—a rake, a shovel, a hoe, and a hose. A tool chest was nearby, with several cardboard boxes stacked in front. I jumped when a mouse scurried across the floor, seeking shelter behind the bales of hay piled high in the corner. I took a few steps back, wondering what else might be lurking inside the shed.

Craig stood up and rubbed his neck. "Glad you came when you did. Otherwise—" He stopped while he cleared his throat. "Carl here might have done me in."

Carl pulled the shade away from the small window with trembling hands and peered out. "Elaine was here earlier with some guy. When they came to the door, I snuck out and ran. I guess they weren't up for a jaunt in the woods. I hid until they drove away. That's when I came to the shed. I thought it would be safer than in the cabin."

"Craig, are you all right?" I rubbed Craig's arm, trying to comfort him.

"I'm sorry," Carl replied in a hushed tone. "Your back was to me. I thought you were the guy with Elaine."

Despite the immediate crisis being over, my head spun as the adrenaline receded in my system. I clung onto Craig's shoulder as I tried to steady myself.

"I got you. Everything's okay," Craig whispered.

"Thanks." I took a deep breath, straightened my stance, and turned to Carl. "Any idea what Elaine wanted?"

"I don't know, but I think it's safe to say it wasn't to pay me a social visit."

I looked at Craig and then back at Carl. "I don't think it's a good idea for you to stay here. Do you have someplace you could go?"

Carl shook his head. "I need to turn myself in to the police and tell them what happened. Even if they don't believe me, chances are I'll be safer in jail than anyplace else."

Craig nodded. "I think you're right. Why don't you grab your stuff, and we'll take you to the station and find Detective Douglas?"

The three of us trudged through the snow to the cabin, Carl apologizing each time Craig rubbed his neck.

I collapsed onto the sofa while Craig helped Carl gather his belongings from the bedroom. I closed my eyes and took a deep breath to steady my nerves, but the sound of an approaching car sent shivers down my spine, ending any serenity I was hoping to gain.

Craig peeked out of the room and cocked his head as if trying to identify the sound.

I ran to the window and yelled, "Oh, no. Looks like we got trouble."

Carl pushed past me and confirmed what I feared. "She's back."

I stared at both men. "What do we do now?"

Craig grabbed my arm. "Run!"

We ran to the back door, and Craig twisted the knob and pulled the door open, only to be met by a man standing in front of us. The inescapable six-foot wall of muscle shouted, "They're back here!"

Our options for escaping seemed nonexistent. The three of us were no match for him, and the footsteps behind us increased my panic. There was no way out.

I turned my head to look behind and saw Elaine wrapped

in her mink coat. Her eyes squinted as she surveyed the tumultuous scene before her. "What's going on?"

"Elaine, let them go. They've got nothing to do with this," Carl pleaded, his voice shaking.

"What are you talking about?" Her eyes drifted from Carl to me and Craig and back to Carl.

"You and your goon here do what you want with me, but leave them alone," Carl said.

"My goon?" She looked at the man standing behind us and started laughing. "That *goon* is my lawyer, John Hathaway."

"What? I don't understand. What do you and your *lawyer* want with Carl?" I asked.

Elaine stepped back, and the corners of her mouth turned up. "I don't know why *you* think I'm here, but I'm here so Carl can sign some papers."

"What papers?" I asked.

"Why don't we all calm down and sit in the other room," said Mr. Hathaway.

Craig and I exchanged a tense glance before we followed Mr. Hathaway, Elaine, and Carl into the living room. Elaine sat in the leather recliner by the front door as Mr. Hathaway stood behind her.

I quickly surmised that if Elaine was telling the truth, the tension between her and Carl at the moment resulted from a misunderstanding. However, if she was lying, we were all in big trouble.

In a panic, I looked around the room. When my eyes rested on a pewter bear figurine sitting on the coffee table, I devised a plan. I could grab the figurine, run for the back door, and throw the bear at anyone chasing us. I knew it wasn't the best idea, but with Craig's help, there was a chance it might work.

Then I saw the deer head hanging above the fireplace. The eyes staring straight ahead reminded me of what happens when you don't outrun your pursuer. Perhaps I needed a backup plan.

Craig broke my train of thought by addressing Elaine. "What are these papers you're talking about?"

She reached into her bag and pulled out a group of papers held together by a paperclip. She got up and handed them to Carl who was sitting in the recliner across from her. As he read through the documents, she faced Craig. "It's none of your business, but I'll explain since Carl has turned this into such a production. I'm loaning money to Sam—Mr. Langford —to keep his gym afloat until he can raise enough capital through investors. I have several leads on potential investors, but it will take time to close the deals, and Sam needs the money now."

Elaine continued, "Mr. Hathaway has prepared all the paperwork for the loan, including an agreement between Carl —the beneficiary of Sam's estate—and me. As per the agree-ment, if Sam dies before the loan is repaid and Carl decides to sell the gym, any proceeds from the sale will be paid to me first. I need Carl to sign the agreement before I can loan the money to Sam."

"I'm so confused." I glanced at Elaine and then at Carl. "Why did you think Elaine was coming here to hurt you?"

Carl looked up from the papers in his hand. "The day of the shooting, Sarah told me Elaine thought I was a liability that needed to be silenced, just like Shelly. After the attempt on Sarah's life, the more I thought about it, the more I figured Elaine was behind it. When she showed up here, I thought she wanted to kill me. What else was I to think seeing her pull up with some guy in the car?"

Elaine's eyes grew wide. "Why in the world would I want to kill you? And—" she added, "I did *not* kill Shelly. How dare you accuse me of murder! We all know you're the one who poisoned her."

"Wait a minute," I interjected. "Why would Carl kill Shelly? You're the one she was blackmailing?"

Elaine squinted her eyes and glared. "You have no idea what you're talking about! Carl here had the most to lose when Shelly threatened to expose their relationship to Sarah. His cash cow would have dropped him on the spot."

While Carl and Elaine bickered about who had the greater motive to kill Shelly, a plan to catch the killer came to me. "Both of you can just shut up. The police will have the answer soon enough about who killed Shelly."

They turned away from each other and stared at me, as did Craig, who clearly wondered what I was up to. "It turns out the university had a new security camera in the lab. They were trying it out for the month of December. When Rick asked his father about the night you *supposedly* surprised him with dinner in his classroom—"

"He did what?" The color drained from Elaine's face.

I ignored her and continued. "During the end of the quarter inventory at the lab, Dr. Spratt discovered the arsenic was missing, so he requested the videotape for the night of your *romantic dinner*, which we both know never happened. Anyway, whoever Dr. Spratt talked to said they would leave the tape in the lab after lunch. He's going back tomorrow to watch it, and if it shows anything suspicious—which I have a hunch it will—he'll turn it over to the police. I'm sure there will be enough evidence to arrest whoever is on that tape on the suspicion of murder."

"Well, you won't find me on that tape!" Elaine exclaimed. "I misplaced Paul's lab pass and couldn't find it, so I had to cancel my surprise dinner. I never told Paul I lost the pass because I found it the next day in the break room at Caroline's gym. I must have left it there. Or—," she paused as she turned toward Carl, "maybe you're the one who took the pass. You were at the fitness center that day."

Carl jumped to his feet. "How dare you accuse me of stealing the pass!"

"Well, if you guys are telling the truth, you have nothing to worry about—" I took a deep breath, "so if you'll excuse us, Craig and I need to go."

Craig stood up and, following my lead, headed for the door. We raced to the car without exchanging a single word.

When the car door closed, Craig asked, "What was that all about?"

"I was planning on getting all our suspects together as Agatha Christie did with her detective Poirot, but when Elaine showed up, I needed another idea fast, so I set a trap for whoever stole the arsenic, which should be Shelly's killer." My hands were shaking. "It was the only thing I could think of." I took a deep breath, running through my options. "When you see a place that might have a pay phone, stop. I need to call Detective Douglas and tell him what I've done."

"Oh, he's going to love you," Craig said sarcastically. "Who do you think will show up?"

"I'm still putting my money on Elaine. I'm not sure I buy that whole story about the pass going missing. Did you see how panic-stricken she was when I mentioned the tape?" I twirled the chain around my neck.

"She wasn't pleased, that's for sure."

I mentally ran through my list of suspects. "If Elaine's innocent, I think she'll call Sarah to vent. So that will let Sarah know about the tape. Carl obviously knows. Who else is on our list? Oh, yeah. Paul. Umm...again, I think Elaine will call him and come clean about misplacing the lab pass. That might be too big of an assumption, but if she doesn't call him, there's a good chance dear Aunt Sarah will warn him if she thinks he's the killer."

Craig momentarily looked out his window, shaking his head. "Sounds like you're pinning your hopes on Elaine and

Sarah making phone calls. I'm not sure that's how it will work out."

"Maybe, but to paraphrase Poirot, 'my little grey cells are following the psychology.' When people are upset, they talk. And if Elaine and Sarah are such good friends, Elaine *will* call her. I'm betting on it. But we need Detective Douglas at the lab before anybody shows up."

"I don't know, Michelle. This could turn ugly fast if we're not careful." Craig sighed.

"Which is why I'm calling in reinforcements. Look, there's a diner. I bet they have a phone." I searched my wallet for Detective Douglas's business card as Craig entered the parking lot.

chapter twenty-eight

Craig parked his car under the covered entrance of the diner. I jumped out, dashed inside, and told the cashier I needed to call the police. She looked at me, startled, and gestured for me to come around the counter. She handed me the receiver from the phone hanging on the wall.

With the receiver on my shoulder, I fished out the detective's business card from my pocket. My hands shook, and my heart pounded as I dialed the number. After five agonizing rings, someone answered, but it wasn't Detective Douglas.

"Lawrence?" I asked.

"Yes."

"It's Michelle. Is Detective Douglas in?" My voice quavered.

"No, he stepped out a minute. Can I give him a message? Is everything all right?"

My words tumbled out in a mad rush as I told Lawrence about the trap I had set for Shelly's killer.

"Michelle—"

"I know, I know…let the police do their job. Well, I'm calling so they can do it. Lawrence, tell him to get to the chemistry lab at Overman Hall as soon as possible. I have no idea who or when they'll show up, but I think someone will."

After hanging up the phone, I sprinted to Craig's car. Time was of the essence, and Craig sailed through every yellow light, swerving past other cars in a mad dash to get to the university before the killer did. I held tight to my seat, trying to keep steady while reminding myself to breathe.

Craig asked, "Where should I park? By Overman?"

I spied a black limo in the back of the lot. *What's a limo doing here? Is that the same—*

"What do you want me to do?" Craig demanded.

"Not here! Try the next lot over."

Craig pulled between two cars, reasoning that his vehicle would not be as noticeable if any of our suspects drove through the lot. I didn't want to question his logic, but I wasn't sure that a silver Jag wouldn't attract attention wherever it was parked. We bundled up and ran to the back entrance of Overman Hall.

Craig flung the door open. "Don't they ever lock these doors?"

"Not during the week. I suppose some of the staff members still have to work. Even Dr. Spratt was here working yesterday." I shrugged. "The janitors probably lock up before they go home at night." I grinned. "Lucky us, it's not that late yet."

We climbed the stairs to the second floor but stopped when we heard footsteps in the hallway. Craig mouthed, "Shh!" with his finger over his mouth. He motioned for me to go back down, where we stood, not moving a muscle, on the step just below the landing.

I whispered. "Do you hear anything?"

After listening for a moment and not hearing anything, we resumed our journey. The silence continued, only broken by the thumping of my heart. I glanced at Craig—cool, calm, and collected Craig. Unlike him, I was terrified, but I didn't want him to know. *After all, if I'm going to be an investigative reporter...*

As we walked down the hall, Craig turned toward me but looked right through me as he focused on the rooms along the wall. Perhaps he was more nervous than I thought.

A noise. I gasped and tugged on his arm to stop. It was a false alarm. A paper had fallen off one of the doors when we walked by. He patted my arm to let me know everything was okay.

When we reached the chemistry lab, I peered through the door window. Convinced no one was in the room, I signaled Craig to follow me as I pulled the door open and crept inside.

"Where should we hide?" I asked, barely above a whisper.

Our eyes, searching for cover, darted across every shadow. Craig's index finger jabbed toward a side door, which I hoped would open into an office, not a tiny closet, but we didn't have time to be picky. It was our only option if we wanted to hide. If we were lucky, the frosted window in the door would allow us to see into the lab from the other side.

Taking a deep breath, I turned the knob. The door creaked open, revealing a dimly lit room. I hesitated for a moment, trying to make out any shapes for movement before entering.

Suddenly, a strong arm reached out from the shadows and pulled me inside. A jolt of fear shot through me, but before I could scream, I made out a face. Detective Douglas—his scowl-etched face inches from mine.

With his other arm, the detective grabbed Craig while Lt. Grogan closed the door.

Glaring at us, Detective Douglas growled, "What are you doing here?"

Still recovering from the shock of seeing the detective, I sputtered, "I didn't know if you would make it in time. I wasn't going to let the murderer escape."

He exhaled deeply, exasperated. "Ms. Kilpatrick—"

Before he could complete his sentence, the sound of the

lab door opening halted his lecture. The four of us froze as the sound of drawers being slammed shut and something crashing as it hit the floor resonated through the lab.

Standing in the cramped office, I felt the walls closing on me. The only way out was through the door in front of me—the one that led to the lab—but judging from the sounds coming from that direction, my one option was not a good one.

Wedged between the detective and Lt. Grogan, I peered through the small window. My mouth dropped open. Although I had set the trap, I was shocked someone had taken the bait and even more shocked that it was Sarah.

Despite being on my suspect list, I found it hard to believe Sarah was the villain, probably because I didn't want her friendship with Caroline to be an act. Maybe in my wild imagination, I had hoped a mysterious madman would appear out of nowhere and confess to the murder. Someone I didn't know. Someone no one in my circle of friends knew—a total stranger.

Yet the glint of metal in Sarah's hand made it clear that the person Rick and his mom considered a friend might also be capable of anything, including cold-blooded murder.

Detective Douglas raised his gun, and Lt. Grogan tensed, ready to surge forward, but stopped when a man entered the room.

"What's going on in here? Who are you? What do you want?" he yelled.

It was Dr. Spratt, and Sarah was pointing her gun at him. To my horror, I realized I was the one who lured Sarah here, and now she might take another innocent life.

Lt. Grogan, ready to pounce through the door, glanced at Detective Douglas for confirmation. To my surprise, the detective responded with a fierce shake of his head and a silent command to "wait."

With a steely grip on the gun, Sarah commanded, "Close the door and move over there...slowly. Who are you?"

"I'm Dr. Spratt, and *you* are in my lab. I demand to know what you're doing here!"

Sarah shouted. "I hardly think you are in the position to demand anything. Where is the tape?"

Dr. Spratt shook his head in genuine confusion. "What tape? I have no idea—"

"Don't play innocent with me. I want the tape you left for the police, and I want it now." Sarah's voice reverberated in the lab. Her finger tightened on the trigger.

The door to the lab flung open, and Carl burst in. "Sarah! What are you—?" His words stopped when he saw the gun in her hand.

"Move away from the door, Carl, or I'll shoot," Sarah barked, her eyes wild with desperation.

"Okay. Okay," he said as he took a few steps toward Dr. Spratt and whispered something to him.

"No talking," Sarah ordered, her voice escalating to a feverish pitch, casting an ominous shadow over the tense tableau unfolding in the lab.

Dr. Spratt met Sarah's gaze. The quick exchange with Carl apparently convinced him to play along with the dangerous charade of a nonexistent tape. "Before I tell you where it is, why did you kill Shelly?"

Sarah's lips twisted into a wicked smirk. "She was getting in the way of everything. She deserved to die. The little social climber was making moves on my man—"

Carl interrupted. "I told you there was nothing between Shelly and me."

"Not you, Carl! You silly little man, did you believe I was in love with you? Ha! You were just a pawn in my game to get rid of Shelly and secure Sam for myself," she hissed.

Carl's face contorted in shock and disbelief. "I...I don't understand."

"Of course, you don't. Someday, I'll explain it to you in simple words," Sarah spat, her eyes blazing with contempt. "But it doesn't matter now. Dr. Spratt, give me that tape."

He stood momentarily and bowed his head as he reached into his pocket, extracting a small key. "It's locked in my desk drawer," he explained as his hand trembled.

Sarah's eyes narrowed into a steely gaze as she slowly and cautiously moved toward the two men, keeping her distance but edging closer. Her muscles tensed as she prepared for any sudden movements. "No tricks," she warned.

Dr. Spratt walked to his desk, and Sarah continued. "Poor, poor delusional, Carl. Why do you think I pointed out the treadmill to you? Sam removed a few screws from it earlier in the day. I thought the police would arrest you for tampering with it, but they missed that little clue. That's why I had to stage the shooting, don't you see, to bring the suspicion back to you and get you out of the way? Going into hiding made you look even more guilty. But then your little friends had to investigate, so I had to throw suspicion on Elaine." She paused and glared at Dr. Spratt. "How are you coming with that key?"

"Give me a minute. I need to unlock the drawer," Dr. Spratt said from behind the desk.

"Well, hurry up!" she yelled, her lack of patience increasing.

"Okay, I got it. The tape should be in that cabinet over there." Dr. Spratt pointed at the cabinet housing the toxic substances.

As the scene in the lab unfolded before our eyes, the tension in the crowded office grew. We were on the precipice of an unpredictable and perilous confrontation, becoming more dangerous by the minute. I stumbled backward and fell into Craig's arms, overcome by my nerves.

Craig steadied me, guiding me back to my spot in front of

the window. His voice offered a fragile reassurance, "Hang in there. It shouldn't be much longer."

Dr. Spratt pivoted, fixing his gaze on Sarah. "I'm just curious, from a scientific standpoint, why increase the amount of arsenic the night of the Open House?"

A wicked smirk stretched across Sarah's face. "Wouldn't you like to know?"

With a sharp click, Dr. Spratt unlocked the cabinet as Sarah continued. "I have no idea where you got your information, but it doesn't matter. The police will never figure it out. My original plan was a slow, drawn-out death, but when *he* called and demanded a quick resolution to our problem, I added a lethal amount of arsenic to Shelly's thermos."

"I can't believe my brother would have any part in a murder," shouted Carl.

"Shut up, Carl," Sarah screamed. "Sam had nothing to do with killing Shelly. He was only concerned about saving his precious business."

Dr. Spratt's eyes narrowed, suspicion etched on his face. "But you said *he* called."

A sneer curled over her lips. "I never said it was Sam, did I?"

"Then who?" he asked as he rummaged through the shelves.

"That's for me to know, not you." Sarah waved the gun in the air before redirecting its focus back to Dr. Spratt. "Now, where is that tape?"

"It's not here," he said in a trembling voice.

I made a mental note that when this was all over, if Dr. Spratt ever wanted to change careers, acting should be at the top of his list. He was a natural, almost convincing me the nonexistent recording was missing from the cabinet.

Sarah yelled, "Then where is it?" '

The question hung in the air, intensifying the suspense that gripped us all.

Dr. Spratt shook his head vigorously. "I don't know. I don't understand why it's not here."

"Well, that's unfortunate." Sarah's words were cold and calculated.

"What do you mean?" Dr. Spratt choked out.

"I mean, it's unfortunate that you now have become a problem I need to eliminate," she said as she placed her finger on the trigger.

Carl pleaded, "Sarah, don't do this."

At that moment, Detective Douglas gave a signal to Lt. Grogan, and they burst into the room, weapons drawn and aimed straight at Sarah. "Drop the gun and put your hands above your head," Douglas barked.

Sarah spun around, facing the detective, and pointed her gun at him, then pivoted toward Grogan. Both men stood their ground, ready to fire.

"Fingers off the trigger," Douglas commanded, his finger twitching on his weapon's trigger. Panic surged in Sarah's eyes as she tightly gripped her sole defense.

"I said, drop it now!" Douglas shouted, his voice echoing through the tense silence of the room.

With a defeated sigh, Sarah let the gun slip from her hand, and it clattered to the floor. As Grogan moved forward to retrieve it, Douglas barked out orders once again. "Cuff her and read Ms. Bentley her rights."

"Sarah Bentley, you are under arrest for the murder of Shelly Gallagher. You have the right to remain silent..."

***

After Craig and I gave our statements to Lt. Grogan at the police station, we found Lawrence at the front desk in the lobby. Before long, Carl and Dr. Spratt's footsteps interrupted our conversation as the two men headed for the door. Dr.

Spratt acknowledged us with a nod, but Carl kept walking, his head hung low.

My heart ached for him, knowing the two people he trusted had betrayed him. I shook my head as the door to the outside world closed behind them.

"Poor Carl," I said. "He was infatuated with Sarah, and it's hard to believe she and Sam Langford were involved all along."

Craig added, "Quite the master plan, wasn't it? Using Carl to divert attention away from the two of them."

My gaze shifted to Lawrence. "Why was Carl at the lab, anyway?"

"He suspected Elaine had dragged Sarah into this mess, and he wanted to warn her. When he couldn't reach her on the phone, he remembered what you said about the tape, so he headed for the lab."

"Unbelievable!"

"Yeah, and don't tell Detective Douglas I told you this, but he said after looking at the supposed crime scene at Sarah's house with you and Craig and finding the bullet in the tree, he had questions about Sarah. On the detective's orders, an officer went through Sarah's trash and discovered gun casings, which made it more likely that the shot originated from inside the house and was fired toward the tree rather than the opposite."

Craig said, "Isn't that the way it always is—a little slip-up unravels the whole story? And think about it, if the doctor hadn't been suspicious about Shelly's cause of death or Shelly's parents hadn't ordered the autopsy for their lawsuit, no one might have ever attributed Shelly's death to the poisoning. I guess it's true, to paraphrase Robert Burns, 'The best-laid plans of mice and men go often astray.' But the real question is, why? What was Sarah's motivation?"

"As usual, it had to do with money. When Detective Douglas got your message, he and Lt. Grogan went to the lab at the university, but he sent a couple of officers to question Sam Langford again regarding Carl's whereabouts. Apparently, seeing the men in blue again scared him enough that he not only told them about the cabin where Carl had been hiding but revealed Sarah and his involvement with the treadmill at Caroline's fitness center."

"What did he say?" I leaned on the counter.

"Langford needed all the money from his father's estate to keep his fitness center going. Even though he could use Carl's share for now, once the gym became profitable, he didn't want to split the proceeds with his brother. When Sarah learned through her son that Rick's mom was looking for a space to lease for a new fitness center, she told Langford, and he panicked. He was already in financial straits and feared the competition would run him out of business. That's when Sarah concocted a plan to befriend Caroline and encouraged her to move forward with the fitness center by promising to put up the capital Caroline needed for it. She thought by dissuading Caroline from getting a bank loan, the fitness center would never open. But when Sarah backed out of investing, Caroline borrowed the money from Rick's father, so Sarah had to devise a new plan."

"Some friend." I sighed. "But what about the treadmill? Did Mr. Langford tamper with it?"

"Yeah, he did. Langford said he and Sarah had been at Caroline's gym the afternoon of the Open House. He removed a few screws from a treadmill, intending to cause chaos and put doubts in people's minds about the safety of the equipment. But Carl almost messed everything up when he found some screws underneath the treadmill and tried to fix it. He warned Shelly not to use the treadmill, but she wouldn't listen. Langford said Shelly dying while on the treadmill was never part of the plan, but Sarah thought it was the pièce de résistance."

"Crazy!" I shook my head in disbelief. "What's going to happen to Sam?"

Lawrence shook his head. "Not sure at this point, but I suspect he will be charged with something related to tampering with equipment and causing bodily harm. That's up to the prosecutor."

"But," I asked Lawrence, "back to Sarah, why did she poison Shelly?"

"She said she didn't like it when Shelly dumped her nephew, Paul. Plus, she said something odd. She mentioned Mae Emerson."

"What did she say?"

"She said *he* wants Mae to pay for the sins of her husband."

"He? He who? And which husband? There are three!" I gasped.

"She wouldn't say anymore," Lawrence added with a perplexed expression. "Got no idea what she meant."

"How strange!" I leaned my chin on my hands as images of the past few months raced through my mind. "The more I think about it, the more it seems everything ties back to Mae."

Craig looked at me, hurt. "You can't think my mother is involved in all this?"

"Oh, no, not in that way."

His face relaxed as I tried to explain. "It's as if someone is trying to get to Mae—maybe send her a message? First, her cousin and his wife kill her sister and also attack her old flame—Bob Lane. And now, someone poisoned Shelly, who had a connection to Mae's second husband. Coincidence? I wonder." My mind raced with theories. "We've got to find out who this mysterious man is and how he's connected to Mae."

chapter twenty-nine

After leaving the police station, I went with Craig to his office and worked on my newspaper article detailing Sarah's scheme to discredit Caroline's gym.

Keeping my promise to Detective Douglas, I refrained from divulging the facts about Sarah poisoning Shelly. To do so would have compromised the case against her, and I certainly didn't want to do that. With each word I penned, I realized how close Sarah had come to destroying Caroline's gym and murdering Shelly.

Someday, the whole story needed to be told. *Who knows, maybe I'll give Craig a bit of competition by writing a book about it once the trial is over.* The thought made me chuckle.

I can not begin to describe the pride that rushed over me as I typed THE END after my last paragraph, except to say it felt wonderful! The article on Professor Ladd's death, published a few months ago, had been a joint effort, but this one was all my own. Except, of course, for Craig's suggestions, which I hated to admit were good and improved my writing.

After a quick rewrite, Craig called his friend, the editor of the city newspaper, and convinced him to run my story in the morning edition.

Tuesday, December 24th

I woke up to find a newspaper slipped under my bedroom door. I crawled out of bed, walked to the door, and looked down to see my article dominating the front page. I rubbed my eyes a few times just to make sure I wasn't dreaming.

To add to my excitement, my parents were beaming when I walked into the kitchen for breakfast. My mom was already on the phone with one of her friends. I overheard her asking Mrs. Cooper to save the paper for her so she could send copies of my article to our family members who lived out of town.

My father peered over his coffee cup and told me, "Nice article." He then chuckled, saying he didn't know what he was going to do with all the newspapers my mom was gathering from her friends. "I might have to add on to the garage if you keep writing like that."

I didn't think my morning could get any better, but I was proven wrong when I walked into the Petersburg Health & Fitness Center. The place was hopping. People were everywhere. Caroline's impromptu Christmas party to celebrate being cleared of all wrongdoing in connection with Shelly's death was in full swing. Sounds of laughter and music filled the air. Christmas was back.

No sooner had I stepped through the door than Rick and his mom rushed to greet me. "Thank you for everything you and Craig did to find Shelly's murderer and for the article you wrote. Because of you, I have a second chance," she said as a tear rolled down her cheek and she threw her arms around me.

Rick smiled and added, "You saved the day again. You're getting rather good at this murder-solving thing."

I laughed. "Well, let's hope I don't get any more practice for a while. I could use a break."

Caroline linked her arm to mine and led me to a dessert table overflowing with delectable treats—each one more decadent and tempting than the last. Trying to be healthy, I focused on the trays of fresh fruit and vegetables on the adjoining table, but my eyes kept drifting back to the cheesecake topped with cherries sitting in the center of the dessert table.

Caroline handed me a white paper plate decorated with red poinsettias and a matching napkin that I recognized as coming from Mae's Gift Shop. "Here's a plate," she said. "Get yourself something to eat. Rick said you have to go to work after this, and I don't want you to leave hungry."

"Thank you." I said, as I succumbed to the cheesecake and placed a small slice on my plate.

Caroline smiled and added three spritz cookies and a handful of dried papaya and pineapple to my plate. "There, that looks better." She grinned before disappearing into the crowd.

As I picked up a plastic fork, a hand reached around me and grabbed two pieces of walnut fudge. I looked to my left and saw Rick with a mischievous grin on his face, chewing on a sweet morsel. After savoring the taste, he asked, "How did Sarah find out about the tape and the lab?"

"Elaine told her. She was upset about what happened at the cabin—Carl thinking she was out to kill him, and me practically accusing her of killing Shelly. Elaine needed to talk to someone."

"Wow, Sarah had Elaine fooled, didn't she? Man, she sure knew how to cover her tracks. It's scary how easily people can deceive you," he said as he reached for a sugar cookie.

I nodded. "Sarah had me convinced Elaine or Carl killed Shelly until I realized her story about the shooting didn't make sense. If it hadn't been for finding the bullet in the tree, I think she would have let the police arrest either Elaine or Carl for poisoning Shelly. Sarah was going to protect herself and Mr. Langford, no matter what. I'm puzzled, though, about something she said."

"What?" Rick raised an eyebrow.

"While at the chemistry lab, Sarah said some man called her and told her to waste no time in killing Shelly."

Rick's eyes widened in shock. "Did she say who this dude was?"

"No, but Lawrence said Sarah mentioned something about Mae paying for the sins of her husband."

"I wonder what she meant." Rick scratched his head.

"I wish I knew." I shrugged, trying to make sense of Sarah's cryptic words. I glanced around the room and spotted Dr. McGuire talking to Caroline, but there was no sign of Elaine. "Where's Elaine?"

Rick sighed. "Talk about not knowing somebody. When Dad found out Elaine had been in prison, he flipped. Not so much because of her time in prison but because she never trusted him enough to tell him about her past. They're taking a break to figure things out. Needless to say—" he smiled, "the wedding is off...at least for now."

"Sounds like you got part of your Christmas wish."

Rick beamed. "I guess I did. Maybe I was a better boy than I thought."

Rick's mom waved at him. "Hey, I gotta go, but you still want to see *Man With the Golden Gun*?"

"Yeah, that'll be fun."

"Great! I'll call you," Rick said as he rushed to his mother's side.

As I watched Rick and his mom talk to a group of people, I noticed T.J. and Meg in deep conversation with Lawrence and his wife. T.J. caught my eye and gave me a knowing look. He whispered something in Meg's ear and made his way toward me.

"I'm glad you're okay," T.J. said, reassuringly touching my shoulder. "Sounds like you had another close call."

"It all worked out," I said.

"This time," T.J. said, his brow furrowed. "Ever since Craig came into your—"

I stopped him. "It's not his fault, only coincidence, nothing more."

He looked at my hand. "You left your ring at home. Is the engagement off?"

I rolled my eyes. "It was never on, remember? And yes, it's in my room. I need to return it to Craig before I lose it or something." I paused. "We're going to tell everyone we're stepping back to reevaluate our relationship because we rushed things a bit."

"I wonder how your mom will take it. She was rather smitten with Craig."

"Oh, she'll survive." I laughed. "Craig says he'll come over to the house from time to time to keep her happy, but I think he enjoys my *normal* family life. Guess that's something he never had growing up."

"Won't that be nice," T.J. said, but his optimistic words did not match his downcast look.

Sensing the need to change the subject, I inquired, "So, how are things with you and Meg?"

"Things are still weird."

"Why?" I reached for my Eiffel Tower charm and twisted it between my fingers.

"Ever since the pageant dress debacle, she's been on edge. I can't explain it, but she hasn't been herself." T.J. stopped and grabbed a chocolate chip cookie. "Meg's met my mom and dad, and I've met her mother. Her dad travels a lot, but with the holidays, I thought it might be a good time to meet him. But when I suggested it, Meg came up with all kinds of excuses about why that couldn't happen. Do you suppose Meg's ashamed of me?"

"Don't be ridiculous. You're a wonderful guy. Any girl would be proud to have you as a boyfriend."

"You think so?"

I could feel my face turning red. "Of course I do. You're the best."

T.J. smiled and put his hand on mine. "There's something I've been meaning to—"

"Hi, T.J. I hope I'm not interrupting." It was Craig.

T.J.'s face sank. He removed his hand from mine. "Guess I better take a few cookies to Meg. Talk to you later."

Craig turned toward me. "Sorry. I didn't mean to run him off."

"That's okay. T.J. just needed some cookies for Meg."

"I've been meaning to ask, have you heard anything about that internship with the *Chicago Tribune*?"

"No, not yet. The deadline isn't until the 31st," I said.

"Oh, I didn't realize that. Hopefully, the letter of recommendation I wrote will do the trick. Let me know when you hear something. Anyway, have you heard that a group of figure skaters and their coach are coming to Petersburg? They'll train at the university's ice rink to prepare for the '76 Olympics." Craig grabbed a paper plate and a napkin, surveying the goodies on the table.

"That's exciting! I love figure skating! Not that I can skate well, but I have fun watching it."

"Well...it so happens the coach and I have the same agent. Suzette suggested he and I meet when he gets to town. Do you want to join us? She said he's got a killer of a team."

"Yes, I'd love to come. Besides, with a lead-in like that, how could I resist?" I grinned.

I glanced over Craig's shoulder and saw Lawrence entering the room, coming toward us while staring straight ahead and clenching his jaw.

"Lawrence, what's up? Everything okay?" I asked.

He said nothing.

"Lawrence, what is it?"

"You remember Sarah mentioned some man gave her orders to kill Shelly?"

In unison, Craig and I both said, "Yeah."

"Well," Lawrence continued, "Sarah left word last night with one of the guards that she wanted to talk to Detective Douglas...she was interested in some kind of plea deal in exchange for revealing the dude's name."

"That's interesting," Craig said. "Do you think the DA will go for that?"

"We'll never know." Lawrence sighed. "I just got a call from the station. Sarah's dead."

I gasped, "How?"

"They claim suicide, but—"

I shook my head. "Why would she commit suicide if she was trying to negotiate a plea deal?"

"Exactly." Lawrence nodded. "And get this, the higher-ups told Douglas not to investigate her death—to leave it as a suicide. I don't know about you, but that makes me want to look into it even more."

I felt Craig and Lawrence's eyes burning a hole through me. "What?" I said, my eyes darting between the two of them.

Craig put his arm around my shoulder and gave me a quick squeeze. "Sounds like we've got some work to do, Sherlock. The next few months just got a lot more interesting."

about sharon kay

SHARON KAY grew up in Ohio, and earned her photojournalism degree from Bowling Green State University. The Michelle Kilpatrick Mysteries are inspired by her life in the 1970s as a college student who commuted to the university.

Sharon is the proud mother of three adult children. She enjoys organic gardening, exploring universal design, and delving into genres outside her comfort zone.

* * *

If you enjoyed *Fashionably Fit, Fatally Flawed*, I'd be thrilled if you would take a few moments to leave a review. Thanks so much!

Visit www.thesharonkay.com for information on releases, events, special promotions, book club questions, recipes, and playlists for the series.
Newsletter: https://thesharonkay.substack.com

facebook.com/thesharonkay

instagram.com/thesharonkay

goodreads.com/thesharonkay

bookbub.com/profile/875097309

www.ingramcontent.com/pod-product-compliance
Lightning Source LLC
Chambersburg PA
CBHW022104310726
48972CB00007B/1870